Tell Me A Secret
Tell, The Detective – Book 1

CHLOE GARNER

Copyright © 2020 Chloe Garner

All rights reserved.

ISBN: 9798638219604

Cover design by Skyla Dawn Cameron

Published by A Horse Called Alpha

For Lyri, whose enthusiasm and faith has never been short of boundless.

Tell Me A Secret

The door.

Strangely enough, it was the door that she remembered best about that night.

The paint was wearing thin right around chest-high, because that's where Tina would always put her hands to push it open, once she'd gotten it unlatched. Two step process, that door. You turned the knob and pressed, and the bolt would get past the frame far enough that it wouldn't latch again, and then you put your whole weight against it to force it the rest of the way open.

Her father had said a dozen times that he was going to fix that door, sand it down, repaint it, get some new weather-stripping to keep the drafts from getting in, in the winter. Tina's mom just bought door blockers for every season and every holiday. She wouldn't have made an investment like that if she'd ever thought Tina's dad would do something about it.

Tina had known something was wrong.

The lights should have been on. The house should have smelled like cinnamon and the one tray of cookies Tina's mom hadn't gotten out of the oven in time.

As she'd fumbled her keys, unlocking the door and giving it a good shove, she'd had no idea that her old life was done. What waited for her on the other side of that door was her new life.

"Miss Matthews, I know that Detective Keller has told you on two separate occasions that he will *call you* when there are developments in the case. You do not need to continue calling."

"It's been six weeks," Tina said. "And he hasn't done a thing. Wandered around the house watching someone else take pictures, drink some coffee, work on the break-ins at the high school. He hasn't made any progress on my parents."

"I understand," the woman said. Tina had the woman's name in her notes, somewhere. Agnes or Mildred or something. Her mother hadn't loved her enough to give her daughter a name that came from this century.

Tina wasn't usually this vindictive. She really wasn't. And she did believe that Ms. Agnes Mildred Beancounter was *trying* to understand. She answered the phones for the police station. Certainly she talked to more than her share of people making impossible demands of her.

"I understand," Beancounter said again. "But the fact that you do not *see* his progress doesn't mean there hasn't been any."

"Has there?" Tina demanded.

"I can't release that information to you,"

Beancounter said. Tina paged through her notes, finding it.

Ethel.

Ethel Brewster.

"Ethel," Tina said. "Please. What can I do? Is there anything you can do to help me?"

"Go home," Ethel said in a fractionally kinder voice. "Grieve. You've suffered a huge loss, and no one is going to be able to fix it. Not me or Detective Keller or anyone else. You need to heal, and you need to find a way forward. Let Detective Keller do his job. I promise… I *promise* the minute I hear anything that he's ready to release, I will call you personally to let you know. I can't *tell* you what it is, because that's his job, but I will tell you that there's something, the minute I know about it. Okay?"

Tina twisted her bottom lip against the top one, calculating.

That turnip was dry.

"Thank you, Ms. Brewster. I'm not going to rest until the man who killed my parents is paying for it, but thank you for doing what you can."

"Have a good evening," the woman said, and Tina hung up, reorganizing her notes. She needed to transcribe and print them to put in a cross-referenced binder, but the sight of her own handwriting on blank pages was stimulating.

It always had been.

It was how she'd always solved everything. Write down all of the facts and reorganize them until they made sense.

She'd bought the binder, though, and it was a productive way of re-inspecting the things she knew, see if the new font, the new spacings, the new format triggered a new thought. It was the creative process, and she was good at it. If there was an intersection between creativity and science, Tina was it. She'd gotten her mother's non-traditional view of the world and her father's scientific rigor. And a serious stubborn streak her mother traced back to her great-aunt, the one who had disappeared in Africa before Tina was born.

The stubborn streak that Ethel Brewster was now on the receiving end of.

Tina glowered at the phone.

Re-paged her notes.

This was stupid.

She knew what she was going to do, and the only thing that was keeping her from it was the choosing. There were any number of methods she could have used to winnow it down, but all of them had downsides, and it wasn't like this was the kind of thing that got thorough, honest reviews online.

She looked back at her laptop, sitting there on the counter next to her elbow, and she rolled her eyes, clicking one of the links at random.

It rang four times, and she had pulled her phone away from her head to hang up and try another random selection when a male voice answered.

"What?"

She jerked her head back.

"Is this Tell... Is your name really Tell?"

"It's a family name," he said. "What do you want?"

"I want you to find someone for me," she said.

"Sweetheart, I know that. That's what I *do*."

She'd made an appointment.

Tell - no other name listed - had tried to tell her to just come by when she felt like it, and he'd be in or he wouldn't, but Tina Matthews didn't do anything important without an appointment, and she resented the idea that he shouldn't need to commit to being there, just because he didn't feel like it.

"I'll be there if I'm there," she muttered, getting out of the car and going to feed the meter. "This is a mistake."

She had her files. Photos, financial information, all of her parents' emails from the six months before *the door*. Tell had had something going on, that afternoon, but he was free for the evening, so Tina had had just enough time to start reorganizing things chronologically, rather than categorically.

She narrowed her eyes at the meter, trying to guess if an hour would be enough, or if she'd want two, then went ahead and fed it the bonus quarters for an extra hour. She hated feeding a device money for something she wasn't going to use, but she'd resent it more if she had to come down here and put more money *in* because she was actually engaged in something useful, up in that building over there.

That building over there.

Tell's office was in a shabby region of downtown, not quit seedy, but certainly run down enough that a hotelier might have looked there for an opportunity to knock a whole bunch of buildings down at once.

Once more, Tina considered going back to her apartment and picking another investigator at random to call, but she'd made *an appointment*, and that mattered to her. That and there wasn't a commitment to pay him until she actually engaged his services. If she didn't like the smell of the place, she could turn around and walk right back out.

Once she shook his hand and introduced herself.

That was what an appointment was.

Everything after that was optional.

She found the door into the building that his address indicated, then went to read the mailboxes to figure out which office was his.

Up six flights of stairs, she came to a door with a half-height frosted glass pane, cracked, and gold stenciling - *Tell Investigates* - with half of the 'g' missing.

Steeling herself up, she turned the doorknob.

Nothing happened.

She tried it again, just to be sure, then looked around.

Could be a security thing. Didn't want people wandering in when he was in the bathroom or listening to music or whatever. Deep in thought.

Investigators should sometimes be deep in thought.

She knocked.

Waited.

Knocked again.

Didn't hear so much as footsteps, inside.

Put her face to the glass, then knocked once more, feeling mislead and mistreated.

She had an *appointment*.

"Sorry," someone said. "Sorry. I'm here."

A man, late twenties, with a fit build and wavy dark brown hair came running up the steps.

"I'm here," he said again. "The thing, it ran late."

"Tell?" she asked.

"That's me," he said cheerfully, pulling out a janitor-style set of keys and thumbing through them to find the one for the office door.

"Do you come with a last name?" Tina asked as he opened the door for her.

"Not usually," he said, going in and waiting for her on the other side of the doorway. She narrowed her eyes at him, and he narrowed his eyes back.

Looked her up and down, tipping his head back slightly and sticking out his chin.

"Tina Matthews," he said. "Parents died six weeks back, breaking and entering, looks like a robbery gone bad. Guy didn't seem to be *there* to hurt them, but he also didn't just stumble in on them and overreact."

"No," Tina said. "He tied them up for at least an hour before he killed them."

She hadn't told him any of this.

He nodded.

"I think the police timeline is probably wrong, but

it usually is. You made good, though. That address, your dad was, what a mailman? Factory worker? Mom taught school or worked as a nurse's aide? You dress well, for that background."

"Dad was a professor at the university," Tina said, going into the office and watching as he closed the door then flipped on a light switch. "Is there something wrong with your razor?"

The carpet needed a serious cleaning - the high-traffic areas showed clearly - but it didn't appear to be grimy or sticky, at least.

The investigator scratched his chin then took off his jacket - just a light duster that would keep the wind off and a bit of rain if it happened - and put the jacket onto a coat rack.

"I'd offer you a coffee, but I don't normally drink the stuff, and it'd be cold, anyway," he said, motioning her through the sitting room and into an office.

There were three chairs in the office - the rolling one behind the desk and two client chairs - but only one of the three was usable.

Tell picked up a stack of folders off of one of the client chairs and thumped them down on the floor next to the desk before walking around and sitting down.

"You want me to find the man who killed your parents," Tell said, folding his hands with his thumbs in front of his lips.

Tina looked around the room, dismayed at the clutter.

The desk was three layers deep in scattered folders

and books, with a desktop computer whose keyboard was somewhere in the midst of it, judging from the cord. The floor had piles of books, folders, photographs, and discarded fast food wrappers, and the wall of filing cabinets had things sticking out of nearly every drawer.

"Did you have a break in?" she asked, and Tell glanced around as though he was surprised to find the place like it was.

"What do you mean?" he asked.

Tina spread her hands.

"This," she said. "It's a disaster zone."

"I know where everything is," Tell said.

"Shouldn't it be locked away?" Tina asked. "Someplace safe?"

"If I'm the only one who can find it, isn't it safe?" Tell asked, bemused. "Tell me about your case."

Tina was irate. She picked up a picture off of the floor.

"Who is he?"

"Neil van Horne," Tell answered simply. Tina shook her head, waiting.

"Don't know what you expect me to say," Tell said slowly. "It's for a case that has nothing to do with you. Would you please put it back where it was?"

"Here on the floor under my chair?" she asked, and Tell gave her a small smile, unamused.

"Do you want my help or not?" he asked. She stood.

"I'm not seeing any progress from the police," she said. "So I wanted another professional to look at it, one who wasn't... completely overwhelmed with the rest of their workload. I'm not sure if you're unprofessional or overwhelmed or both, but I think I can do better."

He leaned back in his chair, weaving his fingers behind his head and putting his feet up onto his desk, which triggered a small avalanche of paperwork.

"Tina Matthews," he said. "Thirty-one, unmarried. Single, from the look of you. Not because you're trying so hard, but because you *aren't*. You're too busy for a serious relationship, but you're too traditional to keep your own name when you get married. Work a good job, take it seriously, but it isn't the kind of job where they *really* care what you look like. The clothes are in good condition, but they're neither new nor high-brand. You haven't gone back to work since your parents died. Bereavement, and you're important enough that you're confident they aren't going to fire you. Good at your job." He narrowed his eyes. "I'm going to guess... Management. Mid-sized company. Mostly working with younger kids straight out of college. Artists? Artsy-types, anyway, and they rub you the wrong way. You're the one who gets things done."

Tina had made it to the doorway into the front room before he started speaking, and she waited, listening.

"All right," she said. "What about my parents?"

"Not a random break-in," he said. "Guy would have run, if he'd been in the wrong place at the wrong time. Skeezy breaking-and-entering stuff, they're trying to do it while no one is home, so they can smash and grab and go buy their drugs or whatever. He hung out way too long for it to be random."

Tina got a chill.

"I'm not cheap," Tell said. "I doubt you can afford me. But I'm the best there is, and you're not going to walk out that door believing anything else."

"I work for a startup," Tina said. "They have a basketball hoop on the wall in the conference room, and the CEO throws a foam basketball at it, through meetings."

Tell smiled slowly.

"Does it make you want to tackle him out of his chair and squeeze the life out of him?"

Tina blinked quickly.

"I fantasize about it," she said.

Now he grinned.

"That, I can work with," he said.

"Somebody hurt my parents," Tina said. "Someone bad. He took them from me, and it's all I can think about."

Tell shook his head, letting his feet drop onto the floor.

"I can't fix that," he said. "I can chase down the guy who did it, and I can turn him over to the police, if you want me to, but I can't fix that you're hurting, and I can't give back what you lost. Sometimes I can, but this ain't it."

He had dark eyes, fair skin, and high cheekbones, a face that was clear and focused.

How could he live in this room?

"I… I know you can't," Tina said. "I just can't stand that they aren't doing *anything* about it."

"I bag on the police, because that's kind of my

bread and butter, but they take murder seriously. If they haven't figured anything out, it's because the legal methods of finding things are coming up dry. They don't have the flexibility that I do, nor the skills that I do, to track down the man who did it."

She should have gone to another detective.

Should have found someone who wasn't twenty-eight and still working out whether or not he was suited to facial hair.

Someone who could find his keyboard when he needed to.

She went to sit in the seat again.

"There's no easy way to deal with loss," Tell said. "You just grow out of it, eventually, leaves a pretty scar. You'd be paying me to catch a guy and make sure he got punished. No more, no less."

"Yes," Tina said. "That's what I want."

He shook his head.

"It isn't, but you don't know that yet."

She rolled her eyes.

"Will you do it or won't you?"

"No," he said, shaking his head and giving her an almost-playful little frown. "I told you, you can't afford me."

"Jerk," Tina said, standing again. "I have money. My parents had money. They lived cheap and they were saving for retirement. I'm funded."

"I charge five hundred dollars an hour," Tell said, tipping his head slightly to the side to observe her reaction.

Various expletives flew through her mind.

"And your office is *here*?" she asked.

The first thing to make it out of her mouth.

Tell laughed.

"It's comfortable," he said. She shook her head.

"What do you do with it all?" she asked. "Stuff it under your mattress?"

He certainly didn't *dress* like he was making twenty grand a week.

"I only work when I feel like it," Tell said, crossing his arms.

"Oh, is that so?" Tina answered, and he grinned.

"I'll tell you what. You go talk to someone else, someone you can afford, and you see what you can get. In the meantime, if I get a minute and I get bored, I'll take a poke around and see what I can find. Let you know. All right?"

"I don't want your free time," Tina said. "I want you to find the bastard and nail his tail to the wall."

Tell's grin widened, and he nodded.

"Then don't call anyone else," he said. "I'll take a poke around and I'll call you if I think it's worth my energy. If you don't hear from me by... Let's say the end of next week, then I'm not interested and you should find someone else."

"No," Tina said, leaning toward him. "It's been six weeks. I'm not waiting any more. I want you to do it *now*."

"If you want me to do it now, you're going to have to pay me," he said. "Five grand retainer, up front."

Tina swallowed.

She'd come in here intending to get references, to

do background checks and a workup on various options before she made a firm decision, but here she was, begging the first one to take her on, ready to write a check.

She hesitated, and Tell raised an eyebrow.

"Too steep?" he asked.

She shook her head, getting out her purse.

"Do it," she said. "I'll be back tomorrow to check in on your progress."

"Hold on, hold on," Tell said. "I do have other things going on in my life, other clients, and, you know *a life*. I can't promise I'll have progress by tomorrow."

"Doesn't matter," Tina said. "I'll be here, anyway. Who do I make the check out to?"

"Check?" he asked, wincing his face to the side. "You can't just send it to me?"

"Who?" she asked.

"You could just *call*," he said. "I won't have anything to say in person that I can't tell you over the phone."

As he said it, a phone rang, and he startled forward, putting his hands over the papers on his desk like he was sensing an aura. Tina stood, listening to the ring for a moment, then started lifting the corners of folders, peering under them, looking for a cell phone.

Tell pulled an entire, wall-wired phone out from under the files, dumping a dozen of them onto the floor in front of Tina.

"What?" he asked the receiver as Tina stooped to collect the papers before they all slid completely out of their manila wraps.

He hung up.

Tina did her best with the folders, stacking them back up on the desk, where Tell smeared them back into a pile.

"Was that a rotary phone?" Tina asked.

"I like it," he said.

"You were saying about calling…?" Tina asked and he pursed his lips.

"Fine. Waste your evening. Whatever."

"Evening," she said flatly. "I'll be here after lunch."

He grinned.

"Bring a chair. I may answer the phone sometimes but I don't unlock that door until night. It's a nighttime business, snooping around after unsavory types, and I sleep most of the day."

Tina hesitated.

It made sense. It just didn't help make him seem any less unreliable.

"Fine," she said. "What time?"

"Eight?" he asked. "Make it nine. I have something else to do, before."

"Check?" she asked, holding up the book. He shrugged.

"Tell Investigates," he said.

"Tell," she muttered, writing the check and handing it to him.

It was a lot of money.

A lot, a lot.

But.

There was no way she was walking out of the office without him committed to finding the man who killed her parents.

She couldn't put her finger on exactly *why* it had to be him, but there it was.

It did.

It had to be him.

He took the check, putting it into a drawer.

"It isn't going to mess you up if I don't get that to a bank sometime soon, is it?" he asked, and she tipped her head to the side.

"You're kidding," she said. He shrugged.

"I sleep through banker's hours, mostly," he said. "Whatever. I'll figure it out."

"You know you can take a picture of it, and they'll process it, if you've got the right bank," Tina said, and he looked up at her with a modicum of surprise.

"The world keeps changing," he said, shaking his head. "Well, unless you change your mind and decide to actually let me do my job, I'll see you tomorrow."

She nodded, going to stand in the doorway between the office and the waiting area for a moment.

"You're going to get him, aren't you?" she asked.

"I never make promises that I can't keep," he said. "But yes."

It didn't hit her until she got back to her apartment, what she had done.

She'd just handed a perfect stranger with an ad

online a check for more than she made in a month.

Sure, her parents *had* money, but now wasn't the time to be an idiot with it.

Now wasn't the time to make *any* big decisions.

They kept telling her that.

That she needed to grieve, to work through it, to learn what the new normal was supposed to look like.

The police had referred her to a grief counselor, and Tina had seen the woman three times in the wake of finding her parents.

It wasn't that the sessions weren't helpful, nor that she didn't like the woman. It was that she was spending all of her time focusing on her parents' deaths, rather than doing normal things like feeding herself or bathing.

When she'd stopped seeing the counselor, she'd been able to pretend - for hours at a time - that everything was normal, and that she was just on a vacation from work.

She'd met a friend at lunch one day, and Sherry had asked if maybe she would be better off *at* work, so that she could distract herself with everything going on, there.

It was a dream job, on paper.

Fast-paced startup with lots of energy and ideas, a perfect place for a creative with rigorous structure to flourish, to *excel*.

And she did excel.

Her ideas were the most grounded and actionable of anyone in the company, and her people were supplied and directed well enough that they actually got stuff done. Jeff said all the time how much he needed her.

As he threw the foam basketball at the hoop in the

conference room again.

He needed her.

He just didn't want to be like her.

Didn't want to *act* like a man running a multi-million dollar company with a ravenous customer base and payroll to meet.

She did a good job for him, but all she did was work. She hadn't seen Sherry in six months, and her old roommate was about the only friend she'd managed to keep up with, out of college. New friends?

Nope.

She worked.

Startup hours.

The kids at work, they went out after work, drinking and carousing. They had office trysts and social drama.

A handful of them had gone skydiving together, and another group went rock climbing twice a week on lunch break.

They *liked* each other. Tina hadn't ever managed to break into their social circles; she was the office grownup, and she ended up doing conflict resolution and mediation when feelings got hurt, and that was about the only way she found out what was going on, with all of them.

She didn't want to go back.

It had taken her four weeks to see it, but that's what it was.

Jeff was still paying her, because he made an obscene amount of money and he *needed* her, but every evening, when she looked at when she was going to go back again, she decided to push it another couple of days.

She wasn't ready to face them all yet.

So she drew a bath and she settled in with her notepad, going through and making notes about the things she hadn't considered yet.

She'd talked to her parents' neighbors, and none of them knew anything that Tina hadn't about what was going on with her parents.

She'd talked to her mom's principal, but the man hadn't talked to her mom more than professionally since the school year had started. She wanted to talk to her mom's students, but she knew better than to ask. Her mom would have been mortified if she'd asked any of them questions about her mom's personal life.

There was another teacher, Glenda Mitchell, who had retired at the end of the previous year, and who Tina's mom had been close with, but Glenda was on a tour of Europe for another week, yet. It was possible Beth Matthews had confided *something* to her, but Tina found it unlikely.

She needed to go through the ladies in her mother's book group, still. It was a long shot, compared to the ones that she played cards with once a week, but the cards ladies hadn't known much of use, even though they knew *lots*.

Her dad was a different issue.

He had coworkers, but he'd never been a *confider*, in the way that her mother was. Her mother, the art teacher, had talked about *everything*. To anyone. Filtering out the important stories from the unimportant ones took effort, and finding what was true... Well, that was another thing, entirely. Beth Matthews told tall tales, expressive ones with big arms and voices.

They weren't always entirely factual.

Sometimes they *were* entirely fabricated.

Glenda had been the music teacher at Mrs. Matthews' school for twenty-five years, and Tina knew more about Glenda than she did about her father.

Winston Matthews didn't tell anyone anything.

Well, about anything personal.

He explained how tidal effects impacted the seasonal migration of everything from orcas to hummingbirds, but Tina didn't even know what his favorite color was.

Quite frankly, Tina had never understood how her parents had met or fallen in love, but she'd been quite sure her daddy hung the moon, and her mama taught her everything there was to know about *being alive*.

They were gone.

Someone had hurt them.

And then he'd taken them away from her.

Focus on the facts.

The facts always win.

The man had been in the house with her parents for a while, from the bruising and other evidence. Had he been looking for something? Or had he wanted to *know* something?

Tell didn't think that it had been a mistake, that a burglar had shown up at the same time that her parents were home. Christmas break.

They got more days off than most people did, so it wasn't unreasonable to think that someone had been breaking in, looking for expensive gifts, and not expected either of them to be home, but that was as compelling as it got.

Tell was right - the man should have just run, if he'd been surprised.

He'd stayed.

But *why*?

Why?

Her parents were fascinating people, but they hadn't been *interesting*.

It didn't make sense.

She needed more information.

Her mind wandered and the bath got cold. She got out and went downstairs to make herself a microwave dinner, then surfed movie channels until after midnight, just to prove that she wasn't going to work tomorrow. She cleaned the kitchen, for what mess there was, then she went up to bed, feeling just as defeated and pointless as she had every night since her parents had died.

Nothing had made any progress today, Tell not withstanding.

He was just a smug guy who overvalued his own time and intellect.

And she'd handed him a huge check.

She was an idiot.

The next day dragged. She wandered the house,

then she went over to her parents' house, doing yard work and trying to keep up the house as much as she could, without going in.

At some point, they had to let her go in, to let her take care of her parents' things, sell what she wouldn't keep, then put the house on the market.

They couldn't hold it forever.

She was going to have to face it, eventually.

She didn't want to.

But her father would have been disappointed if she'd let the house go, so she did her best. It was cold out, like it might snow later, and the trees were still dropping enough leaves that it was worth it to rake. She made sure that the hoses were all disconnected from the house, and she cut back one of the bushes that she knew her dad had been meaning to trim, then she hauled the branches down to the curb and tied them for trash pickup. She didn't know what day the service would come through, but anyone who could read a newspaper knew that the house wasn't occupied; it wasn't like she was giving something away.

That took her to lunchtime, so she got a book and her notebook and she went to one of the indie pizza joints downtown that she liked pretty well, and she tried to lose herself, first in the book and then in reorganizing her notes.

Neither worked, but it burned a couple of hours.

She went back to her apartment and got dressed to go work out, hitting the little in-building gym for an hour, and then going out for a walk.

The weather had turned colder, yet, and the clouds

were heavy and gray, low overhead, and though it rained, bits of ice stuck to her sleeves.

She'd always meant to get a dog. She liked being outside, going for long walks, but it had been years since she'd actually done it, and she'd come to the conclusion that getting a dog would be setting herself up to neglect it, with the hours she worked, so she'd never done it.

At the park, passing the people out with their pets, she was once again sorry that she was alone.

She couldn't focus to eat, so she went driving, ending up across the street from Tell's building, at the parking meters again. She had an hour to burn, if he was even on time, but she couldn't bring herself to start the engine again, so she fed the meter more of her quarters and went upstairs.

She sat on the floor until her butt went numb, then she got up and, on a whim, tried the doorknob.

The office was unlocked.

"Now that inspires confidence," she murmured, going in and taking a seat in one of the waiting room chairs. Tell had magazines on one of the tables, underneath a dusty lamp, and she picked one up, frowning when she recognized one of the celebrities and flipping back to the front cover.

The magazine was eight years old.

She tossed it back onto the table and crossed her legs, just waiting.

At nine-thirty, Tell came in, whistling.

"Did you at least turn on the coffee?" he asked without looking over.

"Your magazines are from last decade," Tina said, standing.

"They came with the office," he answered, flipping his keys around his finger and going to unlock the door to the main office.

"What did you find?" Tina asked.

"Just a minute," Tell told her, getting a stack of pictures out of his pocket and going through them, dropping some of them onto the desk, some onto the floor next to him, and some over his shoulder.

"Is this, like… Some kind of ritual?" Tina asked.

"There," he said, holding one of the photos up. "That's the one."

He put it down in front of his computer, propped up against the screen, then brushed photos off of his chair and sat down.

"Now," he said. "Now it's your turn."

"What did you *find*?" Tina asked.

"I went over to the house," Tell said. "Nosed around a little bit. Found a lead or two, followed one of them for a while." He sat back in his chair, weaving his fingers behind his head. "Here's the thing. I get the distinct impression that, when this is done… You aren't going to like the outcome."

"My parents *died*," Tina said. "Horribly. How could it get worse from there?"

He shook his head.

"See, that you even have to ask means that I'm right. The world is full of dark, terrible things, and people like you? I mean, seriously, if you got the choice to live without ever seeing any of them, why wouldn't you?"

"That's not what I'm paying you for," Tina said.

"No, wait," he said, holding up a finger and letting his feet drop onto the floor. "You're paying me to find the guy who did it and *do* something about it. Doesn't mean I have to *tell* you anything."

"You expect me to just trust you?" Tina asked, skeptical.

He took a breath, then nodded.

"Yes. I'm giving you an option. You don't have to go through this, if you don't want to. I can take care of it, and just let you know it's done."

Tina frowned.

"What did you find?" she asked.

"You need to think about this," he said. "I'm going to keep working, but you... You should take a day and really think about how far down the rabbit hole you're interested in going. Because it is a bad, bad place down there, darling. And you, pretty girl like you with your schooling and your job and your aspirations? You aren't prepared for what I might bump into."

"Like hell," Tina said. "I gave you money, and I expect periodic reports on your progress. That's the only way you stay accountable for the money I gave you and the job I expect you to do."

He looked at her for a moment, then grinned.

"I'm going to let you take a day," he said. "You come back here tomorrow and you tell me if you really want me to tell you what I'm doing and what I'm finding."

He rummaged around under the stack of stuff on

his desk to find the mouse for his computer and he shifted it to wake the machine up. Tina watched as another folder slid onto the ground, but she didn't bother to pick it up, this time.

"You think I'm… leaving," she said. He glanced at her.

"Good night," he answered.

"No," she said.

"Yes," he answered dispassionately, his attention shifted to the computer now. "I'll see you tomorrow."

"This place is a pig sty," Tina said, standing. "And, tomorrow, when I ask you what you found, I expect you to tell me."

"Just so long as you think about it," Tell answered, sounding more like he was talking to his computer than her.

She waited, wanting to try to pry more out of him, angry that he thought he knew best for her, and furious that he thought he was within his rights to keep something from her, but at the same time, drawn like catnip.

He'd found something.

In twenty-four hours, after the police had had six weeks.

He'd found something.

All she wanted was to camp out there on the floor and wait for him to be willing to tell her what it was.

It was all she cared about. She was completely willing to overlook his smug twenty-something face and his patronizing I'm-the-man behavior.

He didn't look up again, and finally Tina went to

the front door, pausing once more to shake her head, then leaving and walking back down to her car.

She got up the next morning and called Sherry.

"Have you got some time on your lunch break?" Tina asked.

"Anything," Sherry answered. "Where can I meet you?"

Tina named a pub they both liked that was close enough to Sherry's work that she wouldn't waste all of her time driving around town, and Sherry agreed to meet her at noon.

"Did the police tell you something?" Sherry asked before Tina hung up.

"No," Tina said. "I hired a private eye."

"I thought you weren't going to do that," Sherry said.

"I'll talk to you about it at lunch," Tina said.

"I haven't heard from you in two weeks," Sherry said. "I've been worried."

Tina wondered how it had been that long, then shook her head.

"You're at work," she said. "I don't want to keep you. I'll talk to you at lunch."

"All right, but if you don't show up, I'm coming looking for you," Sherry said, and Tina nodded.

"Fair enough."

They hung up and Tina went to get her purse and her notebook, then went shopping.

She hadn't bought anything new to wear since before Christmas, and she'd missed the after-Christmas sales. She found herself looking at soft sweaters and jeans that fit well, rather than the button-ups and slacks she wore to work, attracted to rich colors instead of earth tones, and to boots rather than sensible heels.

The guys wore concert tee shirts and tattered jeans; no one at the place cared but her, but she kept to her standards, because it made her feel like a grown up.

She tried things on, buying very little, but managing to burn enough time that she could go to the pub and sit down with a drink to wait for Sherry.

Her friend was ten minutes late and out of breath.

"I'm sorry," she said. "I got caught up in a last-minute meeting. Idiot thinks that his world is ending, and he needs a solution *now*, when what he needs is a plan to fix it for the next launch in six months, and all I needed was an e-mail describing what he was seeing."

Tina smiled.

"I'm sorry," she said. She was a little jealous of Sherry, the same way Sherry was a little jealous of her. At Sherry's work, everyone treated everything like it was the most important thing in the company, and while they *were* always angry, at least they were serious. Sherry thought that Tina's job sounded like a vacation.

"So," Sherry said, sitting down and sliding the menu to the end of the table - who needed that? - "tell me about your investigator. You told me you were going to wait for the police to tell you what was going to happen next."

Tina shrugged.

"I couldn't stand it. Ethel down at the police office couldn't ever tell me anything, the detective *wouldn't* ever talk to me, and they weren't making any progress. It's been six weeks, almost seven, and they have no idea who did it or why."

"It was a break-in, sweetheart," Sherry said. "I'm sorry…" Her friend took Tina's hands and gave her a firm but empathetic look. "Look, we aren't going to know until it's all over, and I wish I knew what to say to you that would help. But you're… Tina, you haven't been back to work, yet. You're *carrying around* the binder you put together for your own investigation. You're trying to find meaning in this, and what you need to do is grieve and move on."

"I can't do that," Tina said. "I don't think it was random. I don't even think the police do. And Tell… Sherry, he knows something."

"Who does?" Sherry asked.

"Tell," Tina said. "The PI I hired. His name is *Tell*. And he knows something."

"Knows something, like he was in on it?" Sherry asked. Tina shook her head.

"No. I went to see him two days ago, and I hired him, and I went back yesterday…"

"… of course you did…"

"… and he told me that maybe I don't want to know what happened."

"What does that mean?" Sherry asked.

"The world is a bad place full of bad people…" Tina said. "I don't know. That maybe I'm too nice to deal with what actually happened to them."

"Isn't that what I've been telling you?" Sherry asked. "That you need to let the professionals deal with it, be sad, and then figure out what to do next?"

Tina slouched in the booth, then turned to lean against the wall, putting her feet up on the leather.

"I don't feel that way," Tina said.

"So, is he telling you that he isn't going to do it?" Sherry asked.

"No," Tina said. "I think he's telling me that he'd recommend that I let him do it without telling me what happens."

Sherry blinked.

"I don't get it. An investigator investigates. What is he going to *do*, if not *tell* you what he finds?"

"See, I don't know," Tina said. "It bothered me at the time, but I couldn't put my finger on it. Maybe he was hinting that he would *take care of it*?"

"Like, tell the police?" Sherry asked.

Tina opened her mouth and stretched it off to the side.

"I don't know," she said slowly.

"What do you mean 'take care of it'?" Sherry demanded. "What kind of man are we talking about here? What did you do, Tina?"

"See," Tina said. She took a breath, not sure what she was going to say next. This was why she had needed lunch. Today. She needed to think it through - she'd promised she would - and going through her binder once more really wasn't going to capture what she was missing.

"I'm waiting," Sherry said. Tina nodded.

"I found him online," Tina said. "I really don't know anything about him."

"And you plan to give him money?" Sherry asked.

"I already did," Tina said.

"Tina," Sherry scolded. "Come on. You... You found a stranger online and you gave him money? And now he's telling you that maybe you shouldn't worry about what happened to your parents at all, and he'll just take care of it without you knowing any more than that? You're smarter than that. This is grief. Do you need me to go with you? You need to get your money back. *Tell?* Do you even know his real name? Did you look him up with the BBB?"

Tina blinked.

"I didn't," she said.

Usually, she would have, but she'd been wavering so hard over whether or not to do it, she'd just *done* it.

Sherry shook her head.

"Do you want me to go with you?" she offered again. "I will, if you want."

Tina shook her head slowly.

"No," she said. "I know where his office is, and I... Sherry, I think he figured something out in a *day*, when the police have nothing after almost two months. A day."

"Have you thought about what he might have had to do, to get that information, if the police couldn't?" Sherry asked. Tina shook her head.

"I don't *care*. He killed my parents, Sherry. Killed them. Hurt them, and killed them. I don't *care* what some strange man named Tell has to do to find the bastard. I want him locked up. Punished."

"But that's all, right?" Sherry asked. "You didn't accidentally hire a hit man?"

"I don't think so," Tina said slowly.

"And if you *found out* that you actually had, you'd tell him *not* to kill the guy, right?" Sherry asked. "Tina. You'd let the police arrest him. Put him on trial. Right? You would *stop* a hit man from killing him."

Tina paused, and Sherry sat straight.

"Promise me," the woman said. "Promise me, right here and right now, that you will *talk to me* before you let him do anything permanent. Right? I know you're hurting and I can't begin to understand it, but… That's not you, Tina. It isn't. I don't care how angry and how hurt you are, you *would* regret it, someday."

"No," Tina said. "No, you're right. You're *right*. He's just an investigator, I'm almost certain, and if I… I'm not going to let him kill anyone on my behalf. Now, if he came across some scum bag that he just couldn't go on his way without killing the guy on the grounds that he's a giant scum bag… You know…"

"Tina," Sherry scolded. "Don't even joke."

"I know, I'm sorry," Tina said. "I'm just… Sherry, it's eating me. I *hate* the man who did this. I *hate* him, and…"

She found that she was crying again as her throat closed, and she put her hands over her eyes. She'd thought she was out of tears.

Sherry put her palms on Tina's forearms.

"I'm sorry, sweetie," Sherry said. "I'm so sorry. I wish there was something I could do."

"No, you're doing it," Tina said. "You're here. My oldest friend. You've stuck with me a long time."

"Don't talk like that," Sherry said. "We're not *old*."

"I feel old," Tina said.

She rubbed her eyes dry and reached for her drink, downing it.

"You're not," Sherry said. "You're young and you're beautiful, and you need to quit your job so that you can go meet a man who actually thinks before he talks, and who isn't obsessed with foam sporting equipment."

Tina laughed, rubbing her face again.

"Thank you," she said. Sherry frowned.

"Seriously, though, how shady is this guy?"

"He's not," Tina said. "That's the weird part. He's kind of like… I don't know. He says he only does it when he feels like it. He isn't hustling, and he isn't, like, trying to get my money. He just… I don't know."

"You think maybe he's warning you because he found something bad?" Sherry asked.

"That's what he was trying to tell me," Tina said.

"And if he is?" Sherry asked. "If he's right?"

"You know what?" Tina asked. "I don't care. I want to know who did it, and I want to know why, and I don't care how nasty or bad it is. I want to know."

Sherry sighed.

"Well," she said. "I hope you aren't making a mistake."

"Yeah," Tina said slowly. "Yeah, me, too."

She was outside of Tell's office at six.

She tried the door and found it unlocked again, and this time she tried the door to the office, as well, finding it also unlocked.

She shook her head, putting her purse down on the floor behind the chairs and putting her hands on her hips.

What kind of *idiot* left his office completely unlocked, with all of this *stuff* everywhere?

She pulled the drawers on the filing cabinets, finding every one of them open, and most of them half-empty. The entire last cabinet was completely empty.

She couldn't bear it.

She started sorting.

She picked up the photos he'd dropped the night before and put them in the desk drawer under the computer, then she started stacking the folders that had *anything* written on them separately from the ones that simply didn't.

Going through the filing cabinets, she found no system at all in evidence, so she started going through those, as well. The files that were in cabinets at least had words on them, most of them, so she alphabetized those, labeling the filing cabinets in pencil as she worked.

It was satisfying, seeing the files move from one place to another, from chaos to order, piles and stacks and drawers of chaos evolve into a system where the words on the files were consistently in *order*.

"You're doing it wrong," someone said, and Tina

jumped, feeling cold shock through her system out to her palms as she turned to find Tell sitting sideways in one of the client chairs.

"How long have you been there?" she asked.

"Long enough to know that you think that alphabetical order is the best way to sort those," he said. "I prefer a hybrid of alphabetical and chronological, if you're going to do it."

"Look, I'm sorry," Tina said. "It was just… It's awful in here. I don't know how you live with it. And I was just sitting here, waiting for you, and I can't stop. I can't *stop* doing *something*, while I'm waiting for my life to start again, because it's *stopped*."

Tell raised his eyebrows.

"Did I sound like I was asking you to stop?" he asked. "I just told you you were doing it wrong, that's all."

"You aren't mad?" she asked. He narrowed his eyes at her, untangling long limbs to stand and walk around the desk.

"You didn't open anything, did you?" he asked. "You're just reading what I've written on the outside."

"Yes," she said slowly. It would have been an invasion of someone else's privacy to do more.

"I'm not going to pretend that I'm not annoyed," he said. "I like the chaos in here. It helps me think. But I'm also not going to pretend that I've never lost anything, or that my clients don't trust me, because of how my office looks. Maybe putting some things away isn't the worst thing in the world. And I'm also not surprised. I've seen your notebook full of *stuff*. All tidy and filed away, in case you need it. You've been itching to do this since the moment you set foot in this office. Maybe you're bolder than I gave you credit for, but it's not a surprise to find you in here."

"How can you just leave it unlocked?" Tina asked. "Anyone could come in here and steal something."

"What's there to steal?" he asked, raising his arms. "The magazines outside?"

"All of your files," Tina asked. He lifted his chin.

"The one you've got there in your hands. What is it?"

She remembered without needing to look.

"Alpaca," she said.

"What does that mean?" he asked. She shook her head.

"Doesn't make any difference to me," she said.

"Open it," he told her.

She did.

She found pictures of fuzzy quadrupeds.

"Those are alpacas," she said.

"They are. Keep going," Tell told her.

She flipped through a dozen pages, frowning as she got past the photos and the diagrams to page after page of…

"It's encoded," she said.

"I speak nineteen languages," Tell said. "Including my own. That's my language, and I guarantee you it would take a team of linguists a decade to figure it out."

"You a savant?" Tina asked, and he grinned.

"What a word," he said. "Covers a multitude of

things, doesn't it, if you're willing to ignore what it actually means?"

Tina tipped her head to the side, frowning.

"You're weird."

"You think people go into this business because they're normal?" Tell answered. She shrugged.

"Fair point. I'm ready."

"I don't know what you're talking about," Tell said, going to sit down in his chair. "Hey, look, my keyboard."

"Yeah, it was there on the desk the whole time," Tina answered. "Do you really need to keep all of these? What's your retention plan?"

"Still don't know what you're talking about," Tell said.

"You don't have a document retention plan?" Tina asked.

"Nope," Tell told her.

"You should have one," Tina said, going around the desk to sit in one of *two* empty client chairs. "I just wrote the one at work."

They hadn't had one, there, either.

"Okay," Tell said, looking at his computer.

"I'm ready for you to tell me," she said.

He glanced at her.

"Tell you what?"

"What happened to my parents," Tina said.

"Oh, I don't know," he said. "I was working on something else, today."

She leaned slowly out over her knees, looking him steadily in the eye. It was a motion that always drew attention, but he seemed oddly unnerved.

"You hinted, yesterday, that something important and *bad* happened," she said. "That I might not even want to know, it was so bad. Was it a con? Were you trying to get rid of me, so that you could tell me it was all *taken care of* and not *do* anything for the money I gave you?"

He held her eye easily, blinking once, then leaning back in his chair and putting his feet up on the desk.

"You know, it is nice to be able to move in here," he said, looking around.

"Bite me," Tina said, and he laughed as she stood.

"It's bad, doll," he said, weaving his hands behind his head. "I just don't know how bad, yet. And I really was trying to give you an opportunity to walk away before it broke your whole life."

"It already broke my whole life," Tina said, barely containing her emotions below shouting level. She put her hand over her mouth to keep more from coming out, and she staggered, grabbing the back of the chair with her other hand and holding on tight for fear of falling over. "My parents are dead. Dead. Gone. I can't even imagine what they went through, how afraid they were. And no one did anything to help them. No one is even doing anything, *now*, to make it right, except me."

"The police are trying," Tell said. "Detective Keller is a good man. He's doing his best, but he doesn't have the leads that I do."

Tina lifted her chin.

"Are you a bad man?" she asked.

He nodded once, still unconcerned.

"One of the worst," he said easily. "But I'm still going to figure out who killed your parents and I'm still going to make sure that they pay for it. It's clear that that's what you want. I just… You're a nice lady, kind eyes, sense of humor. I hate to see that kind of thing go to waste, and this is one of the times that it might happen."

"Just… freaking… tell me," she said, strangling herself.

"They were looking for something," Tell said. "Used gloves and put everything back that they were interested in, but they were all over that house, including the attic, going through things. I don't know if they found it or not, because they would have killed your parents either way, but I don't think that your parents told them where to find it, because the torture wasn't that bad, and it was all early. If they'd spilled it, he would have killed them last thing."

"My parents weren't *interesting*," Tina said. "I told you that."

"Could be mistaken identity," Tell said. "It happens. Could be they had a misadventure and *got* interesting. Could be you really don't know them that well."

"That's it?" Tina asked. "You don't know anything? You're just warning me off because maybe I don't know my parents that well?"

"I'm telling you that someone searched your childhood home for something," Tell said. "And that they might still be looking for it, if they didn't find it."

That struck Tina anew.

"You're saying I might be in danger," Tina said.

"I wouldn't rule it out," Tell said.

"And you wanted me to just pretend like it didn't happen?" Tina demanded, and he gave her a quiet, dry smile.

"They've left you alone, so far, but if you start *acting* interesting, maybe they'll change their mind about you. Just doing what you're doing, now, they haven't come for you. Either they found what they were looking for, they don't *know* about you, or they think you've got nothing to do with it. If they're still on the hunt, though, you don't want to attract attention. And if they catch wind of me, you having constant contact is going to lead them straight back to you."

Tina sat, the wind gone out of her.

"The police didn't tell me I was in danger," she said.

"The police don't know that they searched the house," Tell answered.

She twisted her mouth.

It didn't make sense.

It didn't *compute*.

"I don't understand," she said. "My dad was a professor and my mom taught art."

"I'm still looking into it," Tell said. "A lot of things could be true. What I do believe is that the man who searched your house knew how to find what he wanted and knew how to cover his tracks. That's not a random robbery, nor is it a spur-of-the-moment attack. You're dealing with someone who is calculating and focused.

That's not someone you want to go up against, if you can help it. Not *you*."

"What about you?" Tina asked, overwhelmed.

He smiled.

"I'm weird, and I know how to take care of myself."

"You leave your office unlocked," Tina said. "I could have been in here with a gun."

"Wouldn't have been the first, won't be the last," Tell said. "Don't worry about me. No one's got me yet."

She slouched lower in her chair.

"What will you do next?"

"I've got a few ideas of what they were looking for, based on where they were looking. I want to talk to a couple of dealers and see if they've heard anything interesting, and then I've got a couple of scum contacts who might know about a guy who's this focused on finding something he lost."

"You think they had something that *belonged* to someone else?" Tina asked.

Tell shook his head, as though correcting a remedial student.

"I don't *think* anything. I think it's possible, and that's how I find things. I go check things that are possible until I prove that they aren't possible, or I prove that they're true. Don't write anything off just because you think it's unlikely, and go check the less-likely rocks, first, because Detective Keller will have checked under all of the obvious ones."

"You do this part time?" Tina asked, and he

grinned.

"I do what I like to do," he said. "I like answering questions. Things you don't know; they're what keep life interesting."

"What else do you do?" Tina asked. "Part time private eye."

"Lots of things," he said with another grin. "None I'm particularly interested in telling you about. When are you going back to your job with the prick boss?"

"I don't know," Tina said. "Why?"

"Because the sooner you have something taking up all of your spare time, the better. I don't like how nosy you are. You're going to get yourself into trouble."

"That reminds me," Tina said. "I have notes. I meant to show them to you, but you… Anyway. I have notes."

She went to get her binder, opening it on the desk and turning it to face him. He shook his head, then began to page through it.

"It's worse than I thought," he said, and Tina tipped her head to look at the page he was on.

"What?" she asked.

"You are going to get yourself killed," he said. "If this guy is anything like the pro I think he is, he's going to feel your breath on the back of his neck long before you catch a *glimpse* of him… You need to go back to work. Get in over your head on a project that has nothing to do with this. Let me work."

"No," Tina said. It was out of her mouth before she even thought about it. Tell sat back in his chair, looking at her for a long moment, but Tina held her ground.

"Do you want to die?" he asked, calm.

"I don't know," Tina said. "No. I mean, no, I don't want to die, but I'm… I don't know. I'm not really afraid of it, right now. I'm too angry."

He nodded slowly.

"I can work with that," he said. "You're in danger. Assume that. Carry whatever weapon you're comfortable with, practice with it. If you've ever shot a gun or ever wanted to, now is the time to spend some time at a range. Just be prepared. You married? Live in boyfriend? Roommate? Anything?"

"I live alone," Tina said.

"You have a big dog?" Tall asked.

"No."

"Shame," he said. "None of them are going to stop a guy like this, but they might slow him down long enough for you to get out."

"You would have me sacrifice another human being in order to get away?" Tina asked. "No. Just… No. That's obscene."

"Just saying," Tell said. "What do you have for security at your house?"

"Apartment," she said. "Just, you know, a deadbolt on the door."

"You have a glass back door?" he asked, and she nodded.

"Onto a balcony."

"Even better," Tell muttered. "Climb up there,

break in, no one's even going to care until the place starts to smell."

"Smell," Tina said, and he nodded.

"You're the one who found your parents," he said. "Who do you think is going to find *you*?"

Sherry, maybe? She wasn't sure. There weren't a lot of people who would come looking for her, at this point in her life.

Not even work would know that she'd gone missing.

"I see your point," she said. "But I'm not going back to work. Not until I know what happened."

"Maybe not ever," Tell said. "You really do hate it, don't you?"

She shrugged.

"It's work. You're not supposed to love it."

He grinned.

"I do," he said. "And your parents did, too, didn't they?"

Defeat.

"Yes," she said.

Her father had told her hundreds of times, growing up, that if she found a job she loved, she'd never work a day in her life.

She had no idea what that meant, in her case, but it still lived in her head full time.

"I'm not going to tell you how to run your life," Tell said. "That's not what you're paying me for. But. I'd suggest *considering* a change in routine. Go be somewhere where people know you. Where you can count on them to care what happens to you. Someplace safe. Out of town would be best."

"I don't have any of those," Tina said.

Tell grimaced, then sighed.

"All right. Well, I'm not going to solve this in ten hours, so I need you to stay alive, if I'm going to collect my full rate. So don't die, okay? I hate it when my clients die."

"They have a habit of doing that, do they?" Tina asked, and he grinned.

"It's a dangerous business," he said. "I work on all kinds of things you wouldn't expect, and some of them involve people being in trouble."

Tina drew a slow breath and nodded.

"I'm going to come back tomorrow," she said. "Finish filing. If the phone rings, do you want me to answer it?"

"Um," Tell said. "You're serious, aren't you?"

"It's driving me crazy, the number of folders still just sitting around," she answered. "And it's something to do. No one to bother me by being inept, probably no one to kill me, right? I just… Yes. Unless you lock me out, that's what I'm going to do tomorrow."

He sighed.

"Um. Yes. Answer the phone. Write down whatever they say, verbatim, and leave it here. Don't have any conversations. Okay?"

"I can't believe you don't have a cell phone," Tina said, and he laughed.

"Oh, I do. I just don't give out the number to the likes of you."

He looked over at his computer, then back at her.

"Now, I don't like just hanging out here. I've got stuff to get done, and then people to go stalk. Okay? Don't die. You're too cute to die."

"What?" Tina asked, and he grinned, but he didn't look at her. After a moment, she went to collect her binder from his desk, and he put his hand out to cover it.

"I'll be keeping that," he said without looking at her, and she tugged at it.

"It's mine," she complained.

"It's trouble," he answered. "I'm keeping it."

She tried once more to recover it, but his grip was merciless.

"Fine," she said. "But I want it back. There's a lot of personal stuff in there."

"And it's just written in plain English," Tell answered. "I'll give it to you after everything is over, but not before."

"Fine," she said again. "I'll see you tomorrow."

He scoffed, but he didn't look at her and he didn't argue.

Good enough for her.

She didn't sleep well that night.

She woke up a dozen times, listening to noises in the apartment building and wondering if it was someone coming to kill her. She got up and checked the lock on the door, then she put a windchime from the closet onto the back door, just in case.

It might not have changed anything, but it made

her feel better.

In the end, she went to sit on the couch, holding a pillow and tucking herself in under a heavy blanket, watching the sun come up outside before drifting off for a few hours.

She went out grocery shopping, getting fresh fruit and milk, glad to be out around people, then she went back to her apartment to put it all away, jumping when the deadbolt popped, then shaking her head at herself.

She was stronger than this.

Nothing had happened so far, which meant that it was unlikely that anything was *going* to happen, now or any other time.

Tell had given her the worst-case scenario - probably to mess with her - and it just… It wasn't going to happen.

She was going to be fine.

The problem was, opening the door, she didn't believe that.

There was the memory, in her very arms, of opening the door at her parents' house, the way the light wasn't right, the way the smell…

The apartment was dim.

She hadn't remembered to open the blinds before she left.

With her heart beating in her stomach, Tina forced herself through the door, closing it and locking it behind her.

There was a figure on the couch, and she dropped her groceries on the floor, the milk exploding all over her ankles as she staggered back a step.

She covered her mouth with both hands to hold in the scream as she realized that the figure was just the pile of blankets she'd left there that morning.

"Get a grip," she whispered, taking another step back. "Get a grip, get a grip, get a grip."

She looked down at the mess on the floor, bending over to pick up the fruit sprawling across the wood laminate, then she collapsed, wrapping her arms around her knees and sobbing.

She was so afraid.

It wasn't even Tell's fault.

She'd been afraid since the day her parents died, afraid that something else *bad* was going to happen, that the world, as perfect as she had always seen it to be, was just a sham, a con, something that was waiting for her to get comfortable in order to betray her again.

She was waiting for the other shoe to drop.

This.

This was just more specific than anything had yet been, for what she *should* be afraid of.

She stood, picking her purse up off of the floor and finding her keys where they'd scattered over against the bathroom door, then she walked back out, going to her car and driving to Tell's office.

She didn't know what she expected, but it was the only place she could think of to go.

He wouldn't be there.

And he'd never even suggested that he could *protect* her.

It was just…

She knew what she could *do* there.

He had her binder. Her thoughts, everything about what had happened to her parents.

All of it.

Without it sitting on the seat next to her in the car, she felt lost.

It was all she'd thought about for nearly two months.

She couldn't think *at all* without it.

So she went up to his office and she alphabetized things.

Had he said he wanted them chronological *and* alphabetical?

She thought that's what she remembered, so she started going through folders, looking for dates, and she started sorting things, first by year, then by demi-decade. He had stuff going back almost twenty years, so either he was older than she'd guessed by a fair margin, he had old cases he'd gotten along the way, or he'd inherited the business from someone else.

The *someone else* was her guess. Yeah, he'd translated the files into his odd language, but if his father had done this, or something, it would make sense why he was so odd, and why he was *good at it*, for as young as he was.

She went through the folders in the filing cabinets again, and the stack of unlabeled folders, doing what she could to help sort those, and by the time the orange sunlight started to hit the thick wooden blinds, signaling that evening was coming, she was putting things into filing cabinets.

There was still *so much* that she didn't know where it went, but it was a lot better than it had been, and she at least knew what she needed to ask him, in order to get things put away.

She sat down in the rolling chair, feeling fatigued for the first time all day, and she looked up to find him standing in the doorway.

"You been here all day?" he asked.

"Um," she answered. Looked around. "Yeah, I guess."

"You eat?" he asked. She shook her head.

"No. I forgot."

She had milk on the floor at home.

That was going to be a disaster.

"Come on," he said. "I've got stuff for you, but we can talk over food."

She nodded, numb, getting her purse from against the wall and following him out of the office.

"Shouldn't you be here?" she asked. "In case someone calls or something?"

"If it's important, they call back," Tell said. "If it isn't, they find someone else."

She licked her lips and followed, because it was easier to follow than it was to argue.

"You do a terrible job managing your business," Tina said.

"And yet, you turned up and put a check in my hands," Tell answered, not looking back at her as they went down yet another set of stairs.

"But why?" she asked. "If you're good… and I actually think you are… why not take on more work? Why not *try* to get clients?"

"Because that would mean that I would have to care," Tell told her, getting to the bottom of the stairwell and opening the door for her.

"You have files going back a long way," she said. "Was this… Did you inherit the business from someone else?"

Tell gave her a long, thoughtful look, then shook his head as she started for the front door.

"No, come on this way," he said, waving her toward the back. She followed him down a dim hallway to a small parking lot behind the building, where he unlocked a miniature, red sports car.

"You're a trust fund baby, aren't you?" she asked, finally seeing it. "You do whatever you want because you don't *need* the money."

"I don't need the money," he agreed.

"Then why charge me so much?" Tina asked.

"If it's important, they call back," Tell said. "If it's important, they cough it up. Gotta be selective somehow."

Tina stood as he got into the car, shaking her head at it, then opened the passenger side door and slid in.

"You sleep last night?" he asked as he started up the engine and revved it a couple of times.

"No," Tina admitted, "not really."

"And that's why you spent your whole day looking at encoded files about other people's problems?"

"I needed something to do," Tina said.

"Could go back to work," he said, backing out of the spot and flipping the car into drive with a brief tire squeal. He grinned as the zippy little machine bolted out of the parking lot and onto the side road in between his building and the next.

"I'm not going back until I know that this is handled," Tina said. And maybe not even then, she thought. He nodded.

"Well, I've done some digging. Not a lot, yet, but you provided a lot of interesting detail to the picture of what your parents were up to, and between the fact that you need money to pay your bills and you need something to do during the day, I was thinking that maybe you could be my office manager."

"Now, what now?" Tina asked. "You barely bother to show up at your own office, and you want me to *manage* it for you?"

He shrugged.

"I'm just asking. I mean, it would look better if there was someone actually there during daylight hours, and you can write things down when people call and I can get back to the ones I'm interested in working for. Maybe…" He looked over at her. "Maybe I could stand to be more professional."

She blinked.

"I didn't sleep last night because I was afraid that a hit man was going to break into my apartment and torture me," she said. "And you want me to sit in your office by myself all day, in that shady building, and meet with your shady clients?"

He frowned.

"Basically. Do you want to do it or not?"

"Yes," she said. She surprised herself, being as eager as she was, but she *wanted* to. All of those files to go through, and being able to actually make him sit down with her and go through them, maybe even teach her enough of the language in them to be able to figure out how to file them.

To take the chaos of that office and make it clean.

She wanted to clean it.

"I'm getting you new magazines," she said, and he grinned.

"I'm so attached to the ones I already have," he said. "They're like old friends."

She shook her head, and he turned into a diner parking lot, turning off the engine again.

"We can work out the details when we get back to the office," he said. "Meanwhile, I did some digging into who might have been available to go after your parents, if he was for hire. I'm guessing that it wasn't a hired job, because odds are better that the guy who was doing the looking was the one who went to their house, but it doesn't hurt to turn over some rocks, as long as I'm doing it."

Tina blinked at the diner, her momentary appetite gone.

"Okay," she said.

"I've got a bunch of them that I know where they were, but there are three I'm going to see tonight who could have been there."

She nodded, swallowing hard.

"Okay. What will you do?"

"I'll ask them if they did it," Tell said, and she looked over.

"You'll what?"

He grinned.

"I'll ask them. If they killed your parents."

"And if one of them actually did?" Tina asked. "He'll kill you."

Tell frowned and shook his head.

"I'm harder to kill than that."

"You aren't serious, are you?" she asked. "You're going to go spy on them and talk to their neighbors or whatever? You aren't actually going to *talk* to them."

"You got me," he said with a wink, getting out of the car. He stood waiting for her, and she stared at the diner for another moment.

Could it be that easy?

Finally she got out and closed her door.

"You think you could find the guy who did it tonight?" she asked.

He shrugged.

"I think that every night," he said. "I mean, why not? There's nothing *stopping* me. Every lead I follow could be the last one I need."

She swallowed.

"But what about evidence?" she asked. He motioned for her to follow him into the diner and they sat down at the far-end booth.

"That's part of what we need to talk about

tonight," he told her. "What do you want me to do, when I find this guy?"

"Find a way for the police to catch him," Tina said. "Turn over what you have to Detective Keller and make sure that they catch him."

Tell shook his head.

"I'm not sure you're understanding," he said. "And I think it's because you're choosing not to. There's another option."

"What?" Tina asked.

"I could kill him," Tell said.

Tina stared at him.

He seemed... serious.

What had she gotten herself into?

She'd gotten into *a car* with him, not even thinking about it. Because he smelled good and his clothes were clean and he had a neat haircut and a nice smile, she'd let herself believe that he was a nice guy, a good guy.

He wasn't.

He hung out with underworld men who did bad things, and...

Well, apparently he was willing to kill people.

Sherry had been right.

She was supposed to have brought Sherry, wasn't she?

Or something.

Before she took a *job* with the guy...

Don't make any big decisions, right now.

She was still grieving.

Still irrational.

Very, very upset.

And afraid.

Knowing that the man who killed her parents was *gone. Permanently.*

It was actually tempting.

"No," she finally said, realizing how long he'd been watching her.

The waitress came over and Tina belatedly looked at the menu, ordering a burger and fries because it seemed safe enough, without having looked around at the quality of the restaurant, nor any of its food options.

"Just a coffee for me, Bea," Tell said with a smile, taking Tina's menu and handing it over.

"No," Tina said again. "No."

"Good girl," Tell said, looking out the window.

"You… you wouldn't?" Tina asked. He grinned.

"Oh, I would," he said, turning his head slowly to look at her again, "but I'd have been disappointed in you if you took me up on it. It's not a decision you can ever walk away from. I'm not sure you could live with it."

"Would you stop talking to me like you know me?" Tina asked. "You don't. You barely know anything about me, and, no, I don't want you to do another of those detective-y tricks to try to prove that you can *read* me or whatever. You don't know me."

"Fine," Tell said. "I don't know you."

"And you have to stop patronizing me," Tina said. He looked amused. It was infuriating. "I'm a strong woman who knows her own mind. I don't need you telling me what I should or shouldn't do, and what I can or can't live with."

"So do you want me to kill the guy, if I find him?" Tell asked.

"No," Tina said, exasperated. "And I'll tell you why. First, because you can't know for *a fact* that he did it. There's a risk that you'd kill an innocent man. That's what the *legal* system is for. Second, because he deserves a trial, even if he is the guy who did it, because everyone deserves a trial. Third, because every guy we catch and convict, as a society, is a deterrent to other miscreants who might do bad things, and if you just kill him dead, no one is ever deterred by it…"

"I disagree," Tell said with a wink. "Just with that one."

"Okay, and, four, was I on four? Four. I want to see his face when he finds out he's going to spend the rest of his life in prison. I want to be there for that."

"And it has nothing to do with the condition of your conscience, knowing that instead of a detective, you hired a hit man and made yourself no better than the man who hired this guy to kill your parents?"

"That's a good reason, too," Tina said. He grinned. "You really would?" Tina asked, and he nodded.

"I only kill really, really bad people, because you're right, there's never a way to be one hundred percent sure that they did *this* bad thing. But, you know, if they do *lots* of bad things, anyway, I don't feel so bad, even when I find out I was wrong, later…"

"That happens?" Tina asked, leaning in closer. He shrugged.

"You make enough decisions in life, some of them come up wrong," he said. "I learned a while back that I have to just keep going and keep making decisions. No point in letting the inevitability of one wrong decision paralyze you permanently."

"You aren't eating?" Tina asked, a different neuron firing in her brain. He laughed.

"No. I actually ate breakfast before I came to work today. Shocker."

She licked her lips.

"I thought the blanket on the couch was someone waiting in my apartment to kill me," she said.

He narrowed his eyes.

"If you go back there tonight, will you do better? Was it a one-night thing, or do you think you're going to have a hard time sleeping comfortably until this is over?"

"I don't know," Tina said. "I hadn't thought about it."

"Well, think about it," he said. "Do you have somewhere else to go?"

"I guess I could get a hotel room," Tina said. "I mean, if you could end this *tonight*, that wouldn't be a big deal, but I don't want to live at a hotel if this is going to take another six weeks."

"It could," Tell said. "I can't promise anything about how long it's going to take."

She sighed, nodding.

"I don't… I don't really have any friends who I could ask," she said slowly. Sherry would try, but she lived with her boyfriend in a loft apartment that was full of his artwork. They would clear off the couch for her, if she asked, but it would be awkward. Devon didn't much like Tina. She'd told Sherry early on that she could do better than a failing artist who needed her to pay off his art school loans. He'd found a way to make a business online, doing commercial design work, but he'd never forgotten her assessment of him.

"Well, think about it," Tell said. "If you don't feel safe at your apartment, you should make a different plan."

She nodded, taking the basket of fries from the waitress and reaching for the bottle of ketchup at the end of the table. The burger was somewhere down inside the mountain of fries, and she dug it out, dousing it with ketchup before she filled in the void where it had been in the tray with the same.

Tell sipped his coffee and looked around the diner.

"I like this place," he said. "The hours that I tend to come here, there's never anyone else here, and the waitress, Bea, she's sweet on me, but she keeps to herself. Smells like people, instead of like cleaner or food, you know, people who are going places and doing things. Working people."

"Says the man who only works when he wants to," Tina said, thinking that to her the place smelled like grease and ketchup.

Could have just been the burger, though.

Which was awesome.

"Would you work?" he asked. "If you didn't have to?"

"Are you good at what you're doing?" Tina asked

back, and he shrugged.

"Probably the best alive."

She rolled her eyes.

"Ego much? Do you *help* people, doing what you do?"

He nodded.

"Yes. Sometimes."

She tipped her head to the side.

"I don't work for bad guys," she said, and he grinned.

"What about ones who play both sides of the line, depending on how it entertains them?"

"That might be worse," Tina said, and he smiled, putting one arm out along the back of the booth.

"You aren't going to talk me into being *good*," he said. "You'll just have to make up your mind whether you want to work for me or not. I just like what you're doing with my office. Never thought I *wanted* it clean, but it turns out, it isn't so bad, so long as I'm not the one cleaning it."

"If I decide I don't want to work for you, you'll still find the man who killed my parents?" Tina asked.

"Of course," Tell said, insulted. "I said I would. I mean, I can't *promise* I will, but, yes, I will."

"You're an over-indulged man child," she said. "Spoiled and egotistical. I work with a lot of those, and I'm surprised I didn't see it right off."

He laughed.

"I may be all of those things," he said. "I can't say I'm not. But I'm nothing like the boys you work with."

Tina shook her head.

"We'll see. I need you to tell me what's in a lot of the folders that I have left."

"I'm busy," he said. "Just make your best guess, and then... You know, if I need something, I'll ask."

"You know this is temporary, right?" Tina asked. "I... Look, I don't even know why I'm agreeing to do it, but I have a *job*, and I'm going back to it, eventually. Once you figure out what happened with my parents... You just shouldn't let me hide things away from you where you can't find them."

He lifted his chin and rolled his jaw to the side, grinning.

"I trust you," he said. Tina sighed, exasperated, but he only stole one of her French fries and grinned wider.

She felt better after she ate, but not so much better that she was ready to go back to her apartment. She took a room at a motel for the night, paying with a credit card and then regretting it. And then feeling quite silly.

Who was *actually* going to be able to get her credit card activity to track her down, here? Tell thought that it was someone shady and underworld-y, and they didn't have access to that.

Did they?

She put the bar lock across the door and sat down on the bed, flipping channels without watching them go by until her brain felt numb enough to lay down.

She didn't have toiletries, nor clothes to change into. There was a palm-sized bar of soap in the bathroom and a multi-purpose bodywash/shampoo in the shower, and that was it.

She'd need to get a toothbrush, tomorrow, at least.

Did Tell's building have bathrooms anywhere?

Surely it did.

She just couldn't find them, in her mind's eye.

She was uncomfortable in her jeans, but she wasn't willing to take them off to sleep.

What if she needed to run? Needed to move quickly? She didn't want to have to sprint out to her car in her underwear.

Not in this cold.

She pulled her jacket off of the end of the bed and spread it over top of her, and the extra weight helped her finally fall asleep.

She woke up the next morning confused and disoriented, not remembering where she was, sore almost everywhere from falling asleep in an awkward position and never fixing it, overnight.

She'd slept through the night, though.

She sat up, looking around in the dim, trying to place the furniture, the walls, the shape and smell of the place, and then she remembered.

Someone might try to kill her.

She picked her phone up off of the night stand and frowned.

That couldn't be right.

Could it?

It was almost eleven o'clock in the morning.

The blackout curtains had outdone themselves,

and she'd massively overslept her first day of work at Tell's office.

Not that she *thought* she needed to be on time.

No.

It was just…

Well, if you were going to do something, it was worth doing it the right way, and that meant keeping professional hours.

She got up and did her best to get her hair back into shape, finding a hair band in her purse to put it up when she gave up on it, then she went out to her car and drove to Tell's building, letting herself into his office and going back into the back room, where her work from yesterday lay almost completely untouched.

There were three opened folders on the desk, and she looked at them for a moment, not taking anything valuable away from them, so she closed them and went to put them back away the way the notes on the front indicated - her handwriting, this time.

There was something satisfying, knowing that he'd been able to find what he'd needed, even after she'd filed it.

She settled in to work for a couple of hours, then went and got lunch at the same diner as the night before, just playing around on her phone until she finished eating, and then going back to the office.

When she opened the door, she hesitated.

Something had changed.

The feel off the place had shifted.

She turned her head slowly, looking around the

door to find a burly man sitting in the corner, reading a decade-old People magazine.

She licked her lips.

"Can I... help you?" she asked.

"Just waiting for the freak," the man said, his voice deep, resonating out of his chest. She swallowed.

"The freak?"

"Same one you're here to see," the man said. "Tell."

"Actually," Tina said, closing the door. "I'm working for him, now. Is there anything *I* can do to help?"

The man squinted at her, then set down the magazine and stood, coming to look down at her from much closer.

"Who are you?" he asked. She shook her head.

"Just a client who took an interest," she said. "I, you know, take messages and things."

"You know how to get him to show up?" the man asked.

"Nope," Tina said. "I suspect that that would make me less of an assistant and more of a miracle worker."

The man laughed.

"I like you," he said. "Let's talk."

"Okay," Tina said quickly. "Let's talk. Would you like to go sit?"

She motioned, then followed him into the back office.

"Name's Marcus," the man said, offering her a meaty palm. She shook with him then sat down in Tell's chair, getting out a pad of legal paper from the middle drawer and a yellow pencil.

"Hello, Marcus," she said. "I'm Tina. What can I do for you today?"

"I've had something go missing," Marcus. "Something very valuable to me, and to my confederates, and Tell is just the guy to get it back."

"I see," Tina said, writing down brief notes. "Can you tell me anything about it?"

"How did you end up here?" Marcus asked.

She glanced up.

"Beg your pardon?"

"Here," Marcus said. "Tell. How did you meet him?"

"Picked his name at random from an internet listing," Tina said candidly.

"And what's he doing for you?" Marcus asked.

"That's personal, if you don't mind," Tina answered, and he nodded.

"The item," he said. "It's personal."

"Okay," Tina said, writing it down. "Well, um. Do you know… Is it *missing*, or is it *stolen*? Do you know?"

"Likely I've been betrayed," Marcus said. She nodded, writing that down.

"You think that someone close to you took it," she said.

"I do," Marcus told her. "Which is part of the reason I'm coming here. Tell is the type who can find a thing and turn over the guy who took it without asking too many questions about what happens next."

Tina looked up at him, and Marcus smiled.

She licked her lips again and nodded.

"I see. So you've worked with him before?"

"He's done things for me, yeah," Marcus said.

"So he'll know how to contact you, when he gets in?" Tina asked. Marcus grunted.

"He wouldn't need to *know* me to know how to find me," the man said. "That's what he *does*."

Tina nodded.

"He's… intimated to me that he doesn't do all of the work that comes in the door. If he declines to take this on, how should I let you know?"

Marcus laughed.

"He'll do it. He always does what I pay him to, because he likes what I do for him."

Tina frowned at him and Marcus shook his head slowly.

"Don't ask, sister. You're just some chick off the street. I'm not interested in discussing my business with you."

Tina set down her pencil.

"How about Tell?" she asked. "Would you be willing to discuss him?"

Marcus laughed again, standing.

"You just saved me half a day, hanging out waiting for the freak to show up," he said. "But I'm not going to tell you anything about that man. I like the deal he and I got going, and I'm in no mood to mess it up."

He touched his brow and started for the door.

Pausing, he looked over his shoulder.

"You need to be careful, miss. I ain't the worst of Tell's people, and he makes a lot of *other* people angry. They get wind that he's got someone like you up here? Well, let's just say there are the smart ones who know better than to make him angry, and then there are the dumb ones too stupid to figure out that you're the leverage, but there in the middle? There are some dangerous guys."

Tina frowned, and he touched his brow again, hulking out of the room and then out of the office, closing the door behind him with what seemed like an unintentional thud.

Tina sat quietly at the desk for a moment, considering, then shrugged it off.

She wasn't at all suggesting that the man was wrong.

There just wasn't anything she was going to *do* about it, for right now.

No one knew she was here but Marcus, and for some reason she trusted him - trusted his motivations, anyway - to not put her in danger, no matter what the nature of Tell's business was.

She should have left.

There was no question about it.

But.

The young man who occupied this seat, the way he read her, the easy grin.

She wasn't *mesmerized* by it. Intrigued, even, was too strong a word.

She just liked it.

Liked the *confidence* of it.

Wanted to be around that kind of confidence.

So she stayed.

Went back to the files.

Happily enough.

Tell didn't get in until almost midnight.

Tina had been planning on leaving for two hours, but kept stalling, in case he walked in just after she left and she didn't get to give him Marcus' message.

"Morning," he said playfully, going to turn on his computer.

"Where have you been?" Tina asked, and he grinned at the screen.

"What business of that is yours?" he answered.

"I work for you now," she said. "And you work for me. So. I think I'm allowed to ask."

"Fine," he said. "You can ask."

"A man named Marcus came today," she said, and his face turned.

"Oh?"

She nodded.

"He said that he has something that's gone missing, and he thinks one of his friends took it."

"Marcus Calloway did not use the word *friends*," Tell said, and Tina grinned despite herself.

"No. He didn't. He said something about them being close to him or something. He wouldn't tell me what was missing, but he said that you would take the case and that you knew how to contact him."

Tell resituated himself in his chair, folding his fingers under his chin.

"Marcus told you all of that?" he asked.

"Yes," Tina said. "It isn't that much."

Tell lifted his chin.

"How many words did he use, while he was here?"

"I don't know," Tina said, finding the question quite odd. "A few hundred, maybe?"

"I've seen that man have a conversation in nothing but grunts," Tell said.

"Well, he looked the type," Tina said. "But, then, he called you the freak."

Tell laughed.

"I'll go see him tonight," he said. "I went to see two of my possible leads last night, by the way. Asked about your parents. Neither of them knew anything."

"Are they both still breathing?" Tina asked under her breath, and he turned to look at her again.

"What did you just ask me?" he asked, and she looked up from the folder she was passively holding.

"Um. Just. The way Marcus talked about you. He seemed to… I don't know if he was insinuating that you were dangerous, or if you just hung out with dangerous people, but he said that if the people… I don't know, the ones you hang out with or whatever, if they found out that I was here, some of them would know better and some of them wouldn't put it together at all, but that some of them would try to use me as leverage against you."

Tell nodded slowly.

"Marcus Calloway," he said. "Smarter than he

looks."

"What was he talking about?" Tina asked.

"He's right," Tell said. "I need to get the word out that you're here, working for me. There are people that I want to get ahead of that story before they get it the wrong way."

Tina frowned, setting down the folder.

"I don't understand," she said. "Why would anyone care who you've got sorting folders in your office during the day?"

And, more importantly, should she even *be* here, if her presence made her a target for the kind of people that Marcus Calloway thought were reckless and violent?

"You should come with me, tonight," he said. "I mean, there's stuff I want to go do that there's no way in hell I'd bring you along, but just to go see Marcus. You…" He licked his lips, leaving his tongue peeking through pale skin thoughtfully as he looked at her. "The world I run in, Ms. Matthews, it isn't a pretty one. There are good people and bad people, just like any slice of the world, and honestly I kind of hang out in the middle, because I can't be bothered. But the broader world, it needs people like me who bridge gaps. Between good and bad. Between civil and un-civil. I'm not ever going to apologize to you or anyone for being who I am and where I am. But I think that you… You've stumbled into this at a time where you're not thinking clearly, and it doesn't matter how much I warn you off, it's always going to be too vague to do much good. You need to see a piece of it for yourself, and then you can either go on vacation to the Bahamas or you can stay and work for me until I see this through. I'm not sure there's a middle case."

Tina walked around his desk, putting the stray folder next to the rotary phone there and sitting down in one of the client chairs.

"I work in an office full of twenty-somethings who are preoccupied with how they look and who likes who," she said. "The most dramatic day I've had at work involved a young woman who was trying to date three co-workers at the same time and then tried to break up with all three of them on the same day because she needed some *me time*. I don't… I'm not sure I know how to act like anything you just said is real."

He shrugged.

"Denial makes a lot of the world feel safer than it is," he said. "You could have a brain tumor, right this second, or a bomb sitting under your car, but if you accepted the potential for either one, you'd scare yourself so bad you'd never leave that chair again. You have to deny that bad things could happen in order to *do* anything. I certainly live that, every day. I've also seen it go wrong. Bad, bloody wrong. I'm done trying to warn you off, after tonight, though. You slept in a hotel last night because a pile of blankets made you jumpy. If that's how you feel about your life being in danger, you probably don't belong here. I can't keep you safe, because no one can. That's a promise I wouldn't even hint at. But. I take things seriously, I take people seriously, and I do work that matters to the people involved. And I promise never to engage you in a three-way."

Tina watched his face for a moment, wondering how far past the point where she had been supposed to call Sherry she actually was, then she stood, picking up her purse from the floor next to the desk.

"Let's go," she said.

He grinned.

"Good sport," he said, opening a desk drawer and taking out a gun. He showed it to her.

"You know how to use one of these?" he asked. She shook her head.

"Nope."

"Tomorrow, you learn. I'll give you the address of the shooting range where I practice, and I want you to go there and give them my name. They'll bill your session to me. Figure out what you're comfortable with, and then get *really* comfortable with it. All right?"

"A gun?" she asked. He nodded.

"Tomorrow you apply for your concealed carry permit, too. From here on, you don't go out unarmed."

It was oddly calming, the way he said it.

Matter-of-fact, like this was just how life worked.

She nodded.

"Okay."

"Okay," he said, getting more stuff out of the drawer and shoving it into his pockets. "Let's hit the road."

If Tell's building was in a run-down section of town, Marcus Calloway was in an area that was downright seedy.

Women stood out front of the building where Tell knocked on the door. Tina looked over at one of them, noting the torn fishnets and the belt of a skirt, and the woman licked her lips, sucking on her teeth audibly for a moment.

"Fresh meat," the woman said, and Tina smiled.

Didn't know why she did, hoped she didn't look like an idiot, but it felt like the right thing to do.

A man opened the door and looked Tell up and down, and then Tina, then he moved out of the way and Tell brushed past as though the man was inanimate. Tina followed, unable to resist looking up into the man's face. He narrowed his eyes at her and she kept on, following Tell down a hallway, past a pair of rooms where men were sitting at tables, playing cards. There was loud conversation and laughter, and then they were past.

Tell opened another door, holding it for Tina as she went into a very dim room. As her eyes adjusted, she found herself in a lounge type space, full of couches and low tables and the smell of smoke.

"Ballsy move, bringing her here," Marcus said from out of the gloom.

"You made a fine point," Tell answered, moving past Tina to go talk to a high-backed chair in the corner.

She was in an underworld lair.

This.

This was actually happening.

She took a step forward to stand closer to Tell, who glanced back at her.

"This is my new assistant," he said. "Which means she's under my protection, here and anywhere else. Spread the word, know her on sight."

Marcus laughed quietly.

"You overestimate your reach," the man said. "I can name a dozen men off the top of my head who will *pluck* her off the street to get back at you for something or another."

"You lost something," Tell answered, and Marcus cleared his throat.

"Everyone out."

The men in the room started to shuffle, uncoiling themselves from couches and snuffing out cigarettes.

"He means you, too," Tell murmured to Tina, and she stiffened.

"Where do you expect me to go?" she asked.

"You are a guest under my roof," Marcus said, standing. "No one will harm you, so long as you don't *wander*. Stay downstairs."

She looked at Tell, but she couldn't read his face. She drew a breath and sighed.

"All right," she said. "Just… Okay."

She followed the drift of men out the door and someone closed it behind him as they squinted in the relative bright of the external hallway.

"You want a drink?" someone asked, and Tina turned her head to look at a skinny man with a scar down the side of his face.

"Sure," she said. "Why not?"

"You look like you need a drink," the man said,

going into one of the two rooms and opening a refrigerator. He motioned to a couch at the side of the room, going over to the men sitting there and slapping at them.

"Get," he said. "Go on."

The men got up, complaining, and the one with the scar motioned again for Tina to sit. He handed her a beer bottle and she sat down slowly, very aware that the entire room was watching her.

She got out her keys to open the bottle with a key and the scarred man grinned, opening his on the wooden arm of the couch.

"So how do you know the freak?" he asked.

"He's working for me," Tina said, swallowing. "I cleaned his office."

The man frowned and nodded.

"You stupid?" he asked, friendly enough.

"Don't think so," Tina said, and the man laughed, looking around the room as to an audience.

"Can't you feel it, girl?" he asked. "That man, he ain't natural. Broke in every way that matters. You think we're bad guys? He's a bad guy's bad guy."

"Wouldn't that make him a good guy?" Tina asked, taking a big swallow of her beer and setting it back down on her knee as the room chuckled.

The scarred man shook his head.

"Oh, no," he said. "No, he's the boogie man, darling. The freak."

She couldn't make it fit.

Tell had an athletic build, but he wasn't that much

taller than she was, and he was slender by nature. Was he a ninja? Why did they respect him - fear him - like both he and they seemed to expect?

She drank another big swallow of her beer as the men watched her openly.

"So what is it you guys do?" she asked, and a laugh went around the room, sinister. "Little bit of everything?"

"This and that, this and that," the scarred man said.

"Whatever Marcus says," someone else muttered, and there was another laugh.

Tina tipped the beer back and finished in big gulps, then handed the bottle to the scarred man. He hooted.

"Now there's a girl who knows how it's done," he said. "You want to stay here with us instead of going with the freak, the boys and I could show you a good time."

"I told you, she's with me," Tell said evenly from the doorway, and the scarred man jumped back several feet from Tina.

"Of course," he said. "Of course. I was just teasing. She's so… tasty."

"And off limits," Tell said. He looked at Tina. "I'm done here."

She stood, glancing over at the scarred man and then looking around the room.

They still watched.

They knew things.

So many things she didn't.

She walked to the doorway as Tell took a step away from the front door, giving her a corridor to walk past him so he could follow her out into the night darkness.

"Well, that was... something," Tina said as they reached the edge of hearing range of the scanty women outside.

Tell looked over at her.

"Just a client," he mused, and she frowned.

"What does that mean?" Tina asked, and he gave her a sideways smile.

"That's what Marcus called you. He can't figure out why I've adopted you. Frankly, I can't either. You really are just a client. I should send you home and call you when I've found your guy. But..." He shook his head, shoving his hands into his pockets. "We really don't have many innocents, in this line of work. I think it's that I'm taken with the idea of actually meeting one."

"An innocent," Tina said flatly, and he grinned.

"Don't act so disgusted," he said. "It's a compliment."

"I disagree," she said. "It implies I have no life experience and I don't do anything interesting."

Tell laughed.

"When was the last time you went out and got blackout drunk, or danced on a table, or made out with a guy whose name you didn't know?"

She drew her head back.

"That doesn't make me an *innocent*," she said. He looked over.

"Have you *ever* done those things?" he asked. "I mean, even in your foolish youth?"

"No," she said. "I studied and I went to parties and I had a good time, but innocent and stupid... The fact that I wasn't stupid doesn't mean I'm *innocent*."

"Why is this bothering you?" he asked, going to open the passenger side door to his car for her.

"Because," she said, sitting down and letting him close the door, giving her a moment to think before she answered.

Why *did* it bother her?

He got in the other door and sat, putting the keys into the ignition but not starting the car. He watched her with open curiosity as she struggled.

"I don't know…" she started, then shook her head. "I'm adrift. I shouldn't be here. If… If my best friend knew I was here, she'd strangle me for being so stupid. I don't want to go home, I don't want to face clearing out all of my parents' stuff, I mean, I'm afraid, but… Why am I doing this? I just walked in… *there*… and… It was like, yeah, this is what I do. So what? And… I'm a manager in an office. That's it. I sort folders pretty well."

"Marcus liked you," Tell offered, and she sent him what was intended to be a glare, but that actually turned into a plea for help. He laughed.

"You need me like a hole in the head," he said. "And it's the same for me, right back at you. What the hell, though, right?"

She shook her head.

"What the hell?"

He drove.

She didn't ask where he was driving her.

She would have, six weeks ago, before the door to her parents' house, but tonight? She just put her head back against the headrest and enjoyed the feeling of the car accelerating.

"Give me your keys," Tell said, and she blinked, trying to figure out where she was.

They were downtown.

Not like, take-a-cab-or-get-a-bus downtown.

No.

Downtown downtown.

Buildings stretched up out of sight to either side, and Tell was parked in traffic.

"What?" she asked.

"Keys," he said. "Give me your keys. I'll go get you some basics from your apartment and bring them back in the morning."

She blinked again.

"What are you talking about?"

"I could just break in, wouldn't even know I was there, but I figured the symbolic value of handing them over would be important to you."

She tipped her head forward.

"What are you talking about?" she asked very slowly.

He pointed.

"That's my building. Vince, at the front desk, he'll stop you, but you just tell him that you're here with me, and he'll let you up."

Was her brain foggy and slow, or was he not making sense? She couldn't tell.

"Are you asking me…?" she started, then closed one eye, still trying to work it out. "I don't… I'm not interested in you. At all. Not, you know, like that. I mean, no offense…"

He rolled his eyes.

"I work all night," he said. "I'll be back around sunrise, give or take, and there's no reason you can't sleep in a real bed, tonight, in a building with a doorman and a security staff. I figured you'd sleep better."

"And… You're not making a pass at me," Tina said.

Tell licked his lips.

"You're not my type," he said. "Not remotely. I hate to admit it, but I really kind of like ditzy and vapid. Interested in me for my money and my power."

She looked over at the building again.

"I didn't realize you had *this kind* of money," she said. He laughed.

"It's short term," he said. "But you're safe here. Between whatever is going on with your parents and, damn if Marcus wasn't right, it's a good idea for you do be somewhere safe. Give me your keys, I'll get you some stuff from your apartment, and I'll bring it to you when I come back in the morning. But, seriously, in the morning, you have to go. Marcus really liked having someone actually *be* at my office when he got there."

"This is stupid," Tina said. "I don't know you."

"And you don't go home with strange men," Tell supplied. "I get it. And yet. This is what's going to happen."

He waited.

She reached into her pocket and gave him her keys, then picked up her purse.

"You won't be back until morning?"

"There's a gun in the silverware drawer," he said. "If anyone comes through that door before six tomorrow morning, feel free to shoot them."

"The silverware drawer," she said, and he grinned.

"I take home security seriously," he said. He flipped her keys around his finger once, then shooed her out of the car. She got out, facing the little sports car as it peeled out, then she turned and walked into the building.

A man at a concierge desk came around from behind his desk, holding out a white-gloved hand.

"Ma'am, may I help you?" he asked.

Tina looked down at her clothes, then up at him.

"Um," she said. "Tell told me to say that I was here with him…"

"Of course," the man said. "May I show you up to his penthouse?"

"Penthouse," Tina murmured, following the concierge to the elevator, where he used a keycard to summon it.

"Do you have to… The buttons don't do anything, without a card?" Tina asked.

"You can get down any time you choose, ma'am," the man said. "But, yes, only those with clearance can summon the lift, and only Tell and a few members of staff can access his floor."

He got onto the elevator with her, pushing the

button for the top floor, and Tina stood, watching the numbers count up.

"You're Vince?" she asked. He gave her a polite smile.

"Yes, ma'am," he said.

"I'm Tina Matthews," she said. She didn't know why she told him; it just felt like the right thing to do.

"Ms. Matthews," Vince said. "It's very nice to make your acquaintance."

"I… I'm not… *with* Tell," she said. "Not, like… I'm not a girl he's bringing home."

It bothered her that he would think it of her, but she regretted saying it the moment the words were out. Vince gave her another polite smile, though his eyes twinkled with a hint of humor.

"Yes, Ms. Matthews," he said. "Tell is very open with the women who are here for entertainment purposes. I don't think I've known him to have a woman here at night."

"Because he works at night," Tina said, and Vince nodded.

"You are a guest, and regardless of the situation, we will treat your presence here with utmost discretion. Please, feel free to contact me at the desk, should you require anything."

"This isn't a hotel," Tina said. "Right?"

Vince handed her a card.

"No, Ms. Matthews. This is a privately-owned building with a very well-to-do tenants' association. We are staffed and equipped for most anything you could think of, I think."

"I'd love a toothbrush," Tina said, and once more Vince smiled at her.

"At once," he said. "Can I interest you in a full grooming kit? I assume if you find yourself without a toothbrush, a hair brush, toothpaste, and showering supplies would be welcome, as well."

"Yes," Tina said. "Yes, thank you. I would appreciate that."

The elevator stopped, and Vince used his keycard once more. The doors opened, and Vince motioned with his arm for Tina to precede him into the apartment.

"Does he just leave all of the lights on all of the time?" Tina asked.

"There is a butler program that turns them on when the elevator arrives," Vince said, coming to stand next to her. "Would you like a guided tour?"

"No," Tina said. "No, but thank you very much. I think… I think I just need a minute to get… acclimated."

"Very good," he said. "I will send someone up shortly with your toiletries."

"Thank you," Tina said, belatedly reaching into her purse to tip him.

"Ma'am," Vince said. "Please. The tenants here are very generous. It would insult them and me to imply that a guest to the building owed me anything."

"What kind of place is this?" Tina asked, and Vince gave her a little bow, reaching for the button inside the elevator.

"I've worked desks for a very prestigious career,

ma'am, but I have never worked in a building like this one."

He gave her a nod and pushed the button, bringing the doors to a close.

Tina took her coat off and started to put it on a couch, then thought better of it and went looking for a coat closet.

The place was *obscene*.

The floor under her feet looked for all the world like white marble, and a staircase went up along her left hand, sweeping through an arc to a balcony that spanned the width of the main room, with banks of windows behind, both on the first floor and up on the second. The couches were black leather, and the furniture was mahogany. White marble railings were inlaid with silver in intricate patterns, and a carved lion roared at her from the bottom of the handrail.

"And he took my money," Tina muttered, finding the closet off to her right to be full of heavy fabric jackets, dark colors.

This was not the man that sat behind the desk covered in manila folders and answered a rotary phone.

Not even the man who drove a little red sports car.

She was looking at the coats for a man who went to operas and bought his wife things made out of mink and diamond.

She pulled out a velvet hanger and put her bright purple winter coat onto it, sliding all of the rest of the jackets off to the side to keep from touching them with her coat when she went to hang it back up.

She turned to face the apartment again, sliding her

feet out of her shoes and tucking them there next to the closet door, then she walked in, just a few paces, to lean against the back of the nearest couch.

"He took my money," she said again.

And he'd gone to see Marcus Calloway, today, to take a job to find something another underworld thug had stolen from him.

"Is he Batman?" she asked no one.

She wandered through the parlor and under the balcony, going past a kitchen that was arrayed along the wall under the stairway in a sort of amphitheater style, arranged to show off a chef's skills as he worked. To her right, there was a large dining table with ornate high-backed chairs and origami cloth napkins on bone china. She went past that to stand at the windows at the far wall, looking down at the city below her.

Even at this hour, buildings had lights on, and street lights traced out the road network as it sprawled away from her. Headlights and streetlights danced, and the wind blew by with enough force to whistle.

There were cafe tables there along the windows, with bar-height chairs, and she sat down in one, appreciating the view for several minutes, then she went wandering back into the kitchen to check the refrigerator.

It was empty.

"Bachelor," she muttered, finding the pantry. It was stocked with staples, and she found a box of crackers that looked promising. She set them on the counter, then got herself a glass and poured herself a glass of ice water.

Above the counter, there was a very nice wine rack,

and a wine fridge was underneath the island on one side, but she wasn't going to show up here and drink his wine.

The crackers, though, were another story. She took them back to the cafe table and ate half the box, surprised at how hungry she was.

Breathing, here, was easier than it had been… in weeks, in truth.

Up above it all, with a man downstairs with a keycard, and no one else could even come up. Nothing could touch her.

She could have gone dredging for grief and guilt and anxiety, but she let them be, just eating her crackers and watching the headlights far below.

Eventually, she sated her appetite - at least for crackers - and she folded down the sleeve she was working on, returning the box to the pantry.

There was a gym and game room behind the kitchen, lights off, and there was a hallway going the other direction, but Tina was reasonably confident that the bed she was looking for was going to be upstairs.

And she still felt a bit odd, just openly exploring the place, even if Tell had left her here completely unsupervised and not said a word about keeping to herself.

She went cautiously up the staircase, the marble cold even through her socks, and jumped when the elevator dinged, behind her. She turned to watch a woman in a maid's uniform walk into the front foyer.

"Ms. Matthews," the woman said cheerfully. "I brought these for you."

She offered Tina a cloth-lined wicker basket with a

bounty of toiletries in it, smiling broadly as Tina came down to take it.

"Thank you," she said.

"Have a good evening," the woman answered, getting back onto the elevator and disappearing.

Tina shook her head, looking at the brands on the soap, the shampoo, the conditioner.

They'd included a razor, nail clippers, and a nail file, as well as a sleeping mask and facial scrub.

She tucked the basket under her elbow and started up the stairs again, reaching the balcony and looking down at the entryway from above.

It was startlingly beautiful, elegant, and it made her uncomfortable, so she kept moving, walking the length of the balcony to a wide hallway. On either side, there were a pair of double doors, and another pair of double doors at the end. The ones at the end were open, and while Tina hesitated, she did ultimately go peek through the ones at the end.

Tell's room.

It was dark, a dark carpet and dark furniture, but she could make out large, expensive pieces, including a huge bed with great wooden pillars at all four corners.

She stepped back into the hallway, feeling a touch guilty until she remembered that he was going to be going through her things, tonight, to pack them. Just *looking* at his room was hardly disproportionate.

She went back to one of the pairs of doors off of the hallway and pushed them open, finding a cream-and-rose colored room with a canopy bed and a one wide dresser with a huge mirror over it.

"Sold," she murmured, pushing open another door to find a cream-tiled bathroom with a large walk-in shower and linen closet. She set down the basket on the counter, in there, then went back into the main room, sitting down on the bed. The thick down comforter almost swallowed her whole, and she lay back onto it, just enjoying the cool, slippy soft of it.

The room smelled clean, of fabric softener and fresh air, and the bed was the most comfortable thing she'd ever laid on. She forced herself up and into the bathroom again just long enough to brush her teeth and wash her face, then she went and turned out the lights, looking up at the ceiling as gentle, rose-colored light lit it up from a ledge running all the way around the room.

She went to lay down again, struck by the light and the way it kept the room from being *dark*, while at the same time keeping her from feeling like there were *lights* on. She tucked her feet into the bed, feeling a bit odd, and a bit inappropriate, that she was still dressed, but once she got settled in, it didn't take long for her to forget what she was wearing.

She snuggled in deep to the pillows, closing her eyes.

She should have felt out of place.

She should have felt like she was making a hasty and ill-advised decision.

She should have worried that Tell, a man she hadn't yet known a full week, was giving her access to his apartment, where no one could get in but him.

These were all things that she was aware of, somewhere in the back of her mind, that she should have been fidgeting and worried over, that they should have been keeping her awake.

But the blankets were so nice and the pillows smelled so clean…

She woke up comfortable.

Unrushed.

She remembered where she was, after a time, but it didn't really change it.

Tell didn't use this room. It was clear that it was spare from how pristine everything was, how it didn't smell like people at all, and she was tucked away in it, out of his way, even if he did come home before she left.

She rolled over, finding her phone on a night stand where she'd left it the night before. She needed to plug in the charger she had in her purse, at some point, but she'd let it be, the previous night.

Ten in the morning.

She was late.

Technically.

She rolled back onto her back, just breathing, enjoying the sensation of *not worrying*.

She was still above it all, still up here where her worries didn't seem to rise in elevation by enough for her to consider them.

She sat up and went to take a shower, where the excess was just as excessive as everywhere else. There were six shower heads in the shower, and the back wall had a bench that went from one side of the shower to the other.

You could drown a person in there.

And it never ran out of hot water.

She took her time showering, then got out and dried her hair, getting dressed in the same clothes she'd worn for two days now, and opened the door to the hallway.

There was a suitcase sitting on the floor in front of her, and the doors to Tell's room were closed.

She was curious about when he might have gotten in, if perhaps he wasn't asleep yet, but she just pulled the handle up and rolled the bag into her room, instead, changing out of her worn clothes into fresh ones.

He'd picked a nice selection of sweaters and long-sleeved shirts, but he'd only picked jeans for her. She didn't like the idea of going to work in jeans, but he was the boss and apparently he'd voted.

She found her underclothes in the bag and paused, frowning.

She needed them.

There was absolutely no doubt she needed them.

But.

She really, *really* didn't like the idea of him going through her lingerie drawer and choosing what she would wear.

It was awkward in a way that she hadn't seen coming, and she sat on the bed for a minute, coming to the conclusion that she wasn't comfortable living with a stranger. Yes, he had *fantastic* guest furniture, and he had more than enough space. Yes, it seemed like it might be possible for her to live here at night and never even see him.

Or.

He could be a creepy, clingy stalker type who was moving her into his life in order to latch on and never let her get away.

There was no telling how long the *last* girl had been gone.

It could be anything.

Marcus had called Tell the freak.

And Tina knew almost nothing about him.

She could work for him. She didn't think that that had changed.

She just didn't think that it was wise to contain herself like this.

She didn't like being *exposed* like this.

She packed her things back into the bag and carried it out the door and down the hallway, not wanting the noise of wheels on marble to wake Tell.

She went downstairs and found a breakfast of crackers, then she took one more look around the gorgeous apartment and nodded.

Never again.

Strange as it was, intriguing as it was, she was never coming back here.

She summoned the elevator and waited for it - for several minutes - then she got on and turned to watch as the doors closed.

Down in the lobby, Vince smiled at her from the

concierge desk.

"Ms. Matthews," he said. "Did you have a good evening?"

"Yes, Vince, thank you," Tina said. He tipped his head at the suitcase.

"Mr. Tell had indicated that you might be staying on a bit longer," he said, and she shook her head.

"Any port in a storm, and all that, but I'm better off on my own feet."

He gave her a little nod and came around the desk, offering to take the bag.

"I'm all right, thank you," Tina said.

"May I call you a taxi?" Vince asked. "I assume you didn't bring your own car."

"Actually, that would be very helpful," Tina said. She paused. "Tell. Is that his *last* name, then?"

Vince smiled.

"He doesn't like that I call him Mr. Tell. It's simply my habit."

She nodded slowly and he went back to his desk, making a brief phone call, and then motioning to the door.

"Gerry, outside, will help you with your bag. The taxi should arrive momentarily. I do hope to see you again."

She gave him a genuine smile.

"Thank you, Vince. I haven't felt safe in a few days, and… I really appreciate last night."

He gave her another head dip, and she went outside, finding a doorman standing with his hands behind his back.

"May I help you, Miss?" he asked.

"I'm fine, thank you," she answered. Just as Vince had said, a taxi pulled up on the far side of the parked cars and stopped.

"That will be for you, Miss," the doorman said. "Are you sure I can't help you?"

"I'm very capable," Tina said with a smile. "And not used to having people to help me. Thank you, though."

He touched his cap and she went and opened the back door to the taxi, shoving her bag across in front of her.

She gave him the address of Tell's office and leaned back, glad that the cabbie didn't seem to be the type to try to talk to her.

She was still relaxed - it had been the night's sleep she'd needed desperately - but she'd lost several days, working on what had happened to her parents, and she had the hardest of Tell's files to figure out where they belonged.

She was involved with a man with underworld contacts, probably unsafe even as she rode in the cab, and he expected her to carry a *gun* to be able to keep his enemies from using her against him.

And she didn't even *know* the man.

She was tempted to go home and just pretend none of it had happened, but the truth was she had put a *windchime* on her back door to warn her if someone came in while she was trying to sleep, and she wasn't an awful lot better off, mentally, than she'd been that night.

She could go to another motel, try to find one that

took cash this time, and take showers with her flip flops on until Tell solved the case.

Or she could go to Bermuda.

She didn't like the idea of running away from what had happened. It went against her stubborn nature, and against her curiosity. She wanted to be here when Tell figured it out, *as* Tell figured it out, so that she could see how the pieces fit together.

She didn't want just to know *what*. She wanted to know *why*.

And she believed that Tell was the man who could figure it out.

The only reason she actually considered running away was that she didn't want to deal with where to stay.

She could try to talk Tell into letting her lock the office at night, sleep there, but she got the impression that he would be in and out all night, and that he probably had as many clients - more - turn up during the nighttime hours as he did during the day.

She went up to the office, looking at the remaining stacks of folders, then put her bag underneath the desk and went back down to her own car, driving to the diner and ordering herself a tall stack of pancakes and a coffee. She took her time eating, watching people and letting her thoughts percolate.

She wanted to stay, but she was *afraid*.

She didn't like being afraid. It felt like a cop-out, almost, letting what *might* happen impact how she acted, even though - rationally - that was how she lived every single day. She avoided risk. She did the smart thing. She kept the good job that paid well, and she never even asked herself what she *wanted* to be doing, because... Well, because where she *was* was safe.

She liked the mystery of Tell's files.

She'd liked Marcus Calloway, with his brusque, semi-threatening friendliness.

She liked seeing things that she'd never even thought about, growing up or in her years at college.

She was *really* enjoying the idea of working for Tell.

Could she stomach the risk?

Could she put up with needing to carry a gun?

If something happened. Something *bad*. Would she *regret* doing this?

How *bad* was *bad*?

She tried to imagine, but that got ridiculous quite quickly, and between rationality and denial, she had a hard time actually *believing* that anything worse than being mugged was likely.

She'd never been mugged, but she knew people who had. It meant it was possible.

Being taken as a hostage to try to manipulate Tell?

That was just a silly fear from people who overestimated their own importance.

People didn't actually *do* that.

The police would get involved, and it would show up in the news...

No.

She didn't believe that, no matter how hard she pressed herself to take it seriously.

What if?

'What if' didn't have to be likely. It just had to be possible.

She needed to evaluate her decisions in light of the edge conditions.

Tina paid the waitress for her breakfast and went back to the office, going through files and answering the phone twice, taking close notes for both phone calls.

One was from a woman who was convinced her husband was cheating on her, and she was looking for a quote and a guarantee of results, and while Tina dutifully took down the woman's information, she couldn't help but think that Tell was *never* going to call her back.

The other man asked three times who she was, then refused to leave anything but a phone number.

She had a sense that nothing going on was real, for a moment, as she wrote down the phone number and described the voice, but she went back to filing and cleaning - she had to leave once to get cleaning supplies, and she got new magazines while she was out - and the day slipped past easily enough.

She didn't hear the outer door open or close, but when she looked up later - much later - there was a man standing in the office doorway.

Leaning.

Leaning in the office doorway.

"I'd heard," he said. "But I had to see it for myself."

"Can I help you?" she asked, picking up her phone to check the time. "Tell ought to be here soon."

"I know, because I'm meeting him here," the man

said, taking a step forward. "I'm Hunter."

He offered his hand and Tina shook it, then got out her notepad.

"Are you a client?" she asked, and he motioned for her to put the pad away.

"No, no," he said. "I'm just a friend. Tell works for me from time to time, because he really is the best money can buy, but... No. We're going out drinking, tonight."

Tina crossed her arms.

"He hasn't even *gotten* to work yet, and you're already planning on going out *drinking*?"

Hunter grinned.

"You really are wet behind the ears, aren't you?"

Something about his grin was very similar to Tell.

"Are you two related?" she asked, and he frowned.

"Not really. Just... Came up through the same venues, if you know what I mean."

"Not at all," Tina said, sitting. "He has clients waiting on him."

"Including you, I understand," Hunter said, sitting down in one of the client chairs and swinging his feet up onto the desk. "You've done wonders in here."

"Thank you," Tina said.

"What's he doing for you, again?" Hunter asked.

"My parents were brutally murdered," Tina said, and he grinned.

"Ah, yes. That one. Well, have you figured out what you want him to do when he catches the guy? Make no mistake, he *will* get him."

"Turn over relevant evidence to the detective in the case," Tina said. "What else *would* I have him do?"

Hunter grinned wider.

"Oh, you're going to be fun."

She tightened her arms across her chest, frowning at him as he continued to beam.

"You treat all victims like this?" she asked. He raised his eyebrows.

"Only the ones who aren't going to be tempted to crater my face with their fists," he said. "I have a pretty face. They all think it."

She narrowed her eyes in disbelief, and he laughed.

"I'm going to give you two weeks, tops, before you run screaming back to your suburban whatever life."

She didn't know whether or not she *should* be offended, but clearly she was *supposed to*, and she actually *was*.

"You want to put money on that?" she asked.

She had no idea where that had come from, but his face lit up.

"Oh, I do like a good wager. What do you have in mind?"

"Hundred bucks," she said. "That I'm still working here fifteen days from now."

What?

What was she thinking?

"I'm going to hold you to it," he said. "You go running off, I'm going to come find you and make you pay up."

"Fine with me," she said, still all bluff. He laughed.

"So what do *you* do, Hunter?" Tina asked.

"As little as possible," the man told her. "I don't even know why Tell does this. It's such a big time suck, and he doesn't get to hang out with any of the cool people."

"The cool ones," Tina said, and he grinned.

"Like me."

"He told me that he only works when he feels like it. Is this part of that? You take him out drinking and partying and he decides he doesn't want to work today?"

"Would you?" Hunter asked. "I mean, seriously, if you didn't have to, if you had all of the money and all of the resources and all of the connections, what would you do?"

"Start a charity," Tina said. He tipped his head back.

"Easiest money I ever made," he said, standing. Tina saw Tell walk through the main door and she stood.

"I have messages for you," she said.

"I told you to be here at midnight," Tell said to Hunter.

"I figured your pretty assistant wouldn't be here anymore," Hunter answered.

"That's the point," Tell said.

"Aw," Hunter said. "Are we feeling protective?"

Tell looked over at Tina.

"Vince will let you up into my apartment, tonight," he said. "There's parking under the building. My spot is 321."

"I'm going to figure out my own thing," Tina said.

"Thank you, though. You have messages."

He shook his head.

"I don't think you understand. By letting you be here, I'm letting you put yourself in danger. I want to know that you're safe."

"I sat here all day long by myself," Tina said. "You're that much more worried about where I go sleep than me being in this neighborhood by myself all day?"

Hunter chuckled, going to sit in the waiting area as Tell stepped forward, catching sight of Tina's bag against the wall.

"Look, I'm in a weird place right now," Tina said. "I don't know why you're trying to put me up, and I'm pretty sure that even working here is a bad decision, but it's… I need to make sure that I'm not letting myself do stupid things, just because my ability to evaluate risk is broken."

Tell scratched the back of his head, taking a step forward.

"You're going out drinking tonight, instead of looking for the man who killed my parents," Tina said.

Tell nodded.

"I warned you when I took your case that I only work when I feel like it. Tonight, I feel like drinking with Hunter. But…" He shook his head. "You shouldn't wander off alone, tonight. Or any night. Not until I find the man who killed your parents and you actually go back to your normal life for good. I don't know of any safer place than my apartment…"

"Why do you do this?" Tina asked. "Playing

detective, when you're just some trust fund baby frat bro? Those two lives... They have nothing to do with each other. Why do *this one*?"

"Because I'm good at it," Tell said with an easy smile. "And because the world is full of dark and dangerous things, and the best way I know of to keep myself safe from them is to make sure that I see them and they see me."

"So why not do it, then?" Tina asked. "Why go out drinking with *that guy*?"

Tell laughed.

"Because he's my best friend in the world, and I need that, too. Look, um." He scratched his head again. "I don't know what changed between last night and tonight, but if you'll go sleep at my apartment tonight, I'll stay up in the morning and we can talk and figure out what you actually want to do."

"Why not now?" Tina asked. He pressed his mouth.

"Because Hunter isn't going to wait forever, and because we're meeting people and I don't want to be late."

"You have messages," Tina said, indicating her notebook again, and he shook his head.

"They'll wait. Please? Will you go be safe tonight?"

She sighed.

"I don't understand why this is so important to you, unless you've got some twisted plan to trap me up there or... Or whatever. Why are you pushing this?"

"Ask him what happened to his last *assistant*,"

Hunter called from the next room. Tina frowned.

"What happened to your last assistant?" Tina asked.

"She died," Tell said. "Quite badly. Please?"

"How?" Tina demanded, and he shook his head.

"I'm serious that I need to go," he said. "Please tell me that you'll go back to Viella."

"Viella," she said, then sighed. "Fine, but promise me you won't go through my underwear ever again."

"Is that what this is about?" Tell asked.

"It's weird," Tina said. "I don't really want to go back to my apartment, but I'd rather buy new than…"

He closed his eyes and nodded.

"I promise," he said. "I will let you manage your own belongings from now on. But you really shouldn't go back to your apartment. Probably not ever."

"Ever," Tina said. He shook his head.

"I'm sorry. I need to go. We'll discuss it in the morning. Okay?"

She frowned, then nodded.

"Okay. But I'm taking the gun out of the silverware drawer, and I'm getting groceries on my way there, because there's no milk and there isn't really even any real food."

"Whatever you like," Tell said, turning to walk back into the waiting room. "I'll see you in the morning."

She watched him open the door for Hunter, who arched out of his chair and winked at Tina.

"See you again soon," he said as he left, then Tell waved a hand and the two men were gone.

If she was smart, she would have left.

Just… gone.

She was…

She was making bad decisions because she was where she wanted to be, as close as she could get to the investigation into what had happened to her parents, where she could at least see when things were happening and when they weren't.

She wanted her binder back, wanted to go through everything again to see what she could turn up that might help Tell.

She had hung a lot on this strange man, and it meant that she wanted to believe that she could depend on him.

Could trust him.

It was a sunk cost fallacy.

She was trusting him to investigate the murders, so when she needed to trust him over where she stayed, she felt like she had to.

Even identifying it, she didn't change her mind.

He'd always been elusive, when she'd talked to him, always on the run, brushing her off to go do the next thing, and tomorrow morning, she was going to have his attention, was going to be able to ask him questions and expect him to answer them.

One more day, in order to make him tell her what he was going to do about her parents, what she needed to do to keep herself safe in the meantime, and whether agreeing to work for him had been a mistake.

She picked up the handle on her bag and went

down to the car.

The refrigerator was full of fresh fruits and vegetables, the freezer full of ice cream and microwave dinners - her much more likely go-to. She found a luxurious den below the bedrooms with a pool table and a theater, and she sat down to watch the late news. She ate ice cream out of a crystal bowl with a silver spoon and with a gun sitting on the table next to her.

She didn't *like* having a gun sitting next to her, not really, and she wasn't even really sure she would know how to use it if she needed to, but it made her feel more responsible, being in a stranger's apartment in the middle of the night.

When she finished her ice cream, she put the bowl into the dish washer and went up to the bedroom she'd slept in the night before.

She'd made the bed, but it was still tussled the way that she'd left it; no one had come in to make it more properly.

She kind of appreciated that. She went to brush her teeth and her hair, using the stuff Vince had sent up rather than the things from out of her bag, because it was so much *better*, and then she went wandering back downstairs in her bare feet to the den, where she'd seen a dozen shelves of books. She browsed briefly, finding multiple languages represented, and not much in the way of fluffy reading, but she eventually found an author she knew and liked, and took one of his books up to her room again, lying in bed and reading by rose-colored light for several hours before she put it away and turned off the lights.

She snuggled down deep into her blankets, pulling the comforter tight under her chin and she slept.

The next morning, she woke to a dark room.

"The problem with sleeping with a gun next to you is when you sleep so hard that you don't hear someone come in," a voice said.

She sat bolt upright, trying to remember where she was, why she felt so fuzzy. The bed swallowed her and she battled against it, not knowing which way the floor was, which way to run.

There should have been lights. She hadn't gone to sleep in the pitch black.

"Come on, come on," the voice said, and a hand grabbed her forearm just below the elbow, pulling her up and out of the bed and onto her bare feet. She thrashed against it, getting her arm loose and then striking the body in front of her with fists and knees and feet. It stumbled away, and Tell laughed.

"Best reaction yet," he said. She looked around frantically.

"What do you want?" she demanded.

"To talk to you, like I promised," he said. "But the power went out and they're still getting the generators up and running, downstairs. Emergency services, first."

"What?" Tina asked.

"I've checked it out, and it's the storm that blew the power. Nothing nefarious."

"Storm?" she asked.

"You were hard asleep," he said. "It's supposed to be snow by morning, but for now it's high winds taking out trees."

She took a step back and tripped onto the bed again.

"Why?" she asked, trying to force her panicked, muddled brain into making sense. "What's going on?"

"Come on," he said. "I've got all of the shades drawn, but there's a little more light outside."

He came and took her by the elbow, steering her to a door - she could tell by the sound - and then there was just enough light to see his shadow.

"What time is it?" she asked.

"About eight," he said. "I'm beat, and I want to get to bed, but I promised."

"Why do you have the gun?" she asked, pulling her elbow away from him once more.

"Because I wasn't certain that you wouldn't try to shoot me in the dark."

"It's eight," she said. "Why isn't it light out, yet?"

"It is," he said. "But I don't like dealing with dawn, so I have blinds for all of the windows that come down in the morning. Lets me get to sleep."

"Your day-night sleep cycle is completely messed up," Tina said, feeling her way along the hallway and into the great room. The light there was gray-blue and faint enough that she couldn't pick out colors, but he was right that it was enough to see by.

"I'd offer to make you breakfast, but nothing is going to work without the electricity," he said. "I'm a decent cook."

"Of course you are," Tina muttered, holding on tight to the railing as she went down the stairs.

"You're mad at me," he said.

"You woke me up by threatening me with a gun," she said. "And then you grabbed me. Yes. I'm angry."

"Good," Tell said. "That's the sign of someone who's going to survive."

She went with him to the kitchen, where he opened the refrigerator - no light, inside, but cold enough to keep things fresh - and he pulled out a pitcher of orange juice.

"I didn't buy that," she said.

"I did," he said. "I like it."

She shrugged, and he poured two glasses, propping himself up on his elbows.

He looked menacing in the dark.

"So," he said. "You stayed here. I owe you a conversation."

"I want to know what you've done to find my parents' killer," Tina said. "What progress are you making, what are you planning on doing next?"

He sighed, coming around the wide island and perching on a stool next to her.

"I've ruled out the obvious suspects," he said. "Which means that now I need to dig into your parents' history and figure out where they may have stumbled across something that was worth that much to someone.

If I find him, I'll know him, but if I don't know where to look, this is going to take a lot more time."

"How will you know him?" Tina asked. Tell grinned, a flash of white teeth.

"People have a hard time lying to me," he said.

"So what are you going to do?" Tina asked.

"Your book was a good starting point," he said. "It's got some decent leads on people to talk to. After that, I'll just work through coworkers and people who were *around*, and then things get harder. I'm looking for financial transactions to figure out where they might have been and when, and who was there at the same time that they were. Sales clerks and other customers. People on a bus at the same time…"

"My parents didn't ever take a bus," Tina said.

"Then why does your dad have a commuter pass?" Tell answered.

"He what?" Tina asked, and Tell nodded, drinking his juice.

"Yup. He's had it for fifteen years."

"Fifteen…" Tina said. "I have no idea."

"So I'm going to look into it," Tell said. "There are lots of little, unimportant questions, and you just keep asking them until one of them turns out to be important. That's how this job works."

"And you're just a human lie detector," Tina said. "You'll know him when you find him."

"I have no doubt," Tell said. "Could be I find him in the next few days, just bump into him as I'm shaking things loose. Could be this takes months, yet."

"I can't afford months," Tina said. She didn't want to admit it, but it was the simple truth.

The lights turned on overhead, clean and white, and Tell lifted his face with a smile.

"Power," he said. "I'm going to go turn those off, though. Come sit with me somewhere more comfortable."

"I don't want to take this…" Tina said, touching the glass of juice, and he gave her a dismissive look.

"You think I'm the type to worry about food? I have a proper cleaning crew who goes through this place after I have parties, and the *stains* that they have taken out… No, your OJ is fine anywhere in the penthouse."

"Parties," Tina said flatly as he flipped a lightswitch and the room went dim again. He motioned, and she followed him into the den, where the lights came on overhead, sort of green-and-gold, like in her room. Just against the ceiling, just enough to make the place feel *visible*.

"Yes, parties," Tell said, throwing himself onto a couch. "Sit."

She licked her lips then went and perched on the edge of one of the other couches. They were deep, soft, swallowing couches, much like the bed upstairs, and she'd sat with her shoulders up around her ears to watch television the night before, but now she sat with most of her weight on her toes, just waiting for him to speak.

He twisted his mouth to the side.

"I… I've been feeling guilty about taking your money," he said. She nodded. No kidding. He grinned. "It's how I sort out my clients. If you have more demand for your service than you have time you're willing to commit, charge more. Only the ones who are really committed to employing you will turn up. But something bad happened to your parents, and I don't think Detective Keller is going to crack this one. The guy who did it… He was careful and he was clean and… And I don't think he found what he wanted."

"Why not?" Tina asked.

"Because he's been back to their house, and your apartment, too."

"What?" she asked, letting herself slide back into the couch now. He nodded.

"My people aren't the only ones I'm afraid of them finding you. I… I don't think he's going to get to you at my office, but I don't like the idea of you being alone at night, where he might find you."

"I'm alone all day," Tina said. "What difference does it make?"

"The people in my office, we watch out for each other," Tell said. "You're in stronger company than you think, while you're there."

"I have literally never seen another person there," Tina said, and he grinned.

"That's part of why they're so useful. Anyway, I don't worry about you there. It's when you're out… even when you're just at a grocery store on your own, I feel like…" He paused, taking a long drink of his orange juice and setting it back down in a cupholder on the arm of his couch.

Yeah, it was that kind of a couch.

"I feel like the parts of the world that are *mine*, a

guy like that is going to know to avoid. He's going to be looking for opportunities to come at you, where there aren't people around who know what to do with conflict."

"Vince?" she asked. Tell shook his head.

"Don't underestimate that man. I'm serious. Don't underestimate him at *all*. He scares *me*."

"He's a concierge," Tina said, and Tell shook his head.

"He's so much more. Anyway, I'm going to keep after this. Because… Heck. Because I want to know what happened, as much as anything, and because you're *nice*, and it's been a while since I've been around someone who was genuinely nice."

"Yeah. You investigate cheating spouses," she said, and he shook his head.

"Only when it's truly juicy," he said. "A couple of politicians and a warlord, once. The warlord, I managed to start a regional war, with that one." He grinned. "That was fun."

She shook her head.

"I don't know you, Tell. I don't know why you invited me here, and I don't trust you. And… Look, as stupid as I've been, it doesn't mean I'm going to keep doing it."

"Then go," Tell said. "Far away. A beach someplace where it's always warm. I hear they're lovely. Let me deal with this, and I'll let you know when it's done."

The man had been at her apartment.

Unless Tell was a bastard who was just making it up to manipulate her.

Did she believe that?

She didn't.

She genuinely didn't.

She *could* run, but that would really mean that she was done with her job. She wouldn't have a *life* to come back to. Anything to come back to. If she ran, she was ending her life, right here and right now, and committing to finding a new one, somewhere else. *Being* someone else.

"Why do I trust you?" she asked, and he slouched down to put his elbows on either arm rest next to him.

"I don't know," he said. "Most people don't."

"Why not?" she asked. He shook his head.

"I give off a vibe. Not being one of the normal ones. People see it on me when I walk in the door, and they're either attracted to it, because they think they can use it, or they're repelled. The good people, they're normally the ones keeping out of my way."

"Use it," Tina said. "Use *what*?"

"Money. Power. Intellect. Sex. I'm a goodie basket of things that people are looking for."

"You. Sex," Tina said. "No offense, but you're built like a rail."

He grinned.

"You'd be surprised," he said. "Anyway. Not the point. I've got friends. This isn't me feeling sorry for myself. But they're people I go back a long way with. Everyone else? It's all transactional."

"Why did you go out drinking last night?" Tina asked. "I mean. I can't get my head around it. You're, like, two different people, at least. The sleuth with the underworld contacts, the ones who call you the freak. This guy, whoever he is. With all the money and the luxury and whatever parties. And then the frat guy with the tool of a best friend who goes out drinking when he should be doing something else, because he *can*. The trust fund baby."

He shrugged.

"I'm interested in what happened to you," he said. "And I genuinely don't want to see you get hurt, either because of what your parents were into or because you're hanging out with me. But that doesn't mean I'm going to talk about myself. You either trust me or you don't, and I can see that I'm not giving you much to go on, either way, but I'm not looking for a friend, and even friends, I don't talk about that kind of stuff with."

"How about your last assistant?" Tina asked. Something about the way Hunter had said it. It was mocking him. Mocking him for weakness. Tell shook his head.

"Nope. I don't talk about her, either."

He was in love with her.

Clear as if he'd said it out loud.

"Is that why you're so closed-off?" she asked.

He laughed.

"You don't know me and I don't know you. I run a party circuit and hang out with rich bastards. I was never, ever going to be emotionally transparent with you. Helen or no Helen."

"Helen," she said. He shook his head.

"Don't go there."

She shrugged.

"I feel weird, staying here," she said. "I hired you to look into my case. This is… It's too personal."

He bit the inside of his cheek, nodding.

"Sometimes I forget."

"Forget what?" Tina asked, leaning out over her knees. He shook his head.

"What normal people think is normal. I have women sleep here all the time."

"That bedroom…" Tina said. "It doesn't get much use. I can tell."

"They like the other one," Tell said with an almost-sinister smile. "And they like my room."

"I didn't look in the other one," Tina said. Tell shrugged, picking up his drink again.

"You should. It's worth you knowing." His eyes rose to take her in, intense. "You… You have nothing to fear from me. The women in my life are involved with me willingly, and I am free to gorge on the carnal at will."

This was another man, again, from the ones she'd seen so far. He blinked, slowly, then nodded.

"I can understand that you might find that part of my life distasteful, but it should tell you that you have nothing to fear from me, and that you being here is unremarkable for me."

"No," Tina said slowly, trying to put her finger on it before she put it to words. "No, it tells me that you view women as a commodity to be used, and it makes me like and trust you *less*."

She sighed.

He licked his lips and nodded.

"Yeah. I can see that, as well. And I don't have an argument. Some women just want to be consumed. Maybe you're right to view me as *bad* for being involved, but…" He shrugged. "Your opinion of me doesn't change my opinion of myself. I want you to be safe. You're interesting and kind and… you care about women in a way that they don't care about themselves. And you're my client. Paying or not, you *will be* my client until I figure out everything. That matters, too."

"Should I be working for you?" Tina asked. "I mean, I don't know you. You have a terrible business that puts you in contact with terrible people, and apparently your friends are *worse*. I appreciate that you… That you're doing what no one else *can*, to find the… the guy. You know? But…"

She sighed.

"He was in my apartment?" she asked, and he nodded.

"Went through everything. I don't think he took anything, but I can't be sure."

"Should I go and look?" Tina asked. He raised his eyebrows.

"Certainly not today. I'm beat, and I need to go up and sleep. And in truth, I don't think you're going to find what's missing, if he did take it, because it would have been the first thing you thought of, when I told you that he went through your stuff. But you didn't think of anything. Did you?"

She shook her head.

"I didn't. I don't… I have things that are valuable

to me, but I don't like expensive jewelry or anything…"

He laughed.

"This isn't over things you can buy in a store. I guarantee you that."

She nodded, sitting back again.

"I have no idea," she said quietly, and he nodded.

"But the guy, he doesn't know that. He thinks it's possible you *had* it, and if he thought you might have it, he also thinks you might know where it is."

"Okay," Tina said. "Okay."

Tell raised his eyebrows.

"You'll stay here, then? Let Vince get anything you need. Give him a shopping list, even. I mean it. Here, the diner, and the office. Unless you're with me. Until all of this is sorted out."

"Why…?" Tina started, then shook her head. "You're so soulless about… everything. What about me could possibly be so interesting that you would inconvenience yourself like that? On a *chance* that something bad could happen to me?"

"I do a lot of stuff," he said. "Some good, some bad. I do whatever I want." He smiled with a quiet laugh. "But the first thing you did in the dark was try to punch me. You've got strength in you, and you've got good in you, and… It's like a bird. There's nothing that special about any individual bird, but they *do* something that I can't. They're so fragile, but so *triumphant*, you know?"

"I'm the bird, in this analogy?" Tina asked, and he nodded.

"Yes. A fragile, stupid bird with a propensity to fly

head-first into a window. That's you."

"You make no sense," Tina said.

"I'm going to bed," Tell answered. "Tell the soon-to-be divorcee that I'm not interested, if she calls back, and I've dealt with the other thing."

"But you didn't even look at your messages," Tina said as he stood, taking his glass with him.

"I'm a trained investigator, Ms. Matthews," Tell answered. "I don't have to puzzle over something in order to *see* it."

She pursed her lips, but he was gone.

She finished her orange juice, then went back into the kitchen, getting a bowl of cereal and then going to sit on one of the cafe tables by the windows. The curtains over them were blackout-thick, and they ran down slots in the window box that she hadn't noticed before, so she couldn't just pull them away to sit in the morning sunlight.

It was a shame.

It might have been pretty out.

The day was miserable.

If it had just gone ahead and snowed, that would have been one thing, but it sleeted and rained and hailed all day long, cold precipitation pouring down out of a gray sky.

Tina had mostly finished with the files - she was down to just a few that were truly too obscure for her to figure out anything about them, and she was mostly out of filing cabinet space. She went after the cleaning pretty aggressively for the afternoon, then went and sat in the waiting room, reading the magazines for a few hours.

The divorcee did, indeed, call back, and Tina passed on Tell's message that his client slate was full and he was not going to be able to take her case. The woman had cursed at her and hung up.

Other than that, the phone was quiet, and the door never opened.

Around nine, Tell came in.

"Messages?" he asked.

"None," Tina said. "Unless you want to hear what Mrs. Peese had to say about you turning her down?"

"Not particularly," Tell said.

"Can I get a minute for you to go through these files and tell me *anything* about them?" Tina asked.

"Nope," Tell said, sitting down at his computer.

"How about a new filing cabinet?" Tina asked. "You're out of space."

He looked over.

"That wall is full," he mused.

"I thought you could put one more in that corner, without it looking…"

"Crushed-in?" Tell suggested, and she nodded.

"All right," he said. "Tell Vince."

"Vince… furnishes your office, too?" she asked.

"Vince does whatever I ask him to," Tell told her.

"Charming," Tina answered. "Is that how you treat him all the time?"

He sighed, looking up.

"I didn't sleep well," he said. "Can we push this along to the point?"

"I don't have a point," Tina said. "I'm just saying… he does a lot for you. It wouldn't kill you to show some gratitude."

Tell held up a finger to contradict her, then put his hand on the desk.

"That's actually fair," he said, pinching the bridge of his nose with his fingers.

"Are you… hung over?" Tina asked.

"I might be," he said.

"Were you drunk, this morning, when we talked?" she asked.

He laughed.

"I wouldn't use that word for it," he said, and she shook her head.

"I don't have to meet a guy a lot of times to know that he's a bad influence," Tina said.

"Oh, please tell me she's talking about me," a voice said behind her, and Tina turned to find Hunter standing in the waiting room.

"She's talking about you," Tell said, bored. Hunter clapped his fingertips together.

"Oh, I do love playing the bad influence," he said. "What should we do tonight, Tell? Strip joints? Coke dens? Dog fights?"

"I have work to do, Hunter," Tell said, still bored. "You aren't supposed to be here at all."

"Well," Hunter said. "My plane got grounded by the storm, so I'm stuck here another night. Thought we could tie one on, as long as I've got energy and time to burn."

"You don't live here?" Tina asked.

"Oh," Hunter said, turning to face her, leaning his hips against the desk. "I do. But why let yourself be confined to a single city, when the whole world is out there?"

She actually agreed with the words, but something about the tone just jarred her, like he was heading out on conquest *over* the whole world.

"Don't take him seriously," Tell said. "Hunter has his vices, but he's mostly just a businessman."

"Is that so?" Tina asked. Hunter gave Tell a dour look, then adjusted his shirt, standing straight again.

"I… dabble," Hunter said. "It isn't my fault that I'm simply *good* at it."

"Hunter owns half the undeveloped real estate south of town," Tell said. "And in a dozen cities around the country."

"And a dozen more around the rest of the world," Hunter said, as though Tell was short-selling him.

"Sounds… busy," Tina said.

"Not as busy as you might think," Hunter said. "Land mostly just sits there. What I *do* is wander, looking for new opportunities, as the mood takes me, when this *storm*…"

He shook his head, and Tina rolled her eyes.

"I'm sure the storm did it just to annoy you."

"Took the power out at Viella," Tell said. "Tina just about took my arm off, when I woke her up this morning."

"So you're into the rough stuff?" Hunter asked. "I

approve."

She looked from Tell to Hunter and back, then shook her head.

"This is your best friend?" she asked. "Seriously?"

"Did you tell her I'm your bestie?" Hunter asked. "Oh, sweetie, I thought we were saving the surprise for when we told our families."

"Shut up, Hunter," Tell said, standing. "Tina, you're with me."

"I'm what, say it again?" Tina asked.

"With me," Tell said. "I'll see you later, Hunter. But I do have work to do."

He walked out into the waiting room, and Tina followed, glancing back at Hunter, who hadn't moved.

"What are we doing?" she asked.

"I've got a lead on the thing that Marcus is looking for, but they know me," Tell said. "I need you to go in and get something for me. Easy-peasy, in and out."

"You what?" Tina asked. "No. I don't do that."

"I need this," Tell said. "And you can do it. They aren't going to be watching for you, and no one's going to think anything of it."

"Who?" Tina asked, following him down the stairs. "Who isn't going to be watching for me?"

"Marcus' guys."

"Marcus… What do you mean Marcus' guys? I *did* meet them."

"And it would be really bad luck if one of them was the guy who took Marcus' thing, but I don't think it will be any of them. Best I can tell, there are about three different groups who all know where it is, and they're all waiting on the others to make a move to take it, so that they can bash their heads in and take it, instead."

"Lovely," Tina said. "And you want me to go in and take it, instead?"

"No," Tell said. "I need you to get something else."

"What?" Tina asked. He put his hand into his pocket and then up over his head, holding a key out to her.

"What is this?" she asked, taking it.

"PO Box," he said. "It isn't the one where Marcus' thing is, but I'm pretty sure it's close."

"And what am I getting?" Tina asked.

"Box," Tell said. "About this big."

He motioned with his hands, the size of a brick.

"And then?"

"And then you come out to the car and give it to me, and we drive away," Tell said. "Easy-peasy."

"You keep saying that, and it isn't making me feel any better," Tina said, and he laughed.

"This is what my assistant does," he said. "Answer the phones, file the files, do the milk runs."

"You're the one who just this morning was talking about how you're trying to keep me out of danger."

"And did I or did I not tell you to be at my apartment or the office *when you're not with me*?"

"So it's all better, because you're going to be waiting out of sight somewhere?" Tina asked.

"Exactly," he said jovially. He looked back. "Look. We both know you're going to do it. You got a buzz at the idea of doing something dangerous, the second I said something. You're just trying to be rational. Accept what you are."

"And what's that?" Tina demanded, offended.

"You're an adrenaline junkie," he said. "A hyper-rational one, sure, raised right, but… Come on, did you ever *think* about why you came here in the first place? You want to be involved. The thought of *dying* scared you pretty good, sure, but you didn't run away. You want to be here and you want to be doing dangerous things. You just don't like to admit it to yourself."

She stopped on the landing, looking down at him as he pushed the door open to go into the hallway on the first floor.

"Don't talk to me like that," she said. "You don't know me."

He looked back, letting the door fall closed, and tipped his head at her.

"Don't I?" he asked. "I think I know you better than you know yourself. Because I can tell what's going on in your brain, chemically, when you only hear your own thoughts."

"What?" Tina asked. "What does that even mean?"

"I told you, I'm hard to lie to," he said. "I know that you're so excited to do this that your hands are sizzling, and that you were tired, when I got here, but you don't feel tired anymore. I think you'll have a hard time falling asleep, when I drop you off at Viella, after."

Tina looked at her hands.

They did tingle, and as she reflected and took stock, her breath was short, and it wasn't from the stairs.

"Shut up," she said, and he grinned.

"Just go with it," he said. "You're trusting me, so trust me. I'm not going to put you somewhere that I can't get you back out if it goes bad. It's just better if they don't know I'm involved."

Tina drew a deep breath, then nodded.

"I'm not going to let you push me around," she said. "Even if you're right, I make my own decisions."

"And I respect that," Tell said. "I'm just letting you know where you're going to end up, so we don't waste the whole night to you talking about it. You know, making a binder with upsides and downsides."

She'd actually done that before.

"Shut up," she said again, and he laughed.

"Let's go."

She went out to his car, looking over at where hers was parked.

"I have to take a cab, when you drop me off at the apartment building," she said.

"So?" Tell asked, getting in and starting the engine. She got into the car next to him and looked over.

"They smell bad."

He laughed.

"You want a car service?" he asked. "I'm sure Vince has one he could call."

She frowned.

She just wanted to keep her car local.

"You think I'm going to be riding around with you

a lot?" Tina asked.

He shrugged.

"I find it more convenient than figuring out where to put two cars."

She sighed.

"All right. Yes. Yes, I will take a car service over a cab."

He shrugged.

"No problem."

She glanced at him.

"I still can't believe you took my money."

He laughed.

The post office box was in a little retail cubby, just receiving boxes and a mail slot, and Tell parked down the road from it.

"I'd do a drive-by to let you get a look at it, but that they might see my car," he said.

"You *could* drive something less distinctive," Tina said, and he grinned.

"Could not."

"All right," she said, holding up the key.

"I can see you from here, when you come back out. Your purse. If anything is wrong, carry it on your elbow instead of your shoulder, and I will come and get you. You got it?"

"Elbow," she said, nodding. Her heart rate was way, way up, and her palms were sweaty. "Remind me how you talked me into this?"

"I didn't," he said. "You wanted to do it."

She shook her head.

"Punk."

"Seriously, this isn't that hard," Tell said. "There are a dozen people in and out of that place every day. You don't look interesting at all. Don't look like you think anyone is watching you. Move like you've got somewhere to be, and this is an inconvenience to your day."

"Night," she said, and he shrugged.

"You know."

"I didn't know there were twenty-four hour PO Boxes."

"People have to pick up mail all hours of the day," Tell told her. "Go on."

She nodded, getting out of the car and pulling her purse up onto her shoulder. She held the key in her palm, then she slid her hand into her pocket, walking quickly and pulling her shoulders up to her ears against the cold.

She went from pool of light to pool of light under the streetlights, and it was everything she could do to keep from looking into the shadows for men who were waiting to pounce on her.

A block, a block and a half, she turned, pulling on the door to the little shop.

It didn't give.

She pulled again, with no result, and she started looking for hours.

The sign said twenty-four hours.

She gave the door a hard jerk, and it popped open, crackling with the sound of breaking ice. She looked up where the awning had left a trail of icicles that hit the hinge, then she took a deep breath and went in.

There were two recessed lights up in the ceiling, and the floor was covered with salt that crunched under her shoes. She went to the box listed on the key and she opened it, finding a package wrapped in brown paper of exactly the shape Tell had indicated, and she took it out, turning.

A man came in behind her, going to the opposite wall of boxes and standing there. If he was looking for a box, she didn't stay long enough to find out. She skittered back out onto the sidewalk, walking even faster back down the block. She had to wait at the crosswalk for a cycle, pins and needles between her shoulders the entire time, then she had to *not* run the rest of the way to Tell's car.

She turned to face it, looking back down the block as the other man came out of the shop, then she got in, pulling the door closed behind her.

"See," Tell said, turning the wheel and looking over his shoulder. "Easy-peasy?"

"What is this?" she asked. "And what does it have to do with Marcus Calloway?"

"Open it," Tell answered, pulling into non-existent traffic and turning before they got to the shop.

Tina tore the sturdy paper and found herself looking at a black, metallic box with various speaker grates on it.

"What is it?" she asked.

"Recording device," he said. She raised an eyebrow.

"You recorded the mail?"

"It's a nice, private spot where you can see everyone who's there," Tell said. "There are guys who are watching each other watch that box, and they're all worried that someone's going to walk away with it while they're *not* watching. What better place to have a nice, quiet conversation than standing in front of the box you care about?"

"So you got one nearby and recorded it," Tina said, looking at the box with newfound respect.

"So I rented a box nearby and I mailed myself a recorder."

"And all you had to do was pick it up, and if they said anything interesting…"

"I've got 'em," Tell said.

"Can I listen to it with you?" Tina asked. Tell grinned.

"I'd say that you're plenty far down the rabbit hole as it is, but you did go get it for me, so I owe you that much, if you want."

"You know it's there, and you know they're watching," Tina said. "Why not just go spring it and see who shows up?"

Tell grinned.

"Now there's thinking like an adventurer. No, odds are good that I wouldn't get the guy who *took* it, which is all Marcus is paying me for, and there's also that I haven't made it this long by taking unnecessary risks. They show up and I'm there, acting like I know something they don't want me to know? They're going to try to kill me. And sometimes, even under the unlikeliest of odds, the guy who tries to kill you is going to pull it off. I'd rather do it this way."

"Where I take all your risk for you," Tina said.

"It's not *that* risky," Tell said dismissively. "You're just another person going through the door, picking up their mail."

"Says the man who wouldn't do it," Tina said, settling lower into her seat and watching the streetlights go by.

They got to the parking garage under Viella and Tell parked the car, getting out and walking with her to the stairs that took them up into the lobby.

"Ms. Matthews," Vince said with a smile. "So glad to see you today. And you Mr. Tell."

"How many times do I have to tell you?" Tell asked going to the elevator.

"At least once more, Mr. Tell," Vince replied happily.

"Can you get her a keycard?" Tell asked.

"I'll send you the form for you to sign," Vince answered. "Good evening."

Tell raised a hand, then pushed the button for the penthouse.

"He's very friendly," Tina said.

"I know. And I normally don't trust really friendly people like that, but he's one of the good ones. Don't know why he acts like that, though."

Tina smiled, and Tell put out his hand for the recorder. He put it to his ear and shook it, then nodded.

"What is it?" she asked.

"There are a few little pieces that can get broken if it gets dropped too hard or has something land on it. You never know, when you send something by mail. Seems okay."

She looked over and nodded.

"Are you going to tell me what Marcus lost?"

"Nope," he answered. "He's a client, and you're just my secretary. You don't need to know."

"If you're going to use me to do stuff, I deserve more than that," Tina said. "And I want my binder back."

"I'm not sure I'd give it back, as your friend," he said.

"My friend?" Tina asked.

"I said *would*," he said. "I'm not your friend, no, but if I was? I don't know that I'd give it back to you."

"Why?" Tina demanded as he scanned his card again to make the elevator doors open. She walked back into the gorgeous apartment, shaking her head in disbelief once more. She went to take her shoes off and Tell stood, watching her.

"I told you, I'm not worried about babying this place," he said. "Don't worry about that."

"I take my shoes off at home," Tina told him. "And that's on carpet that someone else's dog peed on."

He shrugged.

"Suit yourself."

"Why won't you give my binder back?" Tina asked.

"Because," Tell said. "You need to move on."

She frowned hard.

"You don't get to say that. You aren't my friend, and even if you were, I get to decide when I'm ready to move on. That's what everyone says."

He snorted.

"Well, not me. I'm saying that you're wallowing in it, because you don't know what else to do. If you're still sad, be sad. I'm not going to stop you. What I will say is that you need to find something to do with your time that doesn't involved what happened to your parents. It's not going to help you, in the end. I promise."

She crossed her arms.

"You see a lot of tragedy," she said flatly, and he nodded.

"I do."

"And you really think that justice and closure aren't going to help?"

"Nope," he said. "Closure when you don't know if someone is *dead* or not? That's one thing. Finding out that your parents had secrets and weren't exactly who you thought they were? You can't ever fix that relationship. Let them be who they were, who you clearly loved, and let them stay like that in your memory. It isn't closure. It blows up everything. And justice? Justice is the guy who killed them dying terrified, alone, and at someone else's leisure. That ain't gonna happen, sister. Best case, you're looking at life in prison or the death penalty, and dying is scary, but it's never going to be what your parents went though. Justice doesn't *happen* in this country, because they're afraid to get it wrong."

"You're seriously advocating torturing him to

death?" Tina asked, and Tell shrugged.

"It's what you're paying me for, not what I'm advocating," he said. "*Justice.*" He blew air through his lips. "I'd settle for knowing that the guy who hunted down your parents isn't going to get to you. I did offer, though."

"Offered what?" Tina asked, following him into the kitchen, where he poured two glasses of orange juice.

"Did you eat?" he asked. Tina frowned.

"Not really."

She'd brought the box of crackers and finished it sometime after lunch.

"Let's see what I've got to work with, then," he said, turning to open the refrigerator.

"What did you offer me, Tell?" Tina asked.

"To torture him to death," Tell said, his back to her.

She stared at him for a long time.

He turned back to the counter, setting several tomatoes onto the granite and getting out a knife to cut them.

"You like spaghetti?" he asked. "I'll have to do the shopping next time, because you really don't know how to stock a cooking fridge."

"You did not," she said.

"Offer spaghetti?" he asked. "Is that offensive somehow?"

"Offer to torture him," Tina said, and he gave her a patronizing, sideways smile.

"Yeah, that was when I knew I was dealing with someone special," he said, then grinned, going back to the tomatoes. She shook her head.

"Do you mean it?" she asked.

"Dead serious," he answered without looking back up.

There was lots of dead time on the tape, but Tell had a computer program that would zip through that, jumping to when things were happening. Even then, it was mostly just the sound of footsteps and boxes opening and closing.

"This is just two days, right?" Tina asked.

"Yup," Tell answered, listening hard.

"How many people use this place?" she asked.

"Plenty."

She glowered, but he ignored her.

She was beginning to believe that he wouldn't have captured anything, when a man on the tape grunted.

"You see Nicky out there?" he asked. "Thinks he's so slick, up there. They rented the room, you know that?"

"Gonna toast his nuts, sitting up there and watching us," another man answered.

"Yeah."

"So I talked to Vee, and he said we're doing it."

"Marcus hired the freak, and he's been nosing around."

"Don't matter. Once we get it sold, there's no way he can pin it back on us. Ginny is solid. No way he breaks her."

"Vee's sure?"

"You questioning Vee?"

"C'mon man, you know what I mean. Don't be like that."

"We're doing it."

"All right. I'll be ready."

Tina waited for a reaction from Tell, but he didn't move any differently than he had, forwarding past doors clicking open and shut.

He got to the end of the tape and sat back in his seat.

"You know all of the people they were talking about?" Tina asked.

"I know who Ginny is," he said. "And I can break her if I have to, but I'd rather not. She likes me."

"She likes you," Tina said, and Tell grinned.

"Is that so hard to believe?"

"If she likes you, why not just *ask*?" Tina asked.

"Because she won't tell me. She has a professional code, as a fence, and if she breaks it, best case is she won't work again. Worst case, she ends up dead. No, I need to get this before it gets to her, so I don't have to go *through* her to get it back."

"What *is* it?" Tina asked.

"Best if you don't know," Tell told her, and she shook her head.

"What about the two guys?" Tina asked. Tell shook his head.

"Couple of grunts," he said. "No importance."

"And Vee?"

"Upstart grunt, I expect," Tell said. "I'll give his name to Marcus when we're done, one way or another, but not until I get his item back. Marcus has tact, but I want to be certain they don't see me coming."

"You just going to sit there and wait for them to open the box?" Tina asked. He shook his head, opening a drawer and putting the recorder away inside it.

"No, I don't want to wait on their timing. I'm going to go nudge them into upping their timeline."

"How are you going to do that?" Tina asked. He grinned.

"I'm going to go walk in and try to take it," he said. Tina let her arms drop to her sides.

"You *just* sent me in there to keep them from finding out that you even knew about it."

"Yes, but now I know where Nicky is hiding," he said, and she tipped her head to the side.

"Does that *really* make that much difference?"

His grin grew and he shook his head.

"Oh, you never know."

She watched as he stood and walked toward the door.

"You should eat and do whatever else you would normally plan on doing at night," he said. "I'll tell you how it goes in the morning."

She pursed her lips, listening to his ever-so-quiet feet on the marble in the hallway, then she stood, pivoting around the arm of the couch.

"Like hell," she said, grabbing her jacket from the back of the couch and throwing it over her shoulders as she chased after him.

She caught up to him before the elevator left, and

he held the door.

"Not sure what you think you're doing, but Vince will let you back up," he said, watching the numbers count down above the doors.

"I'm going to go," she said. "You sent me in there, I want to see what happens next."

He turned his head slowly to look at her.

"You are running my *office*," he said. "This was never my intent."

"See," she said. "You're the one who sold it to me that I *wanted* to do the post office. Told me that I was having the time of my life, *finally*, doing something that had meaning with someone who's actually good at what he does and doesn't act like a twerp. You did this. I'm coming."

He paused.

"In what world was that supposed to change anything?" he asked. "You were afraid of blankets on your couch."

"Oh, I'm staying in the car," Tina told him. "No way I'm getting out. But I want to see how this works, and I want to see what it is Marcus has you after, and who took it and why. It's like reading a murder mystery. You don't get to throw me into the story halfway and then expect me to *leave* before the end."

"Yeah, I'm still not sure why you think words are going to change anything," he said. "You're a liability with no upside."

She shrugged.

"I organized your folders."

"Yes, and that is your single asset to date. The ability to read numbers and letters and put them in an order."

"And I was the one who was there when Marcus came in."

Tell sighed.

"Thus bringing me more work, when I would rather be avoiding it."

She narrowed her eyes.

"You have an *office*. You…" She paused. "You're just like me, aren't you? Hunter is your vapid CEO who plays squoosh basketball while you're trying to have a conversation? You're doing this just to be around someone who *doesn't* own a purple suit."

"Did Hunter mention the purple suit specifically, or was that just an eerily good guess?" Tell asked. She shrugged.

"You're just like me."

"I fail to see why that matters," Tell said, turning back to face the elevator doors.

"You aren't going to say no to me, because you like having me around, because I *get* you. Your clients don't and your buddy doesn't, and I bet none of your other party-party-party friends do, either. Do they? They just like to drink and have a good time and sleep all day. Huh? And you? You work because it's *doing* something."

His nostrils flared and he looked at her once more as the elevator doors opened.

"I'm not going to flatter you with a compliment like 'you suddenly became more interesting', but I might keep you around a bit longer."

She followed him off of the elevator and to the stairwell to go down to his car.

"I want you to drop me off at my car, after this," she said. "I want to drive myself tomorrow."

He sighed.

"I'm going to have to rent another space," he said. "Aren't I?"

She twisted her mouth to the side.

"I can find street parking, I think."

"Not downtown, you can't," he told her. And you'd be walking for blocks in the dark. Viella is well-lit and mostly safe, but this is a rough downtown at night. No. I'll figure something out."

He unlocked the car and waited for her to get in, then looked over with firm eyes.

"No matter what, you stay in the car," he said. "Someone comes and puts a gun to the glass, you stay in the car. You don't unlock the door, you don't roll down the window, and you do not under any circumstance *open* the door. Is that clear?"

"What if I have to pee?" she asked, shocking herself.

She didn't *play* like that. Not ever, and especially not when important things were going on. That was more of a *Brad* thing to do.

"You wait until I get back," Tell said, unperturbed. "As long as it takes."

"All right," Tina said. "Can I have your cell phone number?"

"Why?" he asked.

"If a dude puts a gun to the window, I want to call you and tell you about it," she said. "Gives me something *other* to do than pee myself."

He looked over again.

"This is custom leather," he said. "Do not urinate on it."

"Yes, sir," Tina said.

She was tired.

That's what it was. It was making her goofy, slap-happy.

Had that been why she'd gone after him? She couldn't tell for sure, but the car was running and Tell was backing out of the parking space, so her window to change her mind was expired.

"Hunter is more than he seems," Tell said after a long space of silence. "You should know that, if you're going to be around him."

"More, like… it takes brains to do international land deals, so be nice to him?" Tina asked.

"No, more like, if you underestimate him, he'll take advantage of you, one way or another. He loves to play that game. The shallow playboy. Don't get me wrong, he is shallow and he is a playboy, but he's a lot of other things, too, and stupid isn't one of them."

"Take advantage, like…" Tina prompted.

"Like cheat you out of money or embarrass you or leave you on a street corner, expecting him to show up to take you home and he never does."

"He's done all of those things to you, hasn't he?"

Tina asked.

"More times than I can count," Tell said.

"Sounds like a *great* friend," Tina said.

"We go back a long, long way," Tell said. "He's fun, he knows how to take care of his friends, and he keeps me from going all-in on the private eye thing."

"Would that be so bad?" Tina asked.

"Yes," Tell said. "I need to be a part of that world. It's a big piece of who I am and where I come from, and turning my back on it, I'd never get that back."

"But they're stupid and vapid and shallow," Tina said. "And you're… not."

"It isn't like your office coworkers, as neat an analogy as you think that is," Tell said. "These people are important to me. I just happen not to *like* them."

Tina shrugged.

"Your life," she said.

"Just… Pay attention to how you act and what you say around Hunter. Okay?"

"All right," Tina said.

They were quiet again until he got to a parking spot not far from where he'd let her out, the first time. He parked the car and took the keys out of the ignition, looking at them for a moment and then handing them over to her.

"If I come out at speed, unlock my door and start the car," he said. "All right?"

"Do you *expect* that to happen?" Tina asked, and he shrugged.

"I expect everything. Part of why I'm still alive."

"All right," Tina said. He nodded and got out, locking the door before he closed it behind him, then going to walk down the sidewalk with his hands in his pockets.

Casual.

Didn't matter that it was well after midnight and the only people out… Well, they *all* looked enough like Marcus' people that Tina couldn't tell which of them were staking out the PO Box shop.

He crossed the street and for a moment, Tina lost him behind a car driving past, then she found him again, just walking down the sidewalk like he needed the air.

He dodged into a building, and Tina lifted her chin, trying to see where he ended up, but a pair of men went walking down the sidewalk past the car, cutting across at the same point where Tell had, and heading for the same building.

She picked up her phone and started to call Tell, then she realized that he hadn't actually *given* her his number. He'd just agreed to it.

The two men went into the building after him, and she considered - for much less time than she should have - and then got out of the car to follow.

She crossed the road immediately, going down the far sidewalk as fast as she could, mostly because she didn't want anyone to try to stop her to talk to her - or worse - but also because she wanted to catch up to the men as much as she could, maybe warn Tell that they were coming before they actually found him.

Maybe they wouldn't know where in the building he was going. Maybe *he* didn't know where in the building he was going.

Maybe she could catch him, on the off chance, in a hallway before they even spotted him, and she would be the one to rescue him…

A hand darted out of the darkness and wrapped around Tina's neck, pulling her across the sidewalk as a man stepped out of the shadow of a stairway and grinned down at her.

"You're much too pretty for this neighborhood, you know that."

"I've got…" Tina gasped, trying to force her brain and her mouth to work together. "A box. A box. I've got a box."

She tried to point, but she had no idea which direction she was facing. He narrowed his eyes at her, leering, and she tried to get away. He grabbed her shoulder with his other hand and she tried to point again.

"A PO Box. Over there, across the street."

He nodded slowly.

"Then just what are you doing following Danny and Lub down the street, then?" he asked. She swallowed, shaking her head.

"I don't know what you're talking about. My husband… he's… he'll be… worried… police… call…"

He grinned and shoved her toward the building Tell had gone into.

"Let's just go see what they think about it, shall we?" he asked, pushing her once more, hard enough to knock her off balance and stumbling down the sidewalk. At the front door of the building, he grabbed her elbow, slinging her toward the doors and pulling one open before he shoved her through.

"Tell," she yelled. "Tell, they're coming for you."

The man had his arm around her chest and Tina swallowed as she felt a line of pressure across her throat.

"That right there, missy, is what we call a mistake. Come on, now. You keep your mouth shut, or I'll find myself over-curious about the color pretty little girls have their blood come in."

He pushed her forward with his chest, the knife shifting along her neck with a pulling sensation, and he put his back to a door, letting the knife drop down to rest on her collar bone as they walked one after the other up the stairs.

Three floors.

He pulled a door and dragged her out into a hallway, grunting when he heard shouting.

They walked down the hallway, coming to a door that was open, where they found four men standing in a single-room apartment.

There was light from outside, but it came up and hit the ceiling, orange, and only created shadows out of the men, though Tina could tell from his build that the man next to the window *wasn't* Tell."

"All right, freak," the man with the knife to Tina's throat said. "I got your girl, and we got you. You go quiet, this all gets a lot easier, and she goes loose at the end."

"I thought I gave you exactly one very firm, very specific instruction," Tell said. The man in the far corner.

"They saw you," she said. "They were following

you. I wanted to warn you."

"Can someone get the light, so that we can kill each other like gentlemen?" Tell said, and the man with the knife grunted again.

"Lub, you got it? Don't try nothing funny. I got your girl, here."

Someone flipped a lightswitch and Tina winced her eyes against it, trying to see everything at once.

There was a thump and a groan, and then a voice very, very close.

"You've made a grave miscalculation," Tell said softly, and then the knife was gone from Tina's throat, and the man stumbled backwards, taking her down with him. She lost track of a few seconds as she scrambled, trying to get away from the man, and he did his best to hold her, but she was full-on panicked, now, and he couldn't seem to get a grip on her, as fast and as jolting as her motion was.

The man at the window had a gun out and he pointed it at Tell.

"Hold it there," he said, and the man on the floor grabbed at Tina once more. She snatched her hand away, stepping on him hard in the stomach, and then stomping him again when it felt really, *really* good.

"You're the one I'm here to see, anyway," Tell said, taking a step forward. Tina looked around the room, finding that there was a man by the doorway, laying on the floor, but that there was another man next to him, holding a knife in his hand and looking at Tell's undefended back.

"Tell, behind you," Tina said, and the man threw the knife as Tell turned. Tina put her hands over her mouth as Tell kept coming, walking directly up to the man by the doorway and throwing him into the hallway.

"Everyone down there on the street can see that you're incapacitated," Tell said, his voice still even. "The light in this apartment is never on, is it? And you, they can see you, and that you aren't watching the box. The balance is off, isn't it?"

The man at the window turned and cursed, and Tell looked at Tina once more.

"Did I or did I not tell you to wait in the car?" he asked.

She had her hand on her throat where the knife had been, fighting with the instinct to stomp on the man by her feet again. Tell came to grab her elbow.

"Come on."

"You're hurt," she said.

"No, not really," he answered. "And they're going to get away if I don't go down there and grab the right guy, right now. You turning up was *immensely* inconvenient."

"They *saw* you," Tina said. "I was trying to warn you."

"They were supposed to see me, doll. That was the point. I wanted to get everyone stirred up to do something stupid."

"Why… But why did you send me?" she asked. "If you were just going to do *this*?"

She was shaking hard enough that the stairs were tricky. Tell got a better grip on her arm, but he kept her moving. She looked over.

"There's a knife in your back," she said. "Just…

just stop. Stop. You can't feel it. You have too much adrenalin. You… Please." She jerked her arm away. "You need to sit down while I call an ambulance. No don…"

He reached over his shoulder and jerked the blade out.

"Take it out," she said slowly, wobbling against the rail. She needed to put pressure on it. Get an ambulance here. Get him to sit down.

"He missed me," Tell said. "Just a hole in my shirt. See? No blood."

He patted the edges of the cut with his fingers and held them up for her to see. There really wasn't any blood.

"How are you not right there?" she asked, reaching out to touch his back, but he grabbed her arm once more and started dragging her down the stairs.

"Limited-time opportunity," he said. "Come on."

She felt like she was missing important things, clues that would have explained what was going on, or that - worse - her brain was playing tricks on her, from the stress, but Tell wasn't giving her any time to react, to figure it out.

They were out on the street, under the lights again, and he let go of her arm.

Looked at her.

"Are you okay?" he asked. She shook her head.

"What just happened?" she asked.

He frowned.

"Just… just stay right here, okay? I'm going to go get him, then I'm going to call Marcus and we'll wait for him to get here, and then I'm going to drive you back to the penthouse. Okay? Just…"

He held up two hands and walked backwards into the street like he was trying to teach a dog to stay. She went to lean against the front of the building, wrapping her arms around her elbows. The air had a sour scent to it, like too many cars and too little breeze.

There had been guns and knives and one of them had *hit* Tell with a knife, and the man hadn't so much as flinched, even as Tina stood there with blood on her neck.

Yes.

Yes, there was blood on her hands, and now on her coat.

She put her fingers back to her throat again, finding that it had crusted some, and hurt more. It was a shallow, short cut, but she'd smeared crackling blood all over her neck. She rolled up her sleeve in order to put the back of her wrist across it, then she looked down at the ground, timing her breaths.

Someone came running by, shoes slapping on the concrete as he turned, crossing the road in front of her, and Tina lifted her head to see Tell in the little shop, holding a man at gunpoint as three other men rushed in.

Tell took a step back, motioning for the other three men to move in closer, as he himself came to stand with his back next to the door.

He still wasn't bleeding.

What had the knife *stuck to* if not his back?

Was there some kind of armor or something that it would stick in without getting to him? Could it have gone under his arm and managed to lay against his side like that? She was beginning to doubt everything about what she'd seen, and a pair of men came walking past her, both trained on the PO Box shop and paying no attention to her.

"Just keep walking," one of them muttered. Tina watched them go, wondering if she could identify them, later, in better light.

Maybe twenty minutes later, a pair of cars pulled up and Marcus Calloway got out, along with a couple of other men. He waited outside as Tell stepped out of the building, and Tina jogged across the street, staying out of the way, but not wanting to stand by herself anymore.

"There are cameras in there," Marcus said.

"I'll take care of them," Tell answered.

"And you haven't given it back to me yet," Marcus said.

"It's right there," Tell said casually. "What you do beyond that is up to you."

"I'll be in touch, if anything about this doesn't turn out how I have come to expect, from you," Marcus said, and Tell nodded, putting away the gun as Marcus' men went into the shop after the four bewildered and dark-looking men.

"Wouldn't expect any less," Tell said, turning away from Marcus and looking Tina in the eye.

"Once more, you do not *stay* where I put you," he said, shaking his hand. "You're on the footage from earlier, but you had nothing to do with this. I wanted you off of all of the other cameras, up and down the street, tonight."

She shook her head.

"I'm sorry. I…"

He shook his head.

"Just stay there, okay?" he asked. "Can we do that, this time?"

She looked over her shoulder at Marcus, desperately *not* wanting to be here as they took the men out of the building. Tell sighed, putting his arm around her shoulders and walking her down the block to the intersection.

"Keys," he said, handing them to her. "Stay in the car, okay? I'll just be a few more minutes."

She nodded, clutching the keys against her chest as she walked, stiff and cold and terrified, back to the car and got in.

What had she been thinking?

Why had she done it?

She had no reason, no explanation at all.

Tell came back a few minutes later, and she handed him the keys.

"I have no idea why I did that," she said as he started the car and pulled away from the curb.

"I know exactly why," he said. She waited, but he didn't tell her.

"Okay," she said. "Why?"

"Because you *really* want to be a part of the action. You're just not *ready* yet. Not mentally. You'd do it again, if I gave you a chance, but your system just shuts down when it actually happens." He glanced over at her. "You're gonna be a hellcat when you finally get those two working together, though."

The car thudded, and Tina looked quickly over her

shoulder to see if someone had hit them.

"The hell?" Tell said, and Tina turned back around to find a very large man standing with his hands on the hood of the car.

"Did you just hit him?" Tina asked.

"Be very still," Tell said. "All right? Very, *very* still."

He licked his lips, eyes straight, cold, on the man in front of the car.

"Who is that?" Tina asked.

"Marcus is a nice guy," Tell said softly. "This is one of the bad ones."

The man shoved the hood down, jostling the car, and Tell turned the engine off.

"What are you doing?" Tina asked. "Just *go*."

Tell shook his head.

"You don't know what you're dealing with," he muttered as the man came around to the driver's side. "Very *still*."

Tina might have spoken again, but for the fact that the man outside punched the window. Her mouth dropped open as he punched it again, going through this time and grabbing Tell by the collar bones to jerk him out through the window.

There was a roaring noise that bewildered Tina, and something in her animal brain switched over once more into self-preservation and she froze. Why this time? There was no telling. Maybe it was the way Tell had said it - it was different than his orders had been before.

Before, it had been playful, calculating, casual. This time... this time he'd been short and focused on something else.

He'd meant it.

She watched as the huge man carried Tell over to the sidewalk and across to the building, pushing him up against the wall and shouting at him with something other than *words*. He struck Tell across the face twice with that huge, meaty fist and shouted some more, then tossed him the length of a storefront. Tell landed on his feet in a crouch and the man charged him, grabbing his arm and slinging him into the brick again. Tina cringed, starting to reach for her phone, but the man turned and looked at her.

She froze.

He slammed Tell into the brick twice more, like a rag doll, then he turned to face Tina once more.

Her life.

Was done.

He was going to get here before she could do *anything*, break in her window and smash her to pieces on the wall over there.

Was he *high*?

She'd heard that PCP could do things to people…

He looked in the window at her, leaving a fog on the glass, and she froze like she was hypnotized, looking into eyes so dark they seemed to be all pupil.

And then he turned and he was gone.

Tina shoved her door open, running over to Tell as she fumbled at her purse, trying to get her cell out with one hand.

She tried to find his pulse, but he rolled away.

"You're alive," she gasped. "Just hold on. I'm

going to get an ambulance here and…"

"No ambulance," he said, sounding like his voice was coming from somewhere in the neighborhood of his stomach. "No ambulance."

"Why *not*?" she asked. "You've got to have a dozen broken bones. It's a miracle you're *alive*."

"Just…" he said, trying to push himself up onto his elbows.

"Stop," Tina said, putting her hand under his back and trying to get his arms out again. "You're going to make it worse. I'm going to call the ambulance. You just be still."

"Call Hunter," he said.

"Is he your emergency contact?" she asked. "I can have him meet us at the hospital."

"No ambulance," Tell said, sitting up again and shaking off her hand. There was a pool of blood on the ground underneath him, and Tina's hand was wet with it. "Just call Hunter and…" He grunted. "And drive me back to Viella."

"You're…" Tina started, then shook her head, standing. "You're in shock. No. Just… Will you stop?"

He was standing, his body broken and leaning to one side, but he was on his feet.

"Call. Hunter," he said, limping toward the car.

"You're bleeding all over the place," Tina said. "Please, just…"

He turned around and looked back, then put his hand up to his shoulder.

"I'll be damned," he said. "I guess he did get me,

then. Come on."

"Tell, please, don't let this kill you," she said.

"If you call an ambulance, I won't let them look at me," he said, going to lean against the car. Another car pulled up behind it and honked. Beyond that, the street was abandoned.

"What is wrong with you?" Tina asked as he held out the keys.

"I'm in no shape to drive, in case you didn't notice," he said, turning to put his face down on his arm on top of the car as she took the keys and walked around to the driver's side, stepping on broken glass.

"I should call the police," she said.

"No police," Tell told the ground.

"Why not?" she demanded. The car honked again and she opened the door, getting in and then pushing Tell's door open for him. He slid into the seat bonelessly and lay his head back against the headrest.

"I don't deal with them," he said. "Unless it's to drop something off to get a case closed out. But other than that? I pretend like they don't exist."

"You were just *assaulted*," she said. "I'd call it attempted *murder*. You're just going to pretend like it didn't happen?"

"Oh, no," Tell growled. "No, I'm going to do something about it. Just as soon as I get myself put back together."

"Are you a masochist?" she asked. "I'm taking you to the hospital, at least."

"Nope," he said. "Back to Viella, but calling

Hunter first."

"I don't know how to call Hunter," she said flatly, starting the car and waving at the car behind her in an effort to buy time. The vehicle raced past, honking again, and she shook her head.

"Here," Tell said, getting a phone out of the glove box and handing it to her, then putting his head back against the headrest again.

Tina turned it on and found exactly one contact listed.

Hunter.

She dialed.

"What's up, buddy?" Hunter answered.

"Will you tell him to let me take him to the hospital?" Tina asked, putting the phone on speaker. "Someone just slammed him against a wall and had to have broken most every bone in his body. He's a mess and I'm astonished he's *alive*."

"So you got someone else to drive you around when you get yourself in over your head," Hunter said. "How convenient for me."

"Your fault," Tell muttered, almost a moan. "I'll see you there."

"At the hospital," Tina prompted.

"At Viella," Hunter said. "I'll be there."

Tina gawped.

"What is *wrong* with you people?" she asked.

"Just…" Tell said. "Please? Just."

She sighed.

"Are you absolutely *certain*?" she asked.

"Absolutely," he said, shifting lower in the seat and swallowing.

She sighed, shaking her head.

"Who was that guy?" she asked.

"None of your business," he said, eyes closed, flat tone.

"You bust him cheating on his wife?" Tina asked.

"He's making a point to Hunter, not me," Tell said. "I'm just easier to get to."

Tina shook her head.

"Your land developer has people on PCP out to smash him to pieces, but they decide to go for you, instead?" she asked. "You're *bleeding*."

"It's just the knife wound," he said, and she looked at him, gape-mouthed, again.

"So? *Just*? You… You said it didn't hit you."

"Apparently it did," he said with a half a smile, not looking at her.

"And it just now started bleeding?" she asked. He grinned.

"Apparently."

"Tell, I'm taking you to a hospital," she said.

"If you do, I will refuse any and all treatment," he said. "And then if I die before I get back to the penthouse, it'll be on your head."

"You're absolutely serious," she said, and he nodded.

"Dead serious."

"The freak," she muttered. "What kind of skeezy land deals is Hunter a part of, that a guy like that is involved, too?"

"He wouldn't tell you," Tell said.

"I'm asking you," Tina said. "What kind of company are you *keeping*? I mean, it's one thing when they tempt you out drinking and partying all night, but it's another when just being friends with them is going to get you killed." She frowned. "Besides, he didn't sound that worried about you. I mean, what kind of friend isn't at least a *little* worried when a guy shows up and tries to kill you?"

"Please," Tell said. "I'm kind of in a lot of pain right now, and I'm having a hard time figuring out which question you expect me to answer. Can we just… be quiet until we get back to Viella?"

Tina threw her hands up.

"I'm going to jail for this," she said. "When the police show up at your apartment to investigate what happened to you, I'm going to be the last one who was with you while you were alive."

Tell laughed huskily.

"That's a good point."

"Don't die," she said, and he shook his head.

"Got no plan to," he answered. She drove the rest of the way to Viella, asking him questions from time to time to make sure that he hadn't passed out, then Vince met them in the parking garage.

"Mr. Hunter called me," he said. "He said that you might require some help."

Tina boggled.

"You're just… This has happened before?"

"Mr. Hunter has no trouble getting Mr. Tell into the building, but he wasn't sure you could do it on your own."

Tina looked over at Tell.

"How often does this *happen* to you?" she asked.

"Often enough," Vince said, getting under Tell's arm and pulling him out of the car.

"Be careful," Tina said. "I know he has broken bones. I... I can't believe we're moving him at all."

"Just get me to the elevator," Tell said. "Hunter's on his way."

"Yes, Mr. Tell," Vince said.

Feeling weird that she was just standing and watching - in horror - as Tell limped toward the elevator, she went to support his other arm. Vince got them up the stairs and onto the elevator, then he handed Tina a keycard.

"For you, Ms. Matthews," he said.

"Tell him I didn't do this," Tina said to Tell.

"What?" Tell asked.

"That I didn't hurt you. So I have someone to testify for me when you die from all of this."

Tell coughed a laugh.

"She didn't do this," he said to Vince. "And I'm not under duress."

"No, Mr. Tell," Vince said. "I'm quite confident that she doesn't have the physical ability to do that to you."

Tina shook her head, then Vince gave her a tight-lipped smile and pushed the button for the penthouse as he left the elevator.

Tell leaned against the back of the elevator, just

watching the numbers count.

"You need to go to bed," he said.

"What?" Tina demanded. "No. Not a chance. You…" She looked over at him. "What, exactly, is your plan?"

"Wait for Hunter to get here, and then pass out," he said.

"And what is Hunter going to do?" she asked. He shrugged with a dark grin.

"Don't know, don't care."

"You're smearing blood on the wall," she said. He glanced over his shoulder.

"So strange," he said. "They'll get it cleaned up."

He tipped his head to look at her, then frowned, reaching up to touch his throat.

"He cut you," he said. Tina's fingers found the spot and she nodded.

"This is crazy," she said. "I am *crazy* for being here."

Tina scanned her keycard and the doors opened. Tell staggered forward, letting Tina catch him as he nearly sprawled into the penthouse.

"Couch," he said.

She helped him over to one of the black leather couches and then helped him to lay down on it.

"I need to…" she started, but she had no idea what she needed to do. Look for broken bones? What then? She wasn't able to do anything about it. Check for internal bleeding? She didn't even know *how*. Tell snorted after a moment.

"You need to go get a drink," he said. "A stiff one. Or two. Make it two."

"I'm not letting you *drink*," she said.

"They're both for you," he said and coughed again.

She stood for another moment, then went to find a bottle of bourbon in a cabinet, coming back and sitting down on the floor with it.

"Don't die," she said. "It sucks when people die."

He shook his head.

"Hunter is coming."

She felt her eyebrows go *way* up.

"And what in the world is the frat party boy going to do about it, when he gets here?"

"I'm going to bring in the people who can help," a voice said. Tina hadn't heard the elevator doors open again.

"Will you please talk some sense to him?" she asked, standing.

"Go to bed, little one," Hunter said. "The grown ups have work to do."

"No," Tina said. "I am not trusting his *life* to you."

"You will," Hunter said.

"Who is going to help him?" Tina asked. "Is there a doctor who lives in the building? Do you have a specialist on retainer? A freaking *monster* slammed him into a building by his *arm*. Like, midair. He should not be *alive* right now. He needs trauma care."

"I'm on it," Hunter said, stepping forward.

"What, you're a land developer *and* a surgeon? Is there a sterile OR here in the apartment that I haven't stumbled on, yet?"

"You watch too much TV," Hunter said. "Go to bed."

"I'm not going to *bed*," Tina said. "He's *dying*."

"Hunter knows what to do," Tell said. "All right, man, will you just help her? I need to be done with this. It actually hurts."

"Just waiting for you to ask," Hunter said.

Tina woke up in her bed.

Dressed.

On the blankets.

With drool covering half her face.

She was groggy, trying to remember what had happened, how she'd gotten here. She crawled over to the edge of the bed, finding her feet down onto the floor and sitting for a long moment before she finally remembered.

Tell.

He'd been in danger.

Injured to the point of death.

And she was just… in her bed, like nothing had happened.

She stood up, wobbling for a moment as the world swirled, then she let go of the bedpost again, walking to the door and opening it.

The hallway was dim, but showed evidence that it was daylight outside.

She doubled back to get her phone, checking to find that it was noon.

Noon.

She went out into the hallway again and stepped on something, bending down to pick it up and finding she held a bra.

She checked very, very quickly to ensure that she was still wearing hers, but this had a lacy feel to it that tore too easily and tended to chafe.

Sexy underwear.

She looked back at the doors to Tell's room, finding them closed, then shook her head.

What *happened* here last night?

She got to the end of the hallway and found Hunter decked out across a couch up on the main landing, passed out. There was a woman laying on him - her underwear matched the bra Tina yet carried, though it was blue, and Tina could see now that she was holding red.

There was another woman propped against the couch in black-with-buckles, and Tina turned away, disgusted.

Someone cleared their throat and Tina turned around to find Tell standing behind her in a heavy robe, either black or maroon, she couldn't tell.

She blinked at him once, then let the bra fall on the floor.

"I'm going to leave today," she said. "You do what you want with the case. I..." She paused, sighing, feeling the end of a dream, the death of a dream, and she nodded. "I hope you can find him and tell Detective Keller who did it, but I need to move on. This just proves it."

Tell gave her a half a smile and stepped forward,

craning his neck to look at Hunter.

"He isn't what you think he is," Tell said. "Can I make you breakfast before you go?"

"No," Tina said. "It's noon. I'll get lunch somewhere on my way out of town."

He nodded, going to stand at the railing overlooking the lower floor.

"It's not a bad choice, all things considered. You have an inheritance to spend and an identity to figure out. Being here isn't necessarily the best thing for you."

She looked over at him as she came to lean against the railing next to him.

"What happened last night?" she asked. "I can't remember any of it."

"That's because Hunter drugged you," Tell told her. She blinked once, then looked out at the white marble below.

"I may press charges."

"I don't recommend it," Tell said. "There weren't any witnesses, including you, and nothing happened. You woke up in your bed."

She looked at him again.

"You make me so angry, but… I was really worried last night. How…? How did you survive that? How are you standing here? How did you guys end up with *women* over here? You should have spent months in the hospital learning how to walk again, if you survived at all."

Tell nodded.

"Have a good trip. If you're back through these

parts again, stop in and I'll tell you what progress I've made on the case. Ought to have it solved by the time you wander through, if you go anywhere worth going."

She shook her head, grief, disappointment, something that felt like despair.

"You aren't going to tell me," she said.

"You're leaving," Tell said. "You opened with that."

She licked her lips.

"I liked working with you. Even if I was scared out of my mind and some guy put a knife to my throat."

"You liked it a lot," he said. "And that's part of what scares you about it. You could get *used* to that."

"But that guy tried to *pulverize* you," Tina said. "I wouldn't have survived that, Tell. I wouldn't have survived him pulling me out of the car."

"That's why I wanted you here," Tell said. "Or at the office. He wouldn't *dare* go to my office."

She shook her head, then felt him watching her.

She turned her head.

"I don't think I've ever had someone that concerned over whether I lived or died," he said. "And sure, a lot of it is because Hunter just expects me to live. He takes it for granted, and I don't know how he'd feel if he didn't. But… I was touched, Ms. Matthews."

He gave her a half a smile that was almost sad.

"I'm making some of the worst decisions I've ever made in my life," Tina said. "I need to get away from you and this crazy life. I need to go figure myself out."

"I've wished you the very best," Tell said. "And I

mean it."

She nodded, looking back at Hunter and the two women.

"I can't imagine what this place looks like after a *big* party," she muttered, and she heard Tell laugh softly.

"I can't tell you how long it's been since I've had someone who was willing to be disgusted at me for it," he answered. "It's refreshing. Reminds me who I used to be."

She spun and looked at him.

"Who you *used* to be?" she asked. "You're a twenty-something trust fund baby with a party life. You talk like you have all this life experience, but you *don't*. Yeah, you've seen stuff, but you're a *baby*. Make better decisions. This is just... This is embarrassing. For you."

He bit his lower lip and grinned.

"I can see how that's how you'd see it," he said.

She shook her head.

"I don't know why I'm still here," she said.

"Do you want me to tell you?" he asked.

She rolled her eyes.

He was a *child*. A pretentious one who liked to play at being smarter, wiser than he was.

"Tell me," she said.

"It's because you don't fit anywhere else. But you're smart and you're creative and you've got good instincts, and with a little bit of training, you'd be a really good investigator. Your notebook on your parents? Really, really good work. Better than most of the guys in this industry. You're braver than you give yourself credit for, too. You just ended up starting off in the deep end. You'd be good at this, and…" He paused for a long time, then looked over at her. "And I think that you and I would be friends - real friends - if we'd ever gotten off on a foot that let us."

Tina snorted, looking back at Hunter, but she couldn't say she disagreed with him.

She liked his spirit.

Liked how he made her smile.

That confidence.

"I…" she started, but she didn't know what to say to that. "I don't even know you."

"I know you," he said. "I've met your parents, I've gone through your apartment, and I'm good at people."

She shook her head.

"That isn't how friends work," she said.

He shrugged.

"I know. I guess. Maybe. I'm not sure I have any. Not real ones."

"You got yourself broken to bits last night," she said. "And I called Hunter on your phone and he turned up at no notice. And apparently…" She shook her head. "I still don't know how you're standing there. But that's someone I'd consider a friend. Even if he is a prick."

Tell laughed again, nodding.

"You're right. But he and I go back too far to be friends. We're something else. We're an institution. You can't just split that up."

Tina sighed, thinking how much he sounded like the kids at work. A friend they'd had for six months was a forever-friend.

Tell tipped his head.

"I'm older than you think I am," he said.

She sighed.

"Okay."

"Can I make you breakfast?" he asked. "I bought bacon and eggs and everything. I'm good at pancakes. I can flip them in the air."

She grinned despite herself.

"Tell, what happened, last night?"

He nodded.

"I'll tell you," he said softly. "If you'll stay."

"Are you asking me to stay for breakfast, or to *stay*?" she asked him, and he shook his head.

"They're the same thing," he said. "After breakfast you can stay or you can go. Up to you."

She narrowed her eyes.

"Then they *aren't* the same thing," she said, and he winked.

"Is that a yes?"

She turned, leaning against the railing on her elbows and looked at Hunter.

"I can't stay here," she said. "Not with that being normal. It's disgusting and degrading."

"Come on," Tell said, starting for the stairs, shifting his robe tighter around his waist. "I'm going to heat up a pan."

She followed, going to sit on a stool at the counter as he worked at the stove, every bit the showman that the kitchen was set up for. She'd expected it would be for a celebrity chef, but Tell had the knack. She'd never seen him do it before, but he put on a show, frying eggs and flipping pancakes, launching things over his head and sliding them onto a plate in front of her.

He shut everything down and motioned to the cafe tables against the wall.

"The rest of this," he motioned, "it's for showing off. And you aren't going to be impressed."

She raised her eyebrows and nodded, walking with him to go sit.

"Are you not eating?" she asked.

"It's the middle of the night for me," he said. "And I'm still tired from last night. Going back to bed as soon as I know what you're going to do."

She nodded, spreading a napkin across her lap and then pouring syrup across her pancakes.

"Start with why you let Hunter drug me," she said, and he nodded.

"Because neither of us wanted you to see what happened after that," he said. "And you weren't going to go to bed on your own."

"Why not?" she asked. He nodded again, still the right question.

"Because I don't heal the way everyone else does," he said. "I... I heal pretty well for a while, better than most anyone else you'd ever meet, but then I run out of energy to do it, and I need more."

"Steroids?" she asked, and he shook his head.
"Blood."
She blinked.

"Bite me," she said, and he laughed quietly, putting his hand in front of his mouth.

"Bad vampire joke," he said. "Even if you didn't mean it that way."

"You're not a *vampire*," she said. "That's stupid."

"Then you explain it," he said.

"Steroids," she said. "Biological experiments. Prosthetics. Cutting-edge medicine. You aren't a freaking *vampire*."

He motioned at the curtain.

"I can't take direct sunlight. Not in any real quantity. The sun just being up puts a burden on me that makes me want to go back to bed. I only function *well* while the sun is down."

Tina looked down at her breakfast, licking her lips in thought for a moment, then shook her head.

"Thank you for the show, but I'm going to go."

"It's up to you," he said, "but I'm telling you the truth, and I'm willing to prove it if you want me to."

"Nope," Tina said, getting down. "You're a freak in a blood cult, and I don't know what else you are, but…" She paused. "Okay, how would you prove it?"

He reached across the table to pick up the knife sitting next to her plate, showing her the inside of his wrist and drawing the knife across it. She turned her head in a wince as the skin split, but there was no blood, and the red gash closed as fast as the knife went across his flesh.

Tina gaped, and Tell set the knife down on the table, watching her face.

She shook her head.

"No."

Took a step forward to put her fingers to the spot, pressing at the flesh and trying to find the gimmick to it.

She picked up the knife, putting her thumb across the edge and finding it sharp.

"You can do it if you want to," Tell said, and she shook her head.

"No."

His eyes were amused.

It was a trick.

He was just waiting to see if she'd figure it out.

Of course he'd tell her he was a *vampire*. He worked nights and avoided light. He had an empty fridge. It was a good story. She was sure that some fraction of coeds would find it sexy enough to go to bed with him, just based on that.

He shrugged.

She couldn't find a trick.

The skin under her thumbs felt like skin.

Cool.

But skin.

He'd almost died the night before. He looked a bit pale.

She frowned.

Slid a thumb down the inside of his arm to below his thumb, taking several grips there, trying to find a pulse, but she'd always been bad at that. He lifted his chin, offering her to let him try his neck.

She pushed her jaw forward, considering it.

She didn't want to touch him.

Didn't want to be a part of his icky blood cult and sexification of his dreary lifestyle.

She put two fingers under his jaw.

Probed around for a moment.

"So, I suck and finding a pulse," she said. "I always have."

She put her fingers under her own jaw, finding her heartbeat, then put her fingers back, frowning.

He blinked.

His neck was cold.

"The freak," she whispered. "What, can you stop your heart when you choose to? Is this some big trick, for you?"

He shook his head.

"You saw me get slammed into a wall and have most of my bones broken by an elemental last night," he said. "You knew it should have killed me. Still know that. You find a better explanation, I'll patent it and sell it."

"Is this a game?" she asked. "Why? Why are you doing this? Was that an actor? Is this *all* staged? Are there cameras?"

She took a step back, and he shook his head.

"So you went through with it," Hunter said from behind her, and Tina spun. "How's she taking it?"

"*You* I'll stab," she said.

He held up two hands.

"What'd I do?"

"She doesn't believe me," Tell said. There was the sound of a fork scraping across a plate and Tina looked back at him as he froze with pancakes halfway to his mouth. "What?" he shrugged. "They're good. May as well not waste them."

"I'm leaving," she said.

"Whoa," Hunter said, stepping in front of her. She had a spike of rage and panic at the same moment and she braced herself to slam him out of the way.

"Let her go," Tell said evenly. "She saved my life last night, maybe, and she deserved an explanation."

"Like hell," Hunter said. "The fountains upstairs saved your life. She just dialed the phone."

"Fountains," Tina said, looking back at Tell. "You *bit* them?"

"I heal," he said. "But I don't have an *infinite* ability to do it. I had to tank up."

The number of ideas that blistered through her mind was staggering, things she would try to prove it, things she would try to *disprove* it, things she would do if it was *true*. Questions. Physics. Laws of energy and life and the guiding rules to the whole *universe*.

It was a trick.

She didn't know what kind or to what purpose, but it was a trick, and one of the things she'd known about herself from a young age was that she didn't like being tricked. Her response was to walk away, not to tease it out, because someone who was *tricking* you already had the advantage. Going along just meant they got more opportunity to do it.

So she left.

She walked around Hunter, not looking back as she went up the stairs to get her bag. She passed the lingerie girls once more, refusing to so much as look over, as much as she wanted to search for bite marks, and she went down the stairs, finding Tell and Hunter leaning against the counter.

"She's serious about this," Hunter said. "You're just going to let her go?"

"She isn't a prisoner," Tell answered. "Never has been."

"I'm going back to bed," Hunter said, squinting at the windows. "Sun's oppressive." He glanced back once more. "You don't come back, you owe me a hundred bucks."

Tina frowned after him, then shook her head.

"I'm glad you're not dead," she said to Tell, giving him a little nod and going to push the button for the elevator. It arrived maybe a full minute later - an eternity - and she spent the entire time expecting Tell to come try to talk her into not leaving.

He didn't.

The elevator dinged quietly as it opened and she stepped on, riding down to the lobby, where she gave Vince a quick nod as she left.

She went to a library and researched vampires.

After about an hour of driving around mindlessly, not really seeing where she was.

How was she this lost *again*?

Her parents dying, that was one thing. It made sense that she'd feel like she'd lost her identity after that.

This?

She'd known Tell for *days*, and it wasn't even like it was a real job. She'd gone absolutely bonkers, getting in with people who had *no* concept of reality, probably on a whole *bunch* of drugs, and she'd just gone along with it.

Because she was in a bad place.

Sherry had been right. She shouldn't make any big decisions right now, especially when it came to who she kept company with.

And then she'd ended up in the library parking lot with a grocery bag full of notebooks and pens she'd gotten at the pharmacy across the street, knowing that she had every intention of figuring out what level of *possible* she was willing to accept to the theory that vampires were a real thing.

They weren't.

She was stupid for even thinking it.

But she couldn't think of anything else to do.

She wasn't going back to her apartment. Maybe not ever.

She wasn't going back to her job. That was becoming more evident with every passing day, and she needed to at least do them the courtesy of *telling* them that.

She wasn't going back to her parents' house. Not until all of this was *over*.

She'd pay someone to take care of it, mow the lawn and dust and whatever, but…

She had to go through their things.

She couldn't think about that right now.

So she went and researched vampires.

The root theory of the thing was actually pretty

reasonable, about the way that corpses continue to change once they're buried, bloating and seeping and drying out and all kinds of gross biological processes in a pre-embalming society.

You dig up a body because you think that they might be doing naughty things at night, find it with a bloated belly, elongated canines, and blood pooling out of its mouth?

It wasn't that far-fetched.

The problem was that they weren't any *less* dead, nor any *more* undead.

It was just superstition.

Everything.

No matter how she came at it, despite the constant barrage of blood cults and vampire clubs, everything was just silly. There wasn't anything she could find that was worth taking it seriously.

Were vampires immortal?

Or did they lead mortal undead lives?

The theory of being undead meant being immortal, but *decay* happened to everything. She refused to accept the idea of immortality, because it ran afoul of *physics*.

Her father would have been appalled.

Tell said he was older than he looked…

Was she taking this seriously?

Was she?

Or was she just playing a game to stall from having to make her next grown-up decision? She couldn't actually tell, in that moment.

So she kept doing it.

Through to closing time, she sat at the computer, books open around her on the table, taking notes, references, questions scrawled everywhere.

None of it made sense.

The librarian came over quietly, folding her hands and putting them down on bent knees to tell Tina that they were closing, and Tina looked around at the chaos of books on the table.

"I'm sorry," she said, and the woman shook her head with a dry but friendly smile.

"Don't worry about it," she said. "I'll just put them in the returns pile and I'll let the girl in the morning deal with it. She has so much more *energy* than I do."

Tina helped her gather everything up and they piled it up with a bunch of other sundry books, then Tina took her things and went out to her car.

What time was it?

How long had she been there?

She couldn't even remember.

She didn't know where she was going.

Where she was staying.

What she *wanted* to do.

Working for Tell had been easy.

Fun.

Exciting.

She couldn't remember the last time that she'd done something that she'd been excited about it.

Damn, but he'd been right.

She went and found a motel just outside of town, taking a room at a reasonable rate and sitting down in a reasonably-clean room with geometric-print comforters and beige, textured wallpaper.

It was fine.

She took a shower, thinking of Tell's blood on her hands, the night before.

A knife in his back.

She had no explanation.

None.

The elemental.

Elemental?

What in *the world* was that? And why had it tried to kill Tell?

Had it known it wouldn't kill him?

If it *had*, was it sending a message, or just sadistic?

A message? Best guess.

What was it?

The man… Had it been smarter than he'd looked? *Was* an elemental a *man?* It had looked like a man…

She got out her notebook and scrawled more questions, rolling over on her stomach to look at it.

Hunter.

Hunter had showed up at no notice and he'd taken care of Tell.

Tell had been *fine*.

After all of that.

Maybe he wasn't a terrible friend.

They'd gone out drinking.

She shook her head, her thoughts still scattered, unwell. She needed to *sleep*. Not because she needed *sleep*, but because it would give her a chance to reset from this awful, unsettling day and think more clearly in the *morning*. She'd missed the entire morning.

The shades on the windows.

The hours he worked.

They'd gone out drinking.

She looked at the television, but there was no way that was going to hold her attention well enough to distract her.

Instead, she put the notebooks back away in their bag, changing into her pajamas and laying down in the bed.

After a few minutes, she turned off the lamp.

It was early. She was hungry.

Hungry.

She got up and ordered a pizza, paying for it with some of the final cash out of her wallet, and ate the entire thing sitting cross-legged on the bed, then she lay down again, once more turning off the lamp.

Stared at a ceiling she couldn't see.

Vampires.

No.

Freaking.

Way.

Sleep finally came late, and her dreams were unwell, confused, trying to make sense of what she'd been thinking all day, but she did feel better in the morning.

She took another shower, just to stand in the hot water and feel the way that her body was still recovering from the stress of the previous day.

Her stomach was knotted, almost in pain from a single, huge meal on top of the day's events, and her lower back and up between her shoulders had sharp pain that eased under the water as she found the tension there and stretched it out.

She was tired.

More tired than she'd been the day before.

Whatever Hunter had used to drug her, she'd slept *great*.

She shook her head at the thought, going back into the room and cleaning up the pizza box and packing her suitcase once more.

She wouldn't come back here.

It was *fine*, but it wasn't a plan, and she wasn't going to let herself settle in.

She needed to do better, even if it was going to Myrtle Beach for a month.

Actually, that didn't sound so bad, when she went out and got hit in the face with a gust of frigid, wet air.

Her car had an inch of snow on top of a quarter inch of ice on it, and she took twenty minutes scraping it out before she got in and realized she still didn't know where she was going.

A man had *gone through* her apartment.

She'd believed that.

Did she still?

She did.

Her parents were...

Well, they were. That was a fact. She'd been the one to discover them.

Something *bad* had happened, and…

Either Tell was a lunatic and she shouldn't trust *anything*, or he was…

Or she needed to trust him entirely.

Was that valid?

You didn't trust *anyone* entirely. Even if they *tried* their best, they had their own interests, and they would disappoint you if you were expecting them to come through for you every time. They could be wrong by no fault of their own. You needed to be aware, to be responsible for your own outcomes.

But.

That wasn't this.

He'd done *things*, and he'd told her, with confidence, things about her parents' case that Detective Keller had never even hinted at.

Either he was out of his mind or he was *right*.

Could he be right and *not* be a vampire?

What a stupid, stupid thought.

And yet, it was the right one.

Could he be wrong… be teasing? gaming? tricking her about that, and be reliable as a private detective?

She put her glove in front of the heating vent in the car, then took off the glove to see if she had hot air yet.

Not enough to melt the ice on the side windows, but better than the cold air in the car. She turned on the rear defrost - should have done that five minutes before - and backed out of the spot carefully, still not knowing where she was going.

Breakfast.

That was a plan.

She could go get breakfast.

She drove for twenty minutes before coming to the conclusion that she couldn't decide where to eat, so she went to Marcus Calloway's place, instead.

She actually surprised herself that she remembered how to get there, but thirty minutes after she'd left the motel, she stood in front of the door, looking at the man standing outside.

"I was here with Tell... Tell, the other day," she said.

He shrugged.

"So?"

"I want to talk to Marcus," she said.

He snorted without answering.

"I was there last night," she said. "Denny... Did he make it through the night?"

The man turned his head slowly to look at her, and for a moment Tina worried that she'd over-played her hand.

What in the world was she doing?

He opened the door and shook his head.

"You're some kind of crazy, woman," he said, and she walked down the hallway, looking in at quiet, deserted rooms as she walked to the door at the end of the hallway and pushed it open.

Soft voices stopped as she walked through.

"Who's there?" Marcus asked.

"Tina Matthews," Tina said. "From Tell's office."

"What's going on?" Marcus asked.

Moment of truth.

Was she actually…

… yes, she was actually going to consult with a mobster about a vampire.

Yes, that was going to happen.

"I had a few questions I wanted to ask, and I couldn't think of anyone else to ask," she said. "You were nice to me."

"Get out," Marcus said, and Tina turned for the door. "Not you. Guys, give me a minute."

Tina halted, waiting as three men walked past.

They weren't the same quality of men who had been hanging out in here, the other day. These were leaders, dark, hard men with narrow eyes and scarred faces.

"Come sit," Marcus said, and Tina walked carefully, slowly across the room, going to sit at a small, round table next to Marcus Calloway.

"I won't talk about what happened last night," Marcus said. "If that's what you're here about."

"No," Tina said slowly. "Not exactly."

"What are you doing here?" Marcus asked again. "Where is Tell?"

"I don't know," she said. "Probably sleeping."

Marcus snorted, and suddenly Tina realized that Marcus might not know what Tell was. What if it was a secret, and she was betraying him, bringing it up?

Stupid.

Stupid, stupid.

He *wasn't* a *freaking*. Vampire.

"Why do your men call him the freak?" she asked.

"Better question for him than me," Marcus said, and she shook her head.

"I left," she said. "Yesterday. I... I wasn't going to go back. I still don't know what I'm going to do. No one else... No one else even knows who he is."

Marcus shook his head slowly.

"Not many people do. Especially not the kind *you'd* ever meet."

Tina hesitated.

"I shouldn't be here," she finally said.

"No, but you are," he said. "May as well say what you came to."

She trusted him.

Maybe more than she trusted Tell, right now.

Stupid.

The whole thing...

"One of the men last night stabbed him," she said.

"He's a resilient man," Marcus answered, watching her.

"Yes," she said.

Tell's secrets.

Even when she didn't believe him, even as she sat here, completely doubting every bit of trust she had in him, she wasn't willing to use the word, wasn't willing to *ask*.

"He's a side, isn't he?" she asked.

"I don't follow," Marcus said.

"He's *on* his own side," she said slowly. "And you can either choose to be *on* it with him, or..."

Marcus nodded subtly.

"Or against him," he agreed.

"Would you be on his side?" she asked. He frowned slightly, looking like a smile, and shook his head.

"I'm on my own side, Miss," he said. "But if you're asking if *you* should be on his side? He's going to get you killed. He swims in dark waters. But, yes, it's a good side to be on. Better than mine."

She shivered, standing.

"I shouldn't have come," she said. He shook his head again.

"No. You should either run far, far away or run straight back to him."

She wondered what he knew.

What he *knew*.

The things he might have seen.

If Tell was…

She shook her head, going to the door, tripping on something on the floor and rubbing her arms against a chill, then opening the door and going out into the hallway. The three men were standing there, waiting.

Waiting for *her*.

Because of *Tell*.

Her fingers buzzed.

Vampire.

No.

Just.

Well.

She went through the front door and out to her car, watching over her shoulder the whole way.

The lobby at the Viella was plush.

Red velvet and brass, with mirrors everywhere.

It lacked a carousel horse, but that was about it.

She sat on one of the couches for a long time, seeing Vince watch her and not speaking to him.

She wasn't decided.

Well.

She was.

Same as she'd been decided when she called him the very first time.

She knew.

She just hadn't done it yet.

Vince came over to sit down on an armchair facing her, tipping his head to the side.

"Ms. Matthews, are you waiting for something?" he asked. "Someone?"

"No," she said. "Well, yes. You know Tell. Right?"

He gave her a quick smile, shaking his head.

"I know a great many things *about* him, but I wouldn't say I know him. Perhaps not even as well as you do."

"He gave me a key," she murmured.

"Can I help you, Ms. Matthews?" he asked.

"I don't know him at all," she said. "I worked for him a few days, and then I'm in this… this *world*, and nothing makes sense, and it's *crazy*, and I feel like either I'm on drugs or everyone around me is, and…" She sucked on her lower lip for a moment. "And I don't want it to stop."

The idea of going back to her *life*…

He shrugged.

"I see," he said. "Danger is attractive, sometimes. You have to decide if you can live with the danger or not. Perhaps the question is, would someone who loved you want you to do it? Who *really* loved you?"

She frowned, and he stood, giving her another quick smile and smoothing his mustache with a white-gloved hand.

"It's something my mother taught me when I was young. Doing foolish things, no one who loves you would ever say that you *should* do that, unless it's because you need to learn. But doing things that involve risk? Sometimes, someone who loved you would say that you *should*, either because you'd regret *not* doing it, or because the prize is worth the risk. That voice, of someone who cares about me enough to say that I should take the risk… It's guided me for many years."

She sat back, looking at him for a moment, then smiled.

"Thank you, Vince," she said. "That was… that may have been exactly what I needed to hear."

He gave her a small nod and a smile and motioned.

"If you need anything else," he said. "I'm always here."

He was.

He was *always* there.

Odd.

She stood, looking over at the elevator.

Her father would have said it was foolish.

Her mother would have said that her job was

killing her, and if she'd found something that made her feel alive…

She wanted to understand.

Her father would have understood that.

And Tell said she was good at it.

She believed that, too.

He said that she was safe at his office, and here.

Was that enough?

It was a small world to live in, to open up a huge, new world.

She walked over to the elevator, swiping the key card Vince had given her and getting on.

Yes.

Yes, it was enough.

For today.

She'd decide for tomorrow when the time came.

Hunter and the women were gone.

The door to Tell's room was closed.

She went and put her bag in the guest room, then she went down to the den and turned on the television.

It was still early in the day, barely after lunchtime.

She went and got a box of cereal and sat on the couch in the den, barefoot with her feet tucked under her, eating cereal out of the box with her fingers.

Wasn't like *he* was going to be eating it.

She found a movie that she'd been meaning to go see, when it was in theaters, and hadn't ever gotten around to it, so she sat and watched that, going back to the pantry and looking for microwave popcorn and not finding any.

She briefly considered calling down and asking Vince if he had any, but that felt… abusive.

So she went back and finished the box of cereal, getting a beer out of the fridge to drink with it.

Why not?

There was a vampire sleeping upstairs.

Tell came down halfway through the sequel, sitting down on another couch without comment.

And then he came and sat next to her, taking the box of cereal and putting his hand in, taking out a handful of gold puffs and picking them out of his fingers one by one.

"You eat food?" Tina murmured as she watched.

"When I feel like it," he answered. "Like chewing bubble gum."

She nodded.

And that was all.

They finished the box of cereal as the night deepened outside, and then Tina put the box on the floor as the third movie in the series finished.

She turned off the television, looking over at him in the greenish light.

"You came back," he said. She nodded.

"I went to see Marcus," she said, and he tipped his head a fraction.

"Did you?" he asked. "Why?"

"I wanted to know if he knew you were a vampire," she told him, trying to read a reaction. He gave her a half a smile.

"And what did he say to that?" he asked. She shook her head.

"When I actually came to asking him, I couldn't," she said. "I didn't want to give away a secret. Your secret. If he didn't know."

Tell nodded, shifting.

"I see."

"You were serious, that you thought we would be friends?" she asked. "And that I would be good at being a detective?"

"Yes," he said. "To both."

She sighed.

"I do, too."

He nodded slowly.

"I haven't had a relationship with a human, not a meaningful one, since Helen. It's been fifty years. But she wouldn't like who I've turned into, the last couple of decades, and I don't really like parts of it, myself." He looked her in the eye. "I have secrets. Lots of them. And I'm not always agreeable or easy to get along with. I keep to myself and I keep to my kind, because you just can't *understand*. But… yes. I need to remember myself."

"I'm not looking for a *relationship*," Tina said. "You're *sooo* not my type."

He laughed, a flash-change to his face, and he nodded easily.

"I mean that I haven't spent time around a human in a non-professional and non-feeder context. That's all. You have a type?"

Tina stretched her mouth and looked away,

embarrassed. She'd reacted too quickly.

"Bigger," she said simply and he laughed again.

"Oh, honey, I'm big enough."

"Shut up," Tina said, getting up and shifting to another section of the couch. He grinned.

"Feeders," she said.

"Feeders, fountains, warmbloods, teething rings," he said casually, the look in his eye telling her that he was needling her on purpose.

"How does that work?" Tina asked. He shrugged.

"Would you like to try it?"

She covered her wrists with her hands, tucking her arms in against her chest.

"No."

He lay across the couch, weaving his fingers together on his belly.

"Some chicks dig it," he said. "I have a few men that I'll call when I'm looking for something more casual, but…" He shrugged. "I'm not sure how much of this you want to know."

Tina couldn't help but agree with that.

"How do you find them?" she asked.

"Clubs," he said simply. "Ones you wouldn't ever go to."

"And you just…" She shuddered, shaking her head. The idea of letting someone *do* that… She gripped her wrists tighter.

"Some of us enjoy fear, but most of us… Between animal, retail human, and the fountains, there's plenty to go around."

"Animal?" she asked.

He nodded.

"Has all the vitamins and minerals a growing vampire needs," he said. "Like… tofu. Or kale. It's just not much for flavor. Wouldn't want to live on it, but we have our vegans who do it, after the beginning."

"Vegans," Tina said, and he laughed.

"Indeed."

"And is it a secret?" she asked.

"Yes," he said. "It's not a big secret society with an illuminati board governing what we do, but it's a secret."

"I couldn't find anything about *real* vampires online," she said. "It's a really *good* secret."

"The internet has been an interesting challenge," he said. "Mostly we just let the sex of it run a disinformation campaign for us. No one believes it. Some of the girls don't even believe it. They just think I like role play."

"Role play," she said softly. "I don't know if I believe you, yet. It doesn't make sense. It *destroys* some of the fundamental rules of biology and physics."

He laughed, rolling onto his side and propping his head up.

"Come at me," he said. "Let's have it."

"How old are you?" she asked.

"I don't do the math very often," he said. "After a hundred, it stops mattering so much. I still look like I'm twenty-seven."

"You're older than a hundred?" she asked.

"I'm older than two-hundred," he said.

She squeezed her shoulders in.

"Cellular decay," she said. "You can't stay alive that long."

He looked past her for a moment, sighing.

"We have scientists. Vampires who *are* scientists, who *work* with scientists. Like that. My blood looks like yours, my cells look like yours. I just don't circulate. I'm not that into it, because it works. You know? *I* work? Why do I need to poke at that?"

"Because you could have the secret to agelessness riding around in your body," Tina said. "Like you said, if I could come up with an explanation for what you can do, you'd patent it and make a boatload of money."

He motioned to the room.

"Bored," he said. "Not interested."

"Not even if it revolutionized life on the planet?" Tina asked.

"Look, there are people doing it. If someone was going to manage it, they would have. I just chase down secrets because I like digging things up."

"Chemistry requires heat," she said. "Are you putting off heat?"

"I'm not room temperature," he said. "But I'm not far off. The cold doesn't really bother me until it gets below freezing too far."

"Your blood shouldn't freeze," she said. "It's too salty."

"Frostbite happens to vampires same as humans," he said. "And we don't put off our own heat. PS. Salt isn't the trick to keeping something from freezing. Alcohol is."

She frowned at this.

"That's interesting."

He grinned.

"I don't actually write off believing that some of it is magic," he said after a moment. "Like I said, I don't poke at it, but… Does everything have to have a scientific explanation?"

Tina paused.

"*Yes.*"

He laughed. Tipped his head back to look at her upside down, expression open, friendly.

"Fair enough. But I'm not really going to play with you, trying to figure it out, because I don't *care*."

She narrowed her eyes.

"How do you kill a vampire?" she asked.

"Are you asking for a friend?" he answered.

"It seemed reasonable," she said. "Silver, garlic, stake?"

He shook his head.

"That's offensive."

"Which one?"

"Seriously, who thinks it's okay to walk up to someone and ask about the best way to kill them? It's rude."

She frowned.

"So you aren't going to tell me?" she asked.

"I told you I'm a *vampire*," he said. "Isn't that enough?"

"You were the one who offered to answer

questions," she said, and he grinned.

"I'm answering them. Just not the way you hoped I would."

She sighed with exasperation and settled in, crossing her legs and putting her elbows on her knees.

"Okay, so what's it like?"

He sucked on a back tooth and nodded.

"That one, I'll answer. I'm tired a lot. Any time the sun is up, it's like this weight on my shoulders and on my mind, and all I want to do is sleep. I've lived further north, but the cold isn't much fun, and the people… I like it here, right now. The blood thirst… It's more than being hungry, I guess? I don't really remember what it's *like* to be hungry, but the way people talk about it, like it's an inconvenience or an indulgence, it isn't that. You have to eat and drink to survive, but as long as you do those things, your body kind of takes care of the rest. I feel a bit differently, because my body *needs* blood, and it's not like food or water, where it's broad and generic. It's just the one thing, and if I don't get it, I can feel myself starting to fail. It's about survival in a way that I don't think most people with a healthy body fat ratio would understand."

He sat up, shifting to slouch against the back of the couch and looking at her for a short moment, then he went on.

"I've been around a long time. And my body is adapted to fit in well with normal humans. To be attractive to them. It's fun. I'm not going to lie to you about that. I have a really good time, most of the time, and, like, Hunter? He has a *great* time *all* of the time, but I think he forgets…"

He shook his head. "Anyway, I have money, I have company, I have strength and eternal youth. Downside is that I can't enjoy it while the sun's up, I live a complicated life trying to keep what I am a secret, and… I can hear your heart beat. I can smell how you feel. I think there was a mystery to life, before that, and I kind of miss it, sometimes. Maybe. If I could even remember it."

Tina watched him as his gaze slipped off to the side in thought, and she sighed.

"I still don't believe you," she said softly after a moment. "I mean, I believe that you aren't *lying* to me, but… Denial, maybe. Or a cousin. I don't *believe* you."

He smiled, not looking over at her.

"I think I like that about you."

"It's not much downside for eternal youth," Tina said. "Why doesn't everyone become a vampire?"

"Believe me, they beg. They have no idea what they're asking for, though."

"Why?" she asked. "Why wouldn't everyone want it? Why *shouldn't* they?"

He looked at her again.

"Marcus' people call me *the freak*. When I'm not actively *trying* to be… beautiful, for lack of another word, humans have a sense that there's something wrong with me, and they stay away. I don't have *friends*. Outside of the vampires I know, and believe me, they *are* freaks. You get anyone who isn't afraid of dying, and they're going to turn into something they never would have recognized, before. Yeah, I look good, I feel pretty good for a few hours a day, and…" He motioned to the room around him. "I'm doing okay. Yeah. But I'm hollow inside. I'm not what I was."

"How did it happen?" Tina asked. "How did you become a vampire?"

He shook his head.

"Nope."

"Oh, come on," she answered, and he shook his head again.

"Move on."

She sighed.

"Was it Hunter?" she asked. He tipped his head to the side in exasperation, and she smothered a smile. "Just asking."

"Move on," he said again, less playful, now. She nodded.

"The man the other night," she said. "The one who tried to kill you. The *elemental*. What was that about?" she asked.

"He wasn't trying to kill me," Tell said. "He was sending a message. It's all politics."

"A message," she said. He nodded.

"Politics. I hate politics. I swear, I would go back to being human if I could, just to get away from it."

She twisted her mouth.

"What *is* an elemental?" she asked.

"You'd have to ask him," Tell told her. "I didn't get a chance."

"Are there other… supernatural creatures out there?" she asked.

"Nope. Just vampires and elementals," Tell said, then twisted his face to the side. "Come on. Of course there are. Just you've never heard of most of them, for one reason or another, and they keep a low profile. Vampires have it easy, because we're sexy, and no one takes us seriously. There are guys out there I really feel sorry for."

"Like what?" Tina asked. He shook his head.

"Nope."

"Why not?"

"Because it's telling secrets," he said. "And because there's no reason for you to know about them. You're human. You work in my office and you take messages from clients. I don't want you to be a part of this. I want to hang out with you *because* you're human, not drag you down into all of this mess of freaks and weirdos that I live in the rest of the time."

She pursed her lips.

"I don't know you at all," she said.

He snorted.

"You think?"

"No," she complained. "That's not what I mean. It's that… I don't know. I have a few friends. Not a lot, because I hate my job, and I've never been *great* at making friends, but I have friends, and I *know* them, you know? You don't *want* me to know you. You want us to be friends where I know almost nothing about you and… What? What about that even *makes* us friends?"

He nodded.

Considered.

"I can see your point," he said. "I'll think about it. Okay? You're right, it's just… I'm not normal. I'm the freak. And for some reason that's just not bothering you like it should… Why is that?"

"Why is what?"

"Why did you not go running out of my office that first night? Why did you come back?"

"You promised to find the man who killed my parents," she said. He nodded.

"And I will. I actually have somewhere to be…" He checked his phone. "…in twenty minutes, that's related. I should go soon. But is that really it? Any private eye in the city would have promised you that for the deposit you gave me."

"Still can't believe you took my money," she said, and he grinned. She shrugged. "I don't know. You're smart. I believe you. I think I've *trusted* you basically from the beginning. I mean, why in the world did I *come back*, but that I figured out I've trusted you. I still think I'm going through some nasty stuff, trying to recover from losing my parents, and one of these days I'm going to wake up and be smarter and make better decisions, but… Maybe it's just what you told me. You're exciting, and I'm bored."

"You're not that shallow," he said, standing. "You *are* tired, though. You should go up and get some sleep. I'll check in with you in the morning and let you know if I found anything."

"Does sunlight kill you?" she asked, and he gave her a dour look, then shook his head.

"No. It just makes me feel hungover for hours. Days, if it's too intense and I'm out for too long. Hurts, too, the *direct* light."

She nodded.

"Maybe I need to know so I can save your life from someone who *isn't* just trying to send a message," she said. He grinned.

"I'll take it under advisement," he said. "Get to bed. And don't leave the apartment, okay? I was worried about you."

She nodded.

"This conversation isn't over," she said, and he winked.

"It is now," he told her, trotting out the door. She went to get the box of cereal and picked up the stray bits that had ended up on the couch, listening as the elevator dinged and closed, then went into the kitchen to throw everything out.

She felt light.

Happy.

Absurd.

She was living in a vampire den.

And it was rose and cream colored and smelled like flowers.

How would she ever explain it to Sherry?

She was hard asleep when someone shook her.

Mostly it was her head bobbing violently that woke her, but even that took a while to pull her out from under the weight of dreams.

She finally got her arms up from under the blankets to defend herself, getting the hands off of her shoulders and groggily struggling away.

"What?" she asked. "Who's there?"

"Do you go blind when you sleep?" Hunter asked. She squished her eyes shut to rub them hard, then scooted back to sit up against the pillow.

"Get out," she said.

"Where is he?" Hunter answered.

"What? Who?"

"Tell," Hunter said. "Where is he?"

"Did anyone ever tell him that his name is confusing?" Tina asked, trying to catch up.

"Numerous times," Hunter said. "Where is he?"

"Why would I know?" Tina asked.

"Did you talk to him tonight, or did you just decide to come crash his place because he had you a key made?" Hunter asked.

"What?" she asked. "What is your problem?"

"He's missing, beautiful, and I'm hoping you can tell me where to start looking."

With that, she was awake.

"He said he had something to do that was related to my parents' case," she said. "And that he'd talk to me in the morning. That's it."

"So you two did kiss and make up," Hunter said. "I was only giving you fifty-fifty odds."

"Will you stay on point?" Tina asked. "How do you know he's missing?"

"I'm actually lying," he said. "I was giving him one-in-ten of ever seeing you again. I just really, really want you to like me."

"Hunter," she demanded. "How do you know he's missing?"

"He was supposed to meet me for drinks an hour ago," he said.

Tina lay back against the pillows again.

"Is that all?" she asked. "Maybe he got caught up in what he was working on. Or forgot. Did you call him?"

"He isn't answering his phone," Hunter said. "And he hasn't been late for drinks in twenty years."

Tina frowned.

"Especially now," Hunter sad. "Just got the tar knocked out of him. He needs a few days of binging to get him back on path. He's vulnerable, now."

Tina sat up again.

"Who would want to hurt him?" she asked. Hunter shook his head.

"Who wouldn't? He's got enemies on both sides of the fence."

"How do you find him?" Tina asked. Hunter shook his head again.

"You don't understand. You don't *find* Tell. He finds you."

"Well… Where would he be? Do you know who he talks to to get information?"

"Do I look like the kind of man who would slum it with informants?" Hunter asked. "Do you know how much this suit costs?"

Tina frowned.

"I really couldn't care less," she said. "Are you worried about him or not?"

"Did I or did I not just wake up a sleeping human to *talk* to her?" he asked.

Tina wasn't sure if that was disgusting, so she didn't comment. Instead, she pulled her feet out from under the blankets and got up.

"I'll get dressed," she said. "Does he have other friends he hangs out with? Other places he goes regularly?"

Hunter stood up.

"Nothing happens to Tell," he said. "It happens to other people, and Tell is the one who goes and fixes it."

"Okay," Tina said slowly, wondering if Hunter was having a breakdown of sorts and was refusing to acknowledge it. "Who does he see, regularly?"

"Me," Hunter said. "He goes to his office sometimes, and he hangs out with me."

"Is that *all*?" Tina asked, thinking that it sounded like a rather small existence, to her.

"Tell is… he's pretentious," Hunter said. "Thinks he's too good for the rest of us. Prefers to keep his own company. No telling why he even puts up with *me*. Probably because being *completely* alone is the only thing *worse* than hanging out with me. Anyway. He likes his women, he likes his booze, and people are always coming up to him, looking for him to do stuff. Everyone *knows* him, but… No. It's just me."

Tina drew a slow breath and nodded.

"How about bars? Clubs? Where does he hang out?"

"I'm not taking you," Hunter said.

"I didn't ask," Tina started, but he held up a hand, shaking a finger at her.

"You can't make me. You don't belong there. Tell would kill me. Like, drop me out a window to watch me bounce kill me, and then put me on a blood IV for three days so he could do it again. I won't do it. Fine. Come with me."

He started to walk out the door, and Tina dashed to her bag, dragging out jeans and a sweater, pulling them on over her pajamas and running out the door carrying socks. Hunter was waiting at the elevator, and she leaned against the wall to force on her socks and shoes, then grabbed her coat just in time to get onto the elevator with Hunter.

"Do you have a key?" she asked out of idle curiosity as they watched the floor counter count down.

"No, the man downstairs lets me in every time because he knows me," Hunter answered, looking at her shoes. "Tell wants to be able to cut me off at a moment's notice. Do you know what those are made out of?"

She looked over at him.

"Has he had to lock you out before?" she asked slowly.

"It was just one time, and I swear I didn't know that you can't *actually* train a boa."

"Boa like boa constrictor?" she asked, and he nodded.

"No, like a feather accessory," he said. "Keep up."

She chewed the inside of her lip for a moment, then nodded.

"You know they can probably re-code the card reader in here and give him a new card in about five minutes," she said. Hunter looked over at her.

"You're telling me he wants to be able to cut me off in *less* than five minutes?" he asked. "Ouch."

She nodded, wondering how strange the rest of the freaks were going to be, if this was the one Tell put up with.

"So what happened with the snake?" she asked.

"Got loose," Hunter said easily. "Only like five or six of them. The girls got the rest of them out just fine. I think he was angriest when the one turned up in his bed, though."

Tina turned her head very, very slowly to look at him.

The corner of his mouth went up.

Like he just couldn't keep it down.

She nodded.

"You're an adventure, aren't you?" she asked.

"I'm delightful," he answered.

They drove downtown, walking down an abandoned street to a corrugated metal door under a pink-colored streetlight.

"Stay close, don't talk to anyone, don't drink anything, don't let anyone touch you, and don't make eye contact with anyone with green skin," Hunter said, pulling the door open - it didn't so much as have hinges on it - and pulling it closed behind them. They went down a flight of stairs and stopped at a steel door at the bottom of the stairs, where Hunter knocked.

A slider opened at eye level and a man looked out at them.

"Who's she?" he asked.

"My date," Hunter answered.

The door opened and Hunter took Tina's elbow, drawing her through and into a pink-lit room with black walls and red carpet.

There was music, loud enough that she would have had to shout over it, and women in patent black leather dancing on miniature stages around the room.

She did a quick sweep for people with green skin, but everyone had various shades of pink skin, that she could see.

"You didn't actually believe me, did you?" Hunter asked, his mouth touching her ear.

"Which part was a lie?" she asked without turning her head.

"We all look human," he said. "I wouldn't take you anywhere that they didn't."

She slid her head to the side slightly to look at him, and he grinned.

"Your friend is missing," she said.

"Don't say that too loud," Hunter answered. "There are people in here who would love to hear that."

She nodded, letting him conduct her over to a black-topped bar where a man with no shirt and an abundance of ring-piercings put down a pair of napkins.

"What can I get you?" he asked.

"I'm supposed to be meeting Tell here in about an

hour," Hunter said. "But he told me there was a chance he'd wrap up early and head over. Have you seen him?"

The bartender shook his head.

"You drinking?" he asked. Hunter looked at Tina, who shook her head.

"Is there more to this place than just this?" she asked.

"Why?" Hunter asked, turning to look at the room. "Don't you like it?"

"It's just… loud. And very not private."

He nodded, indicating a black curtain on one of the walls that Tina might have missed.

"Would you like a private accommodation?" he asked, picking her hand up from where it rested on the bartop and turning it over to kiss the inside of her palm at the base of her wrist.

There was a flash of hot that went up to her elbow and Tina only just barely managed to contain the reflex to jerk her arm away.

He wrapped his fingers around the side of her hand, his thumb firm against the back of her hand, and he guided her across the club. Someone reached out to touch her as she went past, just a brushing glance, and Hunter aggressively pulled her against him.

"Get your own," he growled, switching to hold her hand with his other hand and putting his arm around her shoulders.

They went through the black curtain and Tina tried to shrug him off, but he held her yet, going past a half a dozen closed doors, glancing in the small square windows at the tops of the doors as they went past.

At the end of the hallway, he opened a door and pulled her through, closing it behind them.

Tina stayed pressed against the door as he let her go, taking off his jacket and hanging it next to the door.

He rolled up his shirt sleeves and turned to look at her.

"He isn't here," he said.

"Who would he have talked to, tonight?" Tina asked. "Who might know where he was going, if they'd seen him?"

Hunter shook his head.

"Tell doesn't tell you things like that," he said. "Or not me, at least. He just *does* what he *does*."

She looked back at the door again.

"Then why are we here?" she asked.

"Eddie might have seen him," Hunter said. "And if I can find Sid… Sid knows things."

"Things like what?" Tina asked.

"Like who might have finally decided to pull the trigger on taking Tell out."

Tina drew her head back.

"You're afraid he's dead?"

Hunter laughed.

"No, he wouldn't be that lucky. No. If someone got good and mad at him, they're going to take their time, taking it out on him. Or use him as a chip."

"A chip," Tina said. Hunter nodded.

"Look, all of this is way over your pay grade. Come sit."

"No."

His eyes went straight to her face and stayed there as he sat down on one of the over-round couches, letting his arms drape to either side. It was a motion she'd seen Tell make before.

"Let me explain this to you," he said. "There are people here, bad ones, who would really like to get Tell at a disadvantage. If they find out someone has *done* that, it could start a war. Or they could just get into a bidding fight over who gets to torture him. Things are much bigger and much more complicated than you would ever imagine, with your normal human lifespan. So we are not going to give anyone a sign that anything is abnormal. Which means that I have to feed on you."

She put her arms behind her back.

"Not gonna happen," she said. He hooked a finger at her.

"Come sit," he said. "If someone comes by and sees you like that, they're going to know that something is wrong."

"Is this a con?" she asked. "Did you bet someone whether or not you could make me let you bite me?"

"I would never… Okay, I'm actually *probably* going to do that at some point, now, but I don't feed on people unwillingly. Tell thinks I've got no soul left, and maybe it's true, but I do have lines I won't cross."

"But you're going to bring me in here and blackmail me into letting you?" she asked.

"Come sit," he said firmly. "There's someone coming."

His tone had changed.

She walked quickly across the room and sat down next to him, trying not to inch away as he ran a finger up the inside of her forearm where she braced her hand on the couch.

His face was down, looking at her arm.

"Take off your jacket," he said.

"I don't like you talking to me like that," she said. He looked up at her through his eyebrows.

"Do I sound like I care?" he asked. "I told you this was *dangerous*, right?"

She pulled her coat off and put it over the back of the couch, trying not to look at the window as Hunter rolled her sleeve up to the elbow.

She swallowed.

"So how does this work?" she asked.

"I don't know what you mean," he said, tipping his head to the side and licking his lips as he pressed his thumb against the base of her wrist again, lifting her hand.

"Why do people *do* this?" she asked. "Let you *bite* them. I mean… Seriously, if you even try, I *will* punch you."

Hunter laughed without changing posture.

"That's what Tell likes about you," he said. "It doesn't hurt."

"What, if I punch you?" Tina asked. "Then I'll try harder."

"When I bite. When *we* bite," he told her, looking her in the eye again and letting her arm rest on his knee. "And it heals. No marks, no scars. No slurpy blood face."

He licked his lips and narrowed his eyes. "You really are repulsed, aren't you?"

She nodded.

"You would have to be mentally *ill* not to be," she said, and he laughed easily.

"You don't see it," he said. "This is… Come here."

She pulled back again, and he shook his head.

"Never, ever, without permission," he said. "I give you my word, and I don't give my word about much of anything because I lie all the time. But if I give my word, I would rather die than break it."

There was a seriousness in his eyes, and it rang true.

She also got the sense that she was well past the point of saying no to him, if he was *willing* to do something violent.

She blinked, swallowing and looking at her lap.

"Come here," Hunter said again, putting his arm around her shoulders and sliding closer, sitting hip-to-knee next to her. He twisted her shoulders so that her back lay against his chest and he pulled her hair out of the way, running his nose along the back of her neck so that his breath spilled down to her shoulder.

She closed her eyes.

"It's intimate," he said, letting go of her hair and putting his arm around her waist over top of her arm. "Consuming with my mouth the very thing that makes you *alive*." She heard him lick his lips. "There's a reason that we're the ones with all the stories about us. It's raw sex, you see it?"

"You're warm," she realized out loud, and he smiled against the back of her neck, resting his forehead against the back of her head.

"I fed not two hours ago," he said.

"So you aren't hungry," she said.

"Not in the slightest," he said, his lips brushing her skin. "I'm putting on a show for the two men standing outside."

He opened his mouth and pressed it against her neck, and she closed her eyes with a shudder. His arm tightened and he pulled her tighter against him.

But that was all.

No teeth.

She found her eyes fluttering, panic, arousal, the reflex to *look* to see who was out there… watching…

He sucked back corner of her neck, then ran his tongue along her skin and she dropped her head.

"If you think that biting is the only liberty you *might* be taking here, you've been doing this too long," she said. He dropped his nose against the skin of her neck again and nodded.

"I *have* been doing this too long, but I can see it from where you sit," he said. "It probably doesn't help if I tell you that it's nothing personal."

"No, it doesn't," Tina said as he leaned back against the couch again, letting her go. She put her hand to her neck, looking back at him again and sliding away. He had his eyes closed and his face tipped back at the ceiling.

"And no one is going to be looking for *holes* in my

neck after this?"

"I told you, it heals," he said. "The same way that we do. I've heard of vampires using it to heal pre-existing wounds, though I don't know that I see the point. If a human is going to die, you just let them die."

Tina stood.

"That's disgusting," she said. "You would really just stand by and *watch* a human die, if you had the power to help?"

"I'm on a fake buzz," he said. "Leave me alone."

"How is this helping us find Tell?" she asked.

"It's not," he said. "It's helping you get back out of here alive."

She picked up her coat.

"Get up."

He sighed and sat up, tipping his head.

"And here we were getting along," he said, and she shook her head.

"I don't know what he sees in you," she said. He smiled, standing and walking toward the door.

"Two-hundred years of history," he murmured as he went past, looking over his shoulder as he lifted his jacket and put it over his arm as he rolled his sleeves back down again.

"Why did you do that?" she asked, motioning.

"Skin-to-skin contact," he said. She waited, and he shrugged. "It's pretty impersonal to just shove you in a corner and bite your neck. Most girls prefer that you have some foreplay to it."

Tina's stomach turned and she took a step back.

"Have we put on enough of a show, then?" she asked, and he nodded.

"They left."

"Who were they?" she asked. He shook his head.

"Could be a bunch of different people. Don't know what Tell's got himself tangled up in, these days."

He went to open the door, and Tina stepped forward quickly, putting her foot down in front of it.

"He said that the elemental… that there was a message, and it wasn't *for* him."

Hunter blinked once, quickly.

"Did he?" he asked, and she nodded.

"You know who it *would* be for?"

"Me," Hunter said. "I've got… I've got *stuff* with Leopard, and he's got an elemental couple who work for him."

"Then let's go see him," Tina said. "Maybe he's got Tell, and we can just trade you."

Hunter grinned, holding his jacket over his shoulder by a finger.

"You'd really do that, wouldn't you?" he asked. "Mercenary thing, you."

"You're the soulless one," she said. "I'm just getting my employer back."

"It's more than that, though, isn't it?" he asked. "That's why you were so angry when you found out about the girls, the other night. You thought that you and Tell were getting serious, and then he turns up with a girl in his bed…?"

He bit his lower lip, and she shook her head.

"No. Ew. No. There is nothing between Tell and me. I just… I like his job. I like him. I…"

… was having the time of her life?

… couldn't wait to meet the man who was *in charge* of the brute who'd massacred Tell?

… couldn't stop looking at Hunter's mouth?

She swallowed.

The corner of Hunter's mouth moved just a fraction, and she shook her head.

"There's nothing between us," she said, and he smiled.

"Sure. Tell may play a slow game, but I've never seen him fail to close a deal."

"Helen?" she asked, and he frowned, his face suddenly honest.

"I don't think so, actually. But *you*… You are *no* Helen. She was petite and had perfect hair and this little laugh like she was embarrassed that she was laughing in front of you… No. Tell wouldn't have ever bedded that woman, because he would have *broke* her." He licked his lips. "You aren't his type, though."

"What type is that?" she asked.

Sharp eyes. Aware. Very much like Tell's, just for a moment.

"Passing," he said, running his tongue along his teeth, then looking at the door. "You going to let me out, any time soon?"

She moved her foot and he opened the door, holding it for her so she could walk under his arm into the hallway.

She walked ahead of him, not looking back.

"You and your lady have a spat, Hunter? You drink too deep?" a voice asked.

"Think it was something I said," Hunter answered. Tina started to turn, but Hunter's shoulder was against the back of hers, ushering her forward down the hallway.

"Who…" she started to ask, but he squeezed her waist hard, uncomfortably, and gave her the tiniest of head shakes.

Not here.

She let him walk her back out of the club and to the car, where he got in and started the engine.

"Who was that?" she asked.

He looked at her.

"You're in this so much deeper than you know," he told her, and she shrugged.

"Then tell me."

He rolled his jaw to the side, then grinned.

"Pass," he said. "We're going to find Tell, and then I'm going to make him do it."

He grinned wider, putting the car into gear and pulling onto the empty street.

"Okay, so the club was one thing, but Leopard, he's something else, okay? He's the oldest vampire in the city by at least a century, and… Look, you think it's bad that I think that letting a human die is okay? He thinks of humans the way do some countries think of stray dogs. He's going to be mildly offended that I even brought one in. Okay? So you don't talk. I don't care what he says to you or about you, you let me answer."

Tina considered fighting him on it, but Hunter was already out of the car, coming around to her side to get her door.

She wasn't sure how she knew that that was what he was doing, but she stayed in the car until he opened the door and offered her a hand to get out.

He tucked her arm through his and paused, letting her take in the building.

It wasn't like she hadn't been able to see it from inside the car, but she needed a moment, actually standing there.

The man called *Leopard* lived in a house up off of a tiny private road, gated driveway and ten-foot brick wall all the way around it. The house was lit from ground floodlights, and it had a footprint that might have actually been bigger than Viella. Pillars and sconces and gargoyles covered the front of the mansion with a baroque sense of style, and there was a huge fountain in the front pathway, more than a dozen feet tall with cherubs and floral patterns, surrounded by cream-colored rock that gleamed under the reflected floodlights.

"Are all vampires rich?" she asked very quietly.

"All of the ones worth knowing," Hunter answered, tucking her arm more firmly under his and starting toward the towering double doors at the front.

A man in a classic butler's uniform answered the door, stepping out of the way without comment as Hunter led Tina into a sweeping foyer and across pearl-and-cream marble tile. Mirrored walls held candelabra-styled light fixtures, and there were half a dozen chandeliers overhead that flooded the room with golden light.

It was breathtaking, and Tina was very aware of what she was wearing.

"He doesn't leave very often," Hunter told her. "This time of night, he'll be in his study, reading his reports."

She nodded, following him around a corner and into a brass-and-glass room where a man with simple brown hair and a thick brown mustache smoked a cigar over a glass-topped coffee table.

He looked up.

"Hunter," he said. "I wasn't expecting you."

"Yes you were," Hunter said, leading Tina to a tan-colored couch and sitting down with her. "Ritan made sure of that."

Leopard smiled, setting the cigar down on an ash tray and leaning back in his arm chair, crossing his legs.

"Oh, no. He made sure that you knew I was angry at you. I didn't think you'd be fool enough to turn yourself in, like this."

Hunter worked his jaw, maybe masking anger.

"We had a deal," Hunter said.

"Yes, we did," Leopard answered, his tone patronizing. "And then I start hearing rumors that you might be talking to other people to get bids."

"I know that's how it looks…" Hunter said, and Leopard slammed his fist down on the table.

"That's how it *is*. When you take a meeting with

Ginger and then she's off liquidating property in Paris? You think that you can get the whole thing done before I catch wind, and... Frankly, I thought you were smarter, Hunter."

"The situation with Ginger is delicate," Hunter said. "And I'm not at liberty to talk about it until it's *done*, which is why I didn't come to you about it. But I'm not cutting you out, I'm not going around your back. We had a *deal*, and when I make a deal, I make good."

"Tell that to Oak," Leopard said, and Hunter tipped his head, exasperated.

"I swear, I *try* and I *try* and I cannot get my hands around that one. It's like someone's going out and *trying* to make sure that everyone believes Brian's story."

Leopard raised an eyebrow. His eyebrows were about as bushy as his mustache, which made them much more expressive than his mouth.

"You're saying that Brian is *lying*?" he asked.

Hunter sighed, rolling his eyes and shaking his head.

"No. I'm saying that Oak kicked him out not even halfway into the negotiation, and he was *angry*. Yes, we'd had some fun that night, and we'd been joking about some stuff that neither of us would ever do. But, come on, we both know that Brian is an *idiot*. He was chasing around the fountains and making a mess, and Oak sent him home, and all he remembered was the jokes. None of that *happened*."

"So you're telling me that if I called up Oak and asked him whether or not your last negotiation went the way he wanted it to...?" Leopard asked.

Hunter sighed.

"We both know he's going to smear me. I stabbed him in the back with Patrick, and that was just dirty business. I never *told* him that I had the thing going with Patrick, and if he'd known... Look, I kept my word, and I lived up to the deal. The fact that it wasn't as beneficial to him in the end as he'd thought, at the beginning? It doesn't make me a liar."

"But you are a liar," Leopard asked, and Hunter grinned.

"Yeah, but you know that I'm not, when it matters."

Leopard shook his head.

"Is she a tribute?" he asked, indicating Tina.

"No, she was there with Tell when Ritan came by," Hunter said. "Brought her in case I needed to prove that it was Ritan and not some other at-heel elemental in town."

Leopard scratched his mustache and reached out to take his cigar again, putting it into his mouth.

"You think you're a funny man, Hunter. Going to get you killed, one of these days."

"Managed to keep my head this long," Hunter answered. "Leave Tell out of it."

His voice changed. Went from the playful frat boy with the mocking half-a-grin to something much steelier.

"Leave Ginger out of it," Leopard answered, lifting his chin.

"She is out of it," Hunter said. "Has no bearing on your deal with me."

"And you aren't undermining my interests, the way you did with Oak?"

"No faster than you are, mine," Hunter said.

Tina looked over at him, not recognizing this man.

The two men stared each other down, then Leopard lifted his chin again.

"That man, he gets himself into trouble. You need to find a way to get a leash on him. Make him play by the rules."

"You know that I don't run him," Hunter said. "Nor does he run me."

"No, you just run *with* each other, and then claim that you have nothing to do with one another," Leopard said, taking a slow draw on his cigar.

"It's not my fault you've got no friends," Hunter said, returning to his normal posture, his normal speech. "You leave him out of it, or I'll come for you."

"Protective, tonight?" Leopard asked. He narrowed his eyes. "What's happened?"

Hunter leaned out over his elbows and pursed his lips.

"He has friends," he said.

"No he doesn't," Leopard answered. "And he hasn't got elementals, either. He's out there on his own. Doesn't even have your resources to take care of himself."

Tina wondered just how wealthy Hunter was if Tell was poor, by comparison.

"He's one of the last of us who does his own dirty work," Hunter said. "You ought to remember that."

"Oh, I will," Leopard said. "And I'll remind

Ritan."

Hunter stood.

"Is that all?" Leopard asked. "You interrupted me to tell me that Ginger isn't a threat and Tell is?"

"I wanted to look into your eyes," Hunter said. "Let you see that Ritan doesn't put me off closing out our deal, just like we agreed to it."

Leopard gave a little mouth shrug, then turned his attention back to his papers. Hunter reached down to lift Tina to her feet, tucking her hand through his arm and walking back out into the hallway, the foyer, past the butler and outside again.

The air was cold, chilling fast, and Tina looked at the sky for signs of more snow.

"So?" she asked.

"He doesn't have him," Hunter said. "If he took him, it would have been to use as a bargaining chip, and he didn't even consider it."

"So where is he?" Tina asked.

Hunter took out his phone, opening Tina's door for her and easing her down into her seat, then closing the door and coming around the car with the phone to his ear.

"Still no answer," he said, starting the engine.

"You know how to track his phone?" Tina asked, disappointed that she hadn't thought of it before.

"You think he leaves any of that active?" Hunter asked. "We have a guy who goes through and strips all of the tracking stuff out of our phones, hardware, software, all of it. No GPS or anything."

She nodded.

"All right."

He gripped the steering well hard for a moment, then put the car into gear.

"There are little wars going on everywhere," he said. "Tell could have gotten caught up in any of them."

"How?" Tina asked. "I was getting the impression he didn't care."

"Doesn't," Hunter said. "Mostly. Though he does hate the imps."

"Imps," Tina said. Hunter looked over.

"Vampires," he said. "Underworld guys, kinda devolved. Scavengers. Feed on people they can find unconscious, that kind of thing. Sometimes they get out of hand and start actively hunting, and Tell's gone after them every time he's heard of them doing it."

"Why?" Tina asked.

"Because he doesn't like it when vampires get take-y. We pay for what we take, or we get it consensually, but he thinks that just draining blood off of humans because we're *able* is… I don't know, like morally bad, or something. He takes it personally."

"So they'd have a grudge?" Tina asked.

"You say 'they' like there's a club or dues or something," Hunter said. "It's not like that. Especially not with the imps. They're just… You deprive a vampire of blood for too long, he starts to break down. Gets desperate. Turn someone who's in bad shape, you can get the same thing. Get a guy who never really bounces back, thinks more like an animal than a… well, like *us*, and… They're gross."

"How do you find them?" Tina asked. "If they had a communal grudge against him and one of them managed to snag him when he was vulnerable, where would they end up?"

Hunter winced his face to the side.

"It's *gross* down there," he said, and she lifted her eyebrows.

"Is he your friend or not?" she asked.

He sighed.

"Fine."

There was an intersection of three interstates just east of downtown, miles and miles of six or eight lanes merging and looping, on-ramping and off-ramping. Hunter drove to a section approaching the middle of it and pulled off, parking the car on the far side of a guard rail and taking out the keys.

There was a strong scent of rot as Tina got out of the car, swampy urine and washed up refuse.

"Who chooses to be here?" Tina asked.

"There's a lot of shelter and no one bothers you," Hunter answered, walking down an embankment and underneath the roadway, then putting the back of his hand over his nose.

"Stay close," he said. "If they're in open revolt, I'm bringing down sweet meat."

Tina sped up, going to walk behind him and off to the side, barely half a step away. There was a scrabbling noise as they got down closer to the bottom of the rocky foundation under the interstate, and a pair of boys looked up at them.

Tina couldn't see them clearly, but they were thin and wore tattered hoodies.

"Hold it," Hunter said, getting out his phone and turning on the flashlight. The young men winced, holding up their arms to protect themselves from the light, and Hunter continued down the rocks.

"Looking for someone," he said.

There was noise behind her, and Tina turned to see more people climbing up and around her.

"No one to find," one of the men answered.

"That's great," Hunter said. "Then I won't have to stay for long. You got any big-boy vampires down here?"

"No," the other young man said, sullen.

"Now, you're going to have to do better to convince me," Hunter said. "And I'm really not much for this whole conversation-and-interrogation thing. You guys frustrate me, I'll just start tearing you apart until someone tells me something I believe."

Tina wondered if he could do it.

Hard to believe, but at the same time, the two young men in the beam of light in front of them seemed to believe it.

"No, man, it's just us rats," the first young man said, edging sideways.

Tina pressed her mouth, then stepped forward.

"You guys hungry?" she asked. They straightened, easing forward, and she felt Hunter's fingers on her elbow.

"I'm looking for a friend," Tina said. "First person

here to tell me something *useful* about where he is gets a free meal."

She hoped that vampires didn't transmit bloodborne pathogens, but the thought occurred to her too late.

They were closing in.

"That was *very* unhelpful," Hunter said. "They were already thinking about it, but now none of them are thinking about anything *other* than your blood."

"I'm waiting," Tina said for the benefit of the people encircling her.

Hunter jagged abruptly, snatching someone from off to his side and throwing them down onto the rocks in front of them. He put his foot down on the woman's chest and looked around at the rest.

"I will *break* the first vampire who *touches* her," he said.

The woman down on the ground hissed and thrashed.

Tina knelt, looking her in the face.

"How old are you?" she asked.

The woman hissed louder, trying to grab Tina, but Hunter pulled her back out of reach.

"Where is he?" Tina asked. "Where is my friend?"

"Hot, wet, *squish*," the woman said, grasping at Hunter's ankle impotently.

Tina stood, her throat feeling tight.

She looked around at the rest of the vampires, feeling very outnumbered.

"That's enough," someone said. "Get. Go on.

Get."

The woman under Hunter's foot scrambled, and Hunter let her go, watching as she ran away with the rest. He raised his phone to shine light on a man, stooped with apparent age and wearing a long scraggly beard, who was climbing the rock embankment.

"Pyro," Hunter said. "I'd heard you were dead."

"And I'd heard that you were playing the game smarter, these days," the older man said, watching after the vampires as they scrambled and disappeared.

"You're better than these losers," Hunter said.

"Not by much, not by much. Neither are you. Who's the girl?"

"No one," Hunter said.

"Oh, I would recognize *no one*," Pyro said. "She's nowhere near pretty enough to be no one."

"That was backhanded," Tina said.

"The meat does not talk," the man said sharply, narrow eyes cutting into her.

"You never do get any less bitter," Hunter said.

"You indulge them," Pryo said. "Lesser in every way, and you fawn over them."

"They're more fun that way," Hunter said. "Besides, I like the things they bring me, when I shower them with enough money."

Pryo shook his head.

"Shouldn't be here. You'll get your shoes dirty."

"I'm here looking for information," Hunter said.

"Not much of that to be had, these parts," Pyro said, and Hunter nodded.

"Make it worth your while," he said. Pyro shuffled closer, peering up at Hunter.

"I'm listening."

"Look, you guys hate Tell. I get it. Don't really care. What I want to know is if someone bagged him and dragged him home for some revenge."

Pyro settled back a half step, crossing his arms.

"The dissenter turn up missing?" he asked.

"Not saying that," Hunter said. "I just want to know if you know where he is."

"Dissenter?" Tina asked. "You mean he argues a lot?"

Pyro raised a hand and was halfway through a swing that would have smacked her across the face with a clawed hand before she even saw it happening. She jerked away, putting her hands up in front of her face even as Hunter held the man's arm.

"You aren't fed well enough to pick that fight," Hunter said. "Don't do it."

"Soft," Pyro said, hissing with his lips. "Soft."

"You want my money or not?" Hunter asked. "Information or I'm leaving."

"No one's come back with your golden boy. Though if he *does* turn up here, I'm not saying I wouldn't take a poke or two at him. Going against his own kind."

Hunter took out a wallet and counted out bills.

"You're sure?" he asked. "I find out your lying to me…"

"How would you ever know what I know?" Pyro asked. "Yes, I'm sure. He ain't here, pretty boy."

"All right," Hunter said, giving the man the money. Pyro tucked it away and started back down the hill, and Hunter picked up Tina's arm, putting it through his own and going the other direction.

"How sure are you?" she asked.

"You do not offer blood to imps," Hunter said. "You're above that."

"It was an idea," Tina said. "This isn't working."

"They will rip you open just to be sure that you feel it," Hunter said. "That many of them, I can't be sure that I'd get you out before they broke you. You are in *danger* here."

"How many times have you called Tell and had him not answer?" Tina asked.

"Tonight?" Hunter asked. She shook her head.

"Before tonight."

"Never," he said. She nodded.

"He looked out for me. Told me not to go back to my apartment because it might be dangerous. Gave me a safe place to sleep at night. If I can help you find him, I want to."

"You think you owe him?" Hunter asked.

"I think that he's earned me trying," she said. He shrugged.

"You do you," he said.

"He's *your* friend," she said. "Why are you… Why are you like that? You keep trying to talk me out of helping, of even being here, and then you just… I'm still here, you know? You don't take me back to the apartment."

"Truth?" he asked.

"That would be nice," she answered.

"I don't *do* this," he said. "Sometimes Tell talks about work, and it's like *bzzzzzzzz*, and then he finally stops. You actually know what you're doing, *think* like that. And I talk a good game, but I haven't actually ripped someone apart in the better part of a century. That's Tell's thing."

Tina paused, coming out from under the overpass and into a strong, cold wind.

Was Tell a killer?

She wouldn't have pegged him for one. Not even after everything he'd said about it.

He was *funny*.

Light.

Hunter opened her car door and she shook his arm off to get into the car on her own.

He got into the driver's side and backed up until he could get onto the interstate again, waiting for a big enough gap in traffic and then flooring it.

"So where next?" Tina asked.

"You really aren't helping at all," he said. "You don't know anything about us, and I'm spending all of my time trying to make sure that no one kills you. Maybe I *will* just drop you off at Viella."

"Could," Tina said. "What would you do, on your own?"

He twisted his mouth.

"Go back to the club and drink until he showed up."

"Can you get drunk?" she asked.

"Same as you," he said. "Just not for as long. Better if you can get a girl to get herself drunk, and then drink *her*. Tastes better, lasts longer." He paused, glancing sideways at her. "Works the same for getting high."

"You a stoner?" Tina asked.

"I've done most of it," Hunter answered.

She shook her head.

"And Tell?" she asked. "Does he do that?"

"I should tell you that he does," Hunter said. "I mean, you…" He looked over at her. "Tell can read you like your brain has a teleprompter, you know that, right? I'm not Tell, and *I* can tell that it bothers you. No. He's pretty straight-edge for a vampire. One girl at a time, does all of his own drinking, doesn't like drugs."

"He's the best of you, isn't he?" Tina asked, and Hunter smiled sideways out at the dark roadway.

"He thinks so, anyway," he said, glancing over. "What would you do?"

"You know where he was, earlier?" she asked. "Anywhere?"

He shook his head.

"Doesn't tell me anything. Not like I care, anyway. Probably wouldn't have listened, if he *had* told me."

"I can't read his language on the files," Tina said. "Or I'd go through and see if I couldn't figure out what he was working on."

"Can't read it?" Hunter asked. "He has perfect penmanship. Actually had women who swooned over him for his script, back in the day."

Tina raised an eyebrow at that, but moved on.

"He told me it was his own language," she said. "And I can't read but a word of it here or there, where it's got enough of a Latin root to it."

"I could take a look…" Hunter mused.

"Are you good at languages?" Tina asked. He pressed his mouth and shook his head.

"I mean, I pick it up when I have to. Over the years, you get around, you learn that stuff. I speak Japanese and French and Mandarin and… Well, you know. The language of commerce and land deals. But not because I *like* it."

"I mean, if that's the next thing to do…" Tina said.

Hunter's phone rang.

He absently pulled it out of his pocket, then frowned.

"It's him," he said, answering. Tina leaned over to try to hear.

"Where have you been, man?" Hunter asked. "I've lost the better part of a good night, here, looki…" He paused. "Where?" He paused longer. "Just tell me where you…"

He looked at the phone, then dropped it into the cupholder in the center console, leaning forward to get a better view around the car and slamming the brake at the same time that he cut the wheel. Tina slammed into the door as the car careened sideways, and then backwards, and then Hunter had his foot down as the tires screamed, accelerating against headlight-flashing traffic.

As Tina gripped the door and her seatbelt, her teeth clenched and frozen, he darted across a gravel service road that connected one direction of the interstate to the other.

"What?" she demanded when he was finally driving *with* traffic again. "What did he say?"

Hunter didn't answer.

"What's going on?" she asked. "Is he okay?"

"Look, I think that you're going to have to get out and walk," he said. "I'm not taking you to Viella and I… They see you, they'll just rip you to bits. You aren't fast enough and strong enough to get through without them knowing you're there, and you *reek* of blood." He looked down at his suit jacket. "Suppose I do, too, at that."

"What are you talking about?" Tina asked.

He looked over at her.

"Leopard, he's a piece of work," he said. "And he would *absolutely* take Tell if he thought it would buy him an advantage in a deal. And the Imps? They're dirty, nasty guys who wouldn't think *twice* about hurting a vampire just because it felt good. But Bellet? No. Bellet is the guy that they write horror stories about. He doesn't just *think* that humans are inferior. He's been lobbying, coercing, *preaching* an idea that vampires should own everything. Just step up and claim authority over the entire planet, claim humans as slaves and cattle, and…" He shook his head. "The man is an idiot, but he's a *dangerous* idiot, because the vampires with the big egos, they like *hearing* that they should be dividing up the entire planet amongst themselves, doesn't really matter whether or not it would work. "

"What's that got to do with Tell?" Tina asked.

"He's got a gift," Hunter said. "He pisses people off by just always being in the way. Right at the moment when something is *easy* to stop. He goes and puts his foot in the way, and they can't ever get going. Doesn't take a lot, because vampires are like herding cats, anyway, and Bellet's guys… Well, they *all* think they should be second-in-command, and they're always fighting. But Tell turns up, or he does *something*, or he sends Ginger…" Hunter paused, the corner of his mouth coming up. "Damn, that one was clever. Anyway, it's not like he's manning the wall on his own, because we *all* see what a declaration of war against the human race would do to us, but he's the one who's actually thinking about it, day to day. The rest of us?"

"You're doing land deals and drinking coked-up hookers," Tina said.

"See, he said you were sharp," Hunter said.

"So what are you going to do?" Tina asked.

"I haven't got a clue," Hunter said. "I don't even know where he is. He just said that Remmy grabbed him and… Remmy is one of Bellet's guys. If they wanted to kill him, they'd have done it by now, so they're holding him… Anyway, I know where to find Bellet, so I'm going to go *there*, and then figure something out."

Tina folded her arms.

"You're an idiot," she said.

He glanced over, though the car was going too fast for him to look for much longer than that.

"Say it again?" he asked.

"You haven't got the mind for this kind of thing,"

she said. "You're a *businessman*, as involved as you are with all of this *scandal*, but you don't know how to snoop or to figure something out that someone else is trying to keep secret."

"You think business deals don't have secrets?" he demanded, and she shifted.

"But when you need to figure out someone's *specific* secrets, what do you do?" she asked.

"Hire Tell," he said, not fighting her on it.

She nodded.

"Are you trying to tell me that you can do better?" he asked, and she shrugged.

"I'm saying I don't want you to ditch me and run off on a suicide mission."

He glanced at her again, swerving onto an off ramp and stopping at the bottom for a red light. Turning his shoulders to face her with his full attention, he looked her in the eye.

"The rest of this has been a game," he said. "Dangerous, but a *game*. It was fun. I got to see what you're made of, and I'm glad. Tell picked a good one. Shouldn't be surprised, but there it is. This is beyond you, though."

"This has been a test?" Tina asked, and he shook his head, then nodded.

"Yes."

"You were auditioning me to be Tell's friend?" she asked.

"I was auditioning you to be Tell's *human*," he said. "He's needed one, but the whole Helen thing put him off it really bad, and I am *not* going to lose him another one this early. No telling when he'd finally get himself around to picking up another one."

"You say that like I'm baggage," she said.

"More like a touchstone amulet," he said. "One that he wears around his neck."

She raised an eyebrow, and he shook his head, putting out a hand in a *stop* kind of motion.

"Doesn't matter. I need to go try to keep him alive, and you need to go *be* alive. Somewhere else."

"Does he have any other friends?" Tina asked. "Does what's-his-name have other enemies?"

Hunter opened his mouth and then closed it again. Held up a finger.

"It's a very good question. No, Tell doesn't have any other friends. He has plenty of associates, and some of them might go to bat for him against someone *other* than Bellet, but the Bellet-enemies list is a lot more interesting. Aaaand, no. No, Ginger would be willing to *pay* someone to go in after Tell, but it would take her a week to write up the contract. The woman makes glaciers look frisky. Besides, we're in a thing. There are others, but you get the point."

"So you're going in alone and without a plan," Tina said.

"You forget that I'm over two-hundred years old," Hunter told her. "I'm not *stupid*."

"You're up against a fanatic cult leader and a bunch of egomaniacs, many of whom, I assume, are just as old as you are," Tina said. "Or have I missed something important?"

"No wonder they don't like you at work," Hunter said, sitting forward as he watched the light cycle from green to red again.

"Who said they don't..." Tina started, then shook her head.

Probably pretty obvious, if you were Tell.

"You think you'd do better?" Hunter asked.

"I think the two of us couldn't possibly do *worse* than you on your own," Tina answered.

"You *stay* in the car," Hunter said.

"Tell told you about that?" Tina asked as Hunter put the car in gear and turned against a red light.

"Told me about what?" Hunter answered. Tina twisted her mouth to the side.

How in the world was she developing a reputation of *recklessness*?

Hanging out with vampires, for a start.

She needed to consider this.

Put together a list.

Move things around on it, to see how her brain thought things were, compared to how she *knew* things were.

But.

That would have to wait for another time, perhaps a night when her new friend wasn't in danger of being... somethinged to death by vampire cultists.

Right.

"You didn't say okay," Hunter said.

"Okay to what?" Tina asked.

"You stay in the car," Hunter told her, as he pulled to the side of the road and stopped. She glanced over.

"The two of you treat cars like they're some sacred safe space, or something," she said. "I mean, it isn't that vampires can't come inside if you don't invite them, because Tell snooped all over my parents' house and my apartment."

"Very good, little one," Hunter answered. "No. It's that it keeps you off the street, out of scent, and out of direct line of sight, and if I could come up with a way to make you *be* back at Viella instead, I'd do *that*."

"I could hail a rideshare," Tina said. She might be able to figure out how to do that on the phone in the time it took Hunter to rescue Tell.

"You'd do better calling Vince and asking him to send someone," Hunter said. "Actually…"

He took out his phone and dialed, giving the man on the other end an address and asking him to send a car.

"There," he said, putting his phone away.

"Wait," Tina said, pointing. "If they've got Tell in there, what do you want to bet they're all really worked up about it and calling each other?"

"Unless Bellet managed to keep it a secret," Hunter said, and she nodded.

"But I don't see anyone," she said.

Hunter frowned, turning the engine back on and looking around.

"You're right," he said. He put the car into gear and Tina looked over her shoulder, habitually checking for traffic.

"Where are we going?" she asked.

"Bellet's house," he said. "If he didn't bring Tell here, that's where he'll be."

She nodded, settling into her seat again and keeping her eyes open as Hunter drove.

They stayed downtown, going to a section of downtown where the houses were old and surrounded by big lots and fences, and Tina nodded as they got close.

"This is it," she said.

"Yeah, it is," he agreed. There were cars lining the driveway on both sides, and the lights were all on, inside the house.

"What are you going to do?" Tina asked, and he shook his head, looking around.

"How do you like that driveway?" he asked, pointing at one down the road and across the street.

Tina narrowed her eyes. There was a gate across the driveway, but one arm was broken and hadn't closed when the other one did.

"What do you want to bet that drives the neighbors nuts?" Tina asked as Hunter turned, turning off the headlights as he drove up the driveway out of sight of the main road and shut the engine off.

"Stay," he said, and she shrugged.

"Don't die," she answered.

He hesitated.

"Did you have to bring up that that was possible?" he asked, and she turned her face away to hide the smile.

"I'm serious," she said, turning back abruptly. "Is this really the only way?"

"I'm not leaving him in there on his own," Hunter said. "I don't know how they got him…"

"How do you kill a vampire?" Tina asked and Hunter paused, then shook his head.

"Assume you don't know anything about it. Now isn't the time."

He got out of the car and slipped away, disappearing into the dark almost immediately. Tina settled deeper into her coat, feeling like she hadn't really added anything to the night. Feeling like *nothing* about the night had made *sense*.

She shifted into the driver's side seat, turning the keys back on so she could at least turn on the radio to distract herself from what might be a wait that went on until morning, and then she wondered that Hunter had left them.

Was he actually thoughtful enough to want to leave her a way to get away, if he got caught, or had her speaking to him as he was getting out of the car just distracted him and made him forget?

Like Tell, Hunter drove a classic car - Tina didn't know her old cars well enough to identify it, but it smelled of leather and age, and the backseat was inappropriately sized for a toddler, much less a full-sized human being. There was no alarm when she failed to have her seatbelt on, nor to remind him that his keys were still in the ignition.

The radio came in fine, though, and she left it on low, tapping the steering wheel and waiting.

And waiting.

Maybe an hour passed.

Her butt was beginning to hurt, and her fingers were getting cold.

She looked around again, up at the house at the top of the hill, where all of the lights were off. She had a hard time actually distinguishing house from tree, that far away, and in that much dark; the streetlights had no power this far away from the road.

And then the door jerked open and someone pulled Tina out of the car.

"You don't belong here," he said.

"What?" Tina asked. "What's going on? I didn't do anything."

Her immediate instinct was to deny knowing Hunter or Tell, but it was possible that they were completely unrelated, either the people who lived at the house had called… someone - not the police - or Bellet's vampires did a security sweep and had noticed she was there, but didn't know any more than that.

It was possible.

"What are you doing here?" the man asked, holding her by the coat so that her weight barely reached her feet.

"Let me go," she said, wrestling her arms over his hands and trying to extricate herself.

He was strong.

Very strong.

"Answer him," another voice said from the tail end of the car. "Or things to very badly for you, from here."

"Just… listening to the radio," Tina said. "Why? Is that illegal?"

"This is private property," the man behind her said, his voice even. "And the people on this street *really* like their privacy."

"Isn't that his new girl?" a third voice asked. Tina turned her head, trying to see a figure maybe five or six feet off and directly to her left, but it was just a shadow. He sounded young.

"You seen her?" the man holding her asked.

"Yeah, she was at Partridge tonight," he said. "Saw her there, and someone told me."

The man shook Tina.

"You here looking for him?" he asked.

"Who?" she answered.

"Tell," the calm voice from behind her said.

"Do you have him?" she asked.

"She's who he called," the young voice from beside her said. "I betcha."

"She's human," the man who was holding her said with some disdain.

"So?" the young voice asked. "Means she's stupid."

She turned her head.

"Is that what you think?" she asked reflexively. "That humans are stupid? You used to *be* one."

"Cattle think that they're smart or dumb, too," the calm voice said. "But it doesn't make it true."

Tina tried to twist to see the man behind her, but the man holding her shook her again.

"What do we do with her?" he asked.

"Take her in to the boss," the calm voice said.

"He'll decide what to do about her."

"Hope he turns her," the young man said. "She's pretty."

Tina looked in his direction again, but the world spun as the man holding her twisted her to hold her against his chest, forcing her to walk back down the driveway and toward the street.

The way that her shoulder felt against the inside of his forearm told her that thrashing and fighting wasn't going to do her much good.

He was *strong*.

As they got close to Bellet's house, she looked over at the other two men, finding a younger man, maybe in his late teens, wearing a bubble coat and a beanie hat, and a man in a gray trench coat with quick eyes.

They were both frightening, the way they looked at her when they caught her looking at them.

Hungry, cold.

"Why would he turn me?" Tina asked.

"Because you are a problem," the man in the trench coat answered, though she'd been looking at the young man. "Tell likes you, brings you into his business, into *our* business. Humans have no place in any of what we do, outside of the dining room."

"And the bedroom," the man holding her said, squeezing her roughly.

"Same thing," the kid laughed.

They got to the front door, where a number of men and women were standing outside, and someone called to them.

"Who've you got?"

"It's Tell's girl," the man in the trench said. "Call the boss. He's going to want to see her."

They shoved her up the steps and in the front door, then the man who had pulled her out of the car let her go. She looked back, finding a tall, hulking man, built like a lumberjack, wearing no more than a button-up shirt and jeans.

The three of them formed an arc around her as word spread through the house that she was there and other people continued to gather.

Finally, maybe ten minutes later, a man in linen pants, a white shirt, and suspenders came down the main stairs, scratching his head and putting his hands into his pockets.

"Well, well," he said. "I'm told that you have a relationship with the abomination."

"No," Tina said slowly. He hit her across the face with the back of his hand.

"Let's try that again," he said. "And let it be known that we do not tolerate *deceit* in the House of Ascension."

"I don't understand," Tina said. "I'm not…"

He hit her again, with the other hand.

"The *meat* will not speak unless spoken to," he said. "Are you in a relationship with the *abomination*?"

"Do you mean Tell?" she asked.

He hit her again. She tasted blood in her mouth and she sucked on her lip.

"He believes that he has the *privilege* of a name, but I tell you, he does *not*. He sides against his own kind, favoring the *lesser* over the *greater*, and he will see punishment for it, but I tell you, it will be nothing like the punishment that you will experience, so lowly as you are."

She waited.

He lifted his chin.

"Sullen," he said. "And *prideful*. Always so *prideful*, the unbroken humans. Unaware when they are in the presence of their betters."

She waited yet more, angry.

"Are you in a relationship with the abomination?" the man, he had to be Bellet, asked, words dripping slowly.

"No," she said, and he hit her again. The spot was sore already from the first time he'd hit her, and she whimpered involuntarily.

His face was smug.

"Don't lie to me," he said, moving closer, his nose only inches from hers. The lumberjack seemed to sense Tina's mood and she felt him grab her elbows before she could haul off and hit Bellet back.

"I'm not in a *romantic* relationship with anyone," she said.

"I didn't ask you that," Bellet said, stepping back and hooking a thumb through his suspenders. "You *wouldn't* be in a *romance* with a vampire. You are *food* to us. You are in a *relationship* with the abomination in that you *serve* him and you *feed* him."

"No," Tina said, genuinely offended. "No. I work for him."

Once more the man's hand cracked her face, and she let her head hang for a moment, feeling woozy from it.

"I will let him see what it means, to bring humans into our affairs," Bellet said. "Bring her."

The tall man dragged her down the hallway and turned, going down a set of stairs into a musty-smelling basement.

There were men and women down here, in a ring, and at first Tina couldn't see what they were standing around, but she had a good guess.

The ring broke when they realized that Bellet was there, and Tina saw Tell lying on the floor, arms out and legs crumpled underneath him.

"Arise and witness, abomination," Bellet said, and Tell raised his head.

It was worse than what the elemental had done to him. His face was almost unrecognizable for blood and misshapenness, but Tina recognized the look in his eyes.

Clever.

Maybe she was disappointed.

He wasn't *furious* to see her.

He was calculating.

"Over there," Bellet said, pointing, and the big man threw Tina over into a corner against the wall, then went back to stand with the onlookers.

Bellet came to stand in front of Tell.

"This is what happens to abominations. Be warned, we do not forgive those who harbor sympathies for the *least*, for the *weak*, for the *food*. We do not forgive those who sympathize, nor those who plot against us."

He kicked Tell, and Tell went skidding across the unfinished concrete floor, just lying there.

She'd seen it, hadn't she? The clear thought?

He moved like a rag doll.

"What do you have to say for yourself?" Bellet asked. Tell raised his head.

"Vampires aren't made to flock," he said. "Your sheep will scatter."

"*Sheep*," Bellet roared. "Indeed, they are *lions*."

"Turn her," the young man said, pushing his way through the crowd and pointing at Tina. "Turn her and make him watch."

"Is that what you think I should do?" Bellet asked, straightening. "Give her back to him? Allow her to ascend to our level? No. You think that turning her will ruin her for him, will make her an eternal reminder of his *failure*, but this is not the *worst* you can do to an abomination such as this. No. We will drink her dry, and then leave them here alone, so he can decide between taking her life to save his own, or letting them *both* die."

He smiled, then put out a hand toward Tina.

"Bring her to me."

This time, Tina fought.

She thrashed and kicked.

Not that it did her much good.

Bellet seized her by the wrist and pulled her over, grabbing her shoulder and holding her with steely fingers there in front of him.

"Fire," someone called. "There's a fire upstairs."

Bellet's grip on her shoulder tightened, then he threw her back toward the wall, pointing at the man in the trench coat.

"Where did you find her?" he asked.

"In a car, parked across the street," the man in the trench answered.

"By herself?" Bellet demanded as the men and women around them started to step back, away, looking toward the stairs.

"Yes, sir," the man in the trench said, raising his voice, now.

"Did you ever think that maybe she wasn't here *alone*?" Bellet demanded. The vampires broke, turning and running for the stairs as Bellet and the man in the trench held each other's eye for another several seconds. Tina crawled over to Tell, touching his arm. The floor below him was sticky with blood.

"Tell," she whispered.

"You need to go, sir," someone new said, coming and taking Bellet's elbow and coaching him toward the door.

"I will not let this abomination go free," Bellet said, raising his voice once more for effect.

"We'll take care of them," the man in the trench said, and another man in black cargo pants and a black tee shirt nodded, turning in toward Tell and Tina as the rest of the group escorted Bellet toward the stairs.

She could hear the fire, now, smell it.

It was real, whatever was going on upstairs.

She put her hand under Tell's elbow.

"Come on," she said. "Come on."

"Gentlemen," Hunter said, stepping out of the darkness. The two men turned and he hit them one after the other with a pipe, tossing it aside and kneeling next to Tell.

"Is that all it takes?" Tina asked.

"For a couple minutes. I can get us out, but I don't know if I can get us *away*, carrying him," Hunter said confidentially to Tina. "I told you to stay in the car. Why didn't Vince's people come get you?"

"That was at the other place," Tina reminded him, and he wrinkled his nose.

"Right."

"Why did you bring her?" Tell gasped, trying to sit up.

"They bleed you?" Hunter asked, helping Tell up to his knees, where Tell rested for a moment, his head hanging.

"What do you think?" he asked. Tina looked over at the stairs, then at the two men laying on the floor.

"For crying out loud," she said, rolling up her sleeve and extending her arm. "Three days ago, I'd have told you that you needed meds."

Tell raised his head to look at her.

"You don't have to do this," he said.

"Look, I'm offering, don't make it a thing," she said. "You can make me breakfast back at the apartment. Let's just get out of here."

He grabbed her wrist hard enough to jerk her off her feet, and Hunter caught her, moving her to the side so that Tell's grip on her forearm wouldn't pull her off balance again.

Hunter had told her the truth.

It didn't hurt.

Pressure, enough that she knew that he *had* bitten her, but not pain. There was a *drawing* sensation, and Hunter put his arm around her waist, standing behind her.

"The first time, you don't know what to expect," he said.

She was glad he was there.

It was sensual.

Even.

Even in the basement of a madman's house, even in the dark, even as her face hurt, and even as Tell looked like he'd never walk again.

His mouth on her wrist, an electric shooting up her arm, like the brush of skin against skin on a first date.

She turned her face away and the room spun. Her weight found Hunter and he put his other arm around her shoulders.

"You okay?" he asked quietly. "You tell me, I'll cut him off. He knows better, but right now, he's not thinking clearly."

She nodded.

"I'm okay. Just dizzy."

"You ever give blood?" Hunter asked her, and she shook her head - a much smaller, metered motion this time.

"Can't stand needles," she said with humor. He laughed quietly, then pulled his arm from around her waist to touch Tell's shoulder.

"That's it, buddy. You're going to need to get a pro, for any more than that."

Tell let her go, and Tina looked at her wrist.

The light in the basement was dim, and a moment later the lights flickered and went out, but there wasn't a mark on her skin anywhere to suggest damage.

Not even a residue of blood where his mouth had been.

"Told you," Hunter said. "You ready? You need a minute?"

She bent over her knees.

"I'm okay," she said. "We can't stay here."

"You're right about that," Hunter said, moving away. "This is an old house. It's going to come down on us, if we hang out any longer."

She heard motion, scuffling on the floor, and then a hand closed around hers.

"Thank you," Tell said, his mouth close to her ear.

"Let's go," Hunter said.

And then they were moving.

It was pitch dark, just orange shadows up at the top of the stairs, but they didn't go toward that.

They went toward the darker dark where Hunter had come from.

"What about them?" Tina asked, pulling back slightly.

"Who?" Tell asked her.

"The two men Hunter knocked out?" she asked.

"They were going to kill you," Hunter said. "You want to go back for them?"

"The fire department is here," Tell said. "I can hear the sirens. I think they'll get the house put out before it actually collapses on them. And they aren't going to die of smoke inhalation, which is more than I can say for you."

As he said it, Tina felt the wave of smoke come down the stairs and hit them, overtaking them with hot, biting air. She put her sleeve over her mouth, but it didn't help all that much.

Tell pulled her forward again, and she hit her shoulder on a doorway of some kind. There was a small square of moonlight coming through the wall up ahead, and cold air pouring down onto them. She could feel it through her pants, it was so heavy a draft.

"I'm first," Tell said. "Bellet will know this is here, and if he's got any sense at all, he'll have people come watch to make sure we don't get out."

"You sure?" Hunter asked.

"You did your share of the lifting," Tell said. "Let me do what I do."

The light blocked and opened again, and there was a hand on her elbow.

"Are you breathing okay?" Hunter asked. "The smoke thing, I hadn't thought of that."

"It's bad," she said, trying not to cough. "But the fresh air through the window is helping."

"Come on," Hunter said, walking her toward the window. She put her arms up to it - the bottom sill was over her head - and he boosted her up so that her face was even with it.

She could just make out the rippling corrugated metal of an underground window cut-out, but the air was better.

The motion she was going to have to make to get

out of here was beyond awkward. She couldn't picture how Tell had done it.

There was a thud against the house, and then a pair of hands.

"Come on," Tell said. "Quickly."

Tina put her arms through the window and Tell lifted her out like she was a child, setting her on the ground next to him and putting a hand down to help Hunter up and out next.

"Are you okay?" she asked Tell.

"I've got a lot of downtime coming to me," he said. "But I'm at fighting strength, for now. Come on."

He grabbed her elbow and started running. She could see the flashing lights coming up the driveway, the number of scattering bodies between here and there as people ran out of the house. The whole yard was lit up orange as flames roared toward the sky from the other side of the house. They were yet in shadow on this side, but it wouldn't be true for long.

They hit a chain-link fence that was buried somewhere behind five or six feet of untamed brush, and Tell pushed her through to it, then he jumped over and Hunter lifted her.

Tina was growing numb, exhausted and dazed, as they continued moving, not even sure where they were going anymore. There might have been another scuffle, and Tina wasn't sure if someone had caught up to them or if Tell had had trouble going over something.

"Where's your car?" Tell asked.

"Across the street, parked at another house,"

Hunter answered.

"That's where I was when they found me," Tina said.

"No good," Tell answered.

"Where's yours?" Hunter asked.

"A long way from here," Tell said quietly.

"Vince sent a car to get me, it just didn't come here," Tina said.

"Hate to drag him into this," Tell said.

"You got a better plan?" Hunter asked, his face lighting up when his phone turned on.

"No, not right now," Tell said. Tina leaned against Tell, and she felt him lift her face.

"Are you okay?" he asked. "I drank a lot. More than I should have."

She shook her head.

"No such thing as vampires," she murmured, and she heard him smile.

"I'm glad your scientific mind is faring so well," he said. "Are your hands cold?"

"Of course they're cold," she answered. "It's freezing out."

"All right," he said. "We're going to get you home and get you into a hot shower and then bed. You'll feel better in the morning."

"It already is morning," she said drunkenly. The sky was actually beginning to lighten, overhead.

"Vampire morning," he said. "And then we're going to have a conversation about why you were even here, tonight."

She nodded, letting her head fall back onto his shoulder. The world queased and tipped, and Tell and Hunter continued talking. There might have been more walking involved, and then she was laying down across the back seat of a car, her arm under her head as she lay in someone's lap.

She'd never done this.

The crazy college days, drunk and sleepy and inappropriate.

It would have bothered her, if she'd been any less tired.

As it was, the car was warm, and while her face still hurt considerably, she was comfortable enough.

She didn't remember the end of the car ride.

She woke up in the rose-colored room.

In *her* bed.

That was how she identified it, when she opened her eyes.

Hers.

She was still in the same clothes as the night before, and she had no idea what time it was.

Her nights and days were a complete mess.

Fighting against Tell's normal time.

It was confusing.

She went and brushed her teeth, finding her face was bruised in multiple layers and colors, and swollen to the point that getting her tooth brush into her mouth without hurting herself was quite an event.

She looked at the shower, but she was a lot hungrier than she was anything else, so she went looking for her phone - without any luck - and finally just left, going downstairs, where she found two women asleep on the couches and Tell and Hunter sitting at a cafe table.

"Oh, good," Hunter said. "See. I told you she'd be fine."

"You don't get any credit for making that happen," Tell said, dour. "How are you?"

"What time is it?" Tina asked. "I can't find my phone."

"It's in my car, I think," Hunter said. "Tell hacked it, and it's over in that part of town, at any rate."

Tina put her fingers gingerly to her forehead.

"You look terrible," Tell said. "How bad does it feel?"

"Shut up," she said. "You look great."

He smiled.

"I'm not going to say *thanks to you*, because that would trite and obvious. You want pills?"

"Yeah," she said. "Not like, the… you know. Whatever. Yes."

"Regular old painkillers," Tell said, standing and going into the kitchen. He came back with a glass of water and a pair of pills that she recognized.

She nodded, taking them, and Hunter got up, offering her his chair and going to get another one from another table.

"What happened?" she asked, and Tell tipped his head to the side, looking at her face.

"I'd ask you the same thing," he said. "What do you remember?"

"Fell asleep in the car," she said.

"Yeah, you did," Hunter said, with a tone that suggested on a more energetic day she would have smacked him.

"I'm going to kill Bellet," Tell said, with the same tone he'd used to ask her about the pills.

"Can't do it," Hunter said. "We've been over this."

"Why can't he?" Tina asked, and Tell smiled.

"See? She's on my side."

"Because there's nothing that's going to unify a group like that like having someone to chase down and kill for taking out their leader. Yeah, maybe they all fall apart, after, but he *dies* in the meantime."

Tina nodded.

"That's a good point."

"Do you need to see a doctor?" Tell asked. She shook her head.

"No. He just hit me, but I don't think anything is broken. Just hurts. A lot."

Tell shook his head.

"I'm going to kill him."

"Won't get that close again for a long time, anyway," Hunter said. "You know he'll go underground again."

Tell sighed.

"I know."

"What were you doing, last night?" Hunter asked. "Just taking you like that… He wouldn't normally do it."

"I got in a fight," Tell said. "Hadn't gotten properly healed up from Ritan, and one of Bellet's guys saw it. I think he just saw an opportunity."

"What were you *doing*?" Tina asked. Tell shook his head.

"Working."

Hunter waved at him dismissively.

"Don't bother asking any more than that. He won't tell you. He's all hush-hush when it comes to clients."

"But I work for you," Tina said. Tell turned his face toward her, inquisitive.

"Do you?" he asked. "When were you last in the office?"

"A few days," she said. "When were *you*?"

"Tonight," he said. She raised her eyebrows.

"After everything else…"

"Before everything else," he corrected. "I told you when you first came to me that I'm busy, and I only take cases when I feel like it. But I was there. You haven't been."

"Are you firing me?" Tina asked.

"I need someone who's going to be there during the day," he said. "Someone who sleeps at night and lives a pretty normal schedule, for a human. That was what you were doing."

"Not," Hunter muttered, and both of them looked at him. He raised his hands.

"What? I didn't say anything."

Tina ran her thumb over the skin on the inside of

her wrist.

"Are you okay?" she asked Tell. He was watching her face again.

"I will be."

"You were…" She didn't have words.

"I was in bad shape," he said. "Bellet hurt me. A lot. But you came and Hunter came, and you got me out. Isn't the closest I've been to dying."

"Not even this decade," Hunter agreed.

"They know who you are, now," Tell said. "If you're going to run, you have to run far."

"And if I stay?" she asked.

"Then you have to stay close."

"But you don't have allies," she said. "How are you safe without allies?"

Tell looked over at Hunter.

"What have you been telling her?"

"I may have taken her to see the Imps," Hunter said. "Pyro liked her."

Tell shook his head.

"You're more of an idiot than I've ever given you credit for."

Hunter sat up straighter.

"See, I knew if I stuck around long enough you'd accidentally compliment me."

"How are you safe here, if a vampire cult can just pluck you away and no one even cares?" Tina asked.

Tell licked his lips and nodded.

"It's a fine question," he said. "But the answer is that it's complicated. I'm… Vampires are… They're like humans? The have a natural affinity for various things, like regeneration or speed or sensory observation, and then they can learn how to use those things, if they choose to. But life has generally been too easy, for the last few decades, and most vampires… *haven't*."

"He's saying that they're like me, fat and happy," Hunter said casually.

"You're not fat," Tina murmured, and he grinned. "You noticed."

She shook her head, looking at Tell again.

"I practice," he said. "I kill… a lot of people. I hunt a lot. It makes me more *able* than a lot of vampires, a lot of *anything*, but it's not… I don't have vampire superpowers. I'm just a vampire who works out. Does that make sense?"

"Not remotely," Tina said. "But keep going anyway."

He nodded.

"It's the money," Hunter said, and Tell shot him a look. Hunter shrugged. "You're teasing this out like it's a big reveal. It isn't."

Tell shrugged.

"It's the money."

"What does that mean?" Tina asked.

"It means I can buy security," Tell said. "Good security. That works on vampires. And quite a lot of other things, too."

"But the elemental pulled you out of the car," Tina said. "He knew where you were going to be."

"Or he made a really lucky guess," Hunter said.

"He'd been following us," Tell said. "I traced him back to a vampire named Leopard, which means that he was *communicating* with Hunter."

"I met him," Tina said, and Tell's eyes widened.

"You took her to see *Leopard*, too?"

"She was…" Hunter started, then put two hands flat on the table. "I think I'm just going to go, because anything I say from here on out is just going to get me in trouble."

"It's day out," Tina said. They both looked at her.

"What time do you think it is?" Tell asked.

"I don't know. Noon. *Two*?"

Hunter snorted.

"It's past eight, baby, and it's time for the vampires to go out and play."

"You're going *out*?" Tina asked. "After last night?"

"I have work to do," Tell said.

"And I have beautiful women to bed," Hunter said.

"You're disgusting," Tina said, pointing at Hunter without looking at him. "But you?" Tell. "You were on the verge of *death* last night, and the people who did that to you, they're all still out there."

"I've fed," he said. "And I'm actually planning on going with Hunter to feed again."

"At Partridge?" Tina asked. Tell dropped both hands on the table, and Hunter sprang out of his seat.

"Look at the time," he said. "I'm late for an excuse I haven't even made up yet."

He kissed Tina's cheek on the way by, which felt completely natural for some reason, and then he was out of her line of sight, headed for the elevator.

"So you two had quite a night," Tell said, weaving his fingers behind his head and looking Tina over.

She nodded.

"Yeah. I guess so. Kind of a crash course in *not everything makes sense*, you know?"

"Yeah. How do you feel about it?"

"Not everything makes sense?" she said. "You promised me breakfast."

"So I did," he said, slapping his knees and standing. "Bacon? Eggs? Toast? Pancakes?"

"All of the above?" Tina asked, and he motioned her to come sit at the counter with him.

"I don't actually know why he kept me with him all night," Tina admitted as she sat down on one of the barstools. "Partially, he just wasn't asking the right questions to figure out where you were…"

"Don't underestimate him," Tell interrupted. "I know he plays the whole pretty-and-dumb thing to the hilt, but he's *really* a lot smarter than he lets on."

"I'm relieved," Tina said. "I'd been questioning your taste in friends. He told me later, though, that it was a test. That he was auditioning me for you."

Tell nodded slowly, heating a pan on a burner and digging milk and eggs out of the fridge.

"That does sound like him," he said. "You know that there's nothing between us, you and me, romantically. I know that, too. I just want to say it out loud so that it doesn't ever come up as a surprise. But…" He gave her a tight little smile. "Hunter likes the world to work a certain way. I think it comes with living as long as we have. And part of the way that our world has worked is that I have a human assistant of one kind or another who kind of… balances out the rest of the crazy. After what happened to Helen, though, I… I've been full-bore vampire for a while, now."

"Do you consider yourself partially human?" Tina asked, and he frowned, breaking an egg with the spatula and cracking it into the pan one-handed.

"You know, I think I probably do. I think that, if I can keep that piece of myself *alive*, I won't turn out like the rest of them do. I mean, we *are* human. The elementals *aren't*. And there are a bunch of other things… What else did you *see* last night?"

She shook her head.

"Nothing that didn't *look* human, I don't think," she said, and he nodded.

"He took unacceptably big risks, taking you out like that, but I shouldn't be surprised. Anyway, there are a lot of things out there that have never *been* human. They don't think like humans, they don't *work* like humans. Vampires are humans. They're just powerful, immortal, and blood-dependent. I honestly think that the human world would *turn into* the vampire world, just by making humans immortal. I really do."

"That's interesting," Tina said, and he nodded.

"A lot of it is, if you take a step back." He paused. "I like being around you. It reminds me… Who I used to be. Who I still am, sometimes, when I'm not paying attention and I'm not hunting anything." He smiled, maybe the first genuine smile she'd ever seen from him. "I like that guy."

"I think I do, too," Tina said, and he shook his head.

"You need to be careful," he said. "There's a lot of stuff about this world that *looks* romantic, but it's mostly over-sized egos and creatures that will not hesitate to kill you if you get inconvenient. I feel bad, using you like this, and I've been trying to scare you off, but… You're kind of made for this."

"I didn't find you, last night," Tina said, and he shook his head.

"No, but you and Hunter actually went to some really useful places. You just didn't have anything pan out before I got hold of my cell while they weren't looking."

She watched him cook for a few more minutes, just appreciating how well he moved, how happy he seemed to be.

"Do you still want me to work for you?" she asked. He nodded.

"I do."

"And you want me to stay here?" she asked.

"At least until we figure out something else that's just as secure," he said. "You're welcome here as long as you want to be, but I understand if you'd prefer to have your own living situation."

"And you're still going to figure out what happened with my parents?" she asked.

He nodded.

"Actually had someplace I was going to be, last

night, working on it, except that I got waylaid."

"Waylaid," Tina murmured, and he grinned.

He slid a plate in front of her and tipped the pan as the plate stopped so that the eggs landed at the same time, then he tossed a fork to skid underneath the edge of the plate.

"Eat," he said. "Take some time. Then get some sleep. I want you at work in the morning."

She nodded slowly.

"I still have questions," she said. He nodded.

"And I'm still unlikely to answer any of them," he answered.

"How do you kill a vampire?" she asked, then held up a hand. "I need to know, because there are apparently vampires out in the world who are willing to kill you. Which means I need to know what you can survive and what you can't."

"Compelling," he said. "All right, there's the easy way and the hard way." He laid strips of bacon across the pan, touching it with quick fingers to get it to lay flat. "The easy way is to starve them to death. Takes a few weeks, depending on temperature, but what's nice about it is you still win if you get interrupted, and there's very little work involved."

"All right," Tina said. "And the hard way?"

"You bleed them out," he said. "You hurt them until they can't keep healing, and then you bleed them. It's an energy-intensive process, but you can get it done overnight, depending."

"Stakes, silver, garlic?" she asked. He shook his

head.

"Not even sure where garlic came from," he said. "But a stake is a good way to *bleed* a vampire. Nothing special about silver."

"And sun?" she asked. He shuddered.

"Bleeding a vampire is torture," he said. "But exposure is worse. You need two or three days of solid exposure, and…" He shook his head. "We don't have *rules*, because that's not how we work, but that's against the rules."

She nodded, twisting the fork in her fingers.

She looked at him.

"If everyone hates you, why don't they just kill you?"

He smiled, picking up the spatula and separating the bacon again.

"I'm useful," he said. "There aren't as many vampires - or anyone else, for that matter - who are interested in killing me as it might look like, and I solve problems. Problems like Bellet." His voice turned dark for a moment, then he shook his head. "It leaves the more powerful vampires space to go about their lives the way the like. Because I still care."

She chewed on a mouthful of eggs for a moment, then nodded.

"That makes no sense," she said, covering her mouth with her hand. "I mean, it sounds clever and stuff, but…" She shook her head. "You're assuming that everyone who might ever decide they'd like you dead is going to be rational and consider the consequences."

He grinned.

"Anyone else would have taken that as a complete explanation," he said. "But you're right. Vampires are like cats. Even as they're attracted to power, they tend to do it on their own path, not in groups, and they don't care what anyone else thinks. They don't kill me because I'm hard to kill, and they all think they can use me, eventually, against the others."

"Useful," she said, and he nodded.

"I do bad things," he said, his voice changing again, softer. "Really bad things, sometimes. I don't have alliances or allegiances, and when it comes to vampires and other stuff that goes bump in the night… I do what I need to. People like knowing there's someone out there who *can* do what I do…"

"But you still *care*," Tina said. He nodded.

"I do. It's just… It's complicated. Sometimes I care more than others. The vampires in the basement last night? Sure, I could hear the sirens, but I lied when I said that the house would stay up until they put it out. I didn't know and I didn't care."

She looked away, considering this.

"I know it doesn't change it for you," Tell said, "but they would have, either one of them, killed you the moment you stopped being useful."

"I know," she said. "But they were still…"

He shook his head slowly as she searched for a word.

"They weren't human, and they weren't alive," he said. "*People* depends on your definition."

"Do you think you're evil?" Tina asked, and he gave her a sad smile. Thoughtful.

"No," he said. "But I'm not *good*, either."

"And am I?" she asked.

He gave her a little mouth shrug, draining the bacon into a can behind the sink and flipping it onto a paper towel.

"I don't know," he said. "But probably. You cared about whether they lived or died, even after how they treated you... how they treated me."

"You think I'm betraying you, for feeling that way," she said, and he shook his head quickly.

"Not at all," he said. "You're reminding me... who I used to be."

He came around the island, sitting down on a stool next to her and putting the bacon on the counter.

"I told you that I thought we could be friends, and I meant that. I still mean it. But the minute you decide you need to go, I'm going to let you, because... You only get the things out of this that *you* get, whatever they are. I don't ask for your loyalty. I don't *want* your loyalty. Loyalty, when you're human and I'm vampire, just means that you die and I live, and I don't want to live with that on me again. I *won't*. Do you understand?"

"You don't want me to be loyal to you, or you don't want me to *stay* because I'm loyal?" she asked.

He narrowed his eyes.

"You're very specific," he said, nodding slowly. "I think I like that about you."

She narrowed her eyes back in a quasi-mocking

expression.

"You're very evasive," she answered. "I think I'm going to beat that out of you."

He grinned.

"I need to get to work," he said. "I left things unfinished last night, and it just stacks up."

"Take care of yourself," Tina answered. "I can't bail you out again tonight."

His face changed and he reached out to touch the inside of her arm with his thumb, letting his fingers close around her forearm.

"You shouldn't have let it go that far," he said.

"How far is that?" she asked. "Going out with Hunter, meeting the kingpins of the bastard vampire world, getting myself caught, or letting you feed on me?"

He twisted his mouth to the side.

"I'll let you know when I figure it out," he said. "But I could have hurt you. You *never* owe me that, and I don't *want* it. I don't care if I die. I would *rather* die than hurt someone because they offered me their blood."

She nodded.

"I have no idea what my limits are, and I have no intention of learning them."

He smiled and stood.

"Good girl. I'll see you in the morning."

She nodded and watched him leave, wondering how long the women in the front room were going to stay, then going into the den to watch TV.

Tina went in to the office the next morning.

Tell was already in bed by the time she got up, so she didn't actually get to talk to him, but she assumed he'd have stayed up or left a note or something if there was anything he needed her to know.

So she went in.

There wasn't a lot to do, but she felt a bit more comfortable in his space, actually turning on the computer and cruising the internet for a while. She fielded three calls, one from a telemarketer trying to sell professional services, one from a company interested in hiring an 'unaffiliated outside professional', and one from a woman whose college-aged son had gone missing on his way home from a visit.

"I don't get to pick his cases, but I'll tell him about it," Tina said. "And if I can talk him into it, I will."

"Is he good?" the woman asked, and Tina nodded.

"He's very good," she said. "He's expensive, but he's very good."

"It isn't the money," the woman had said. "I just want my son back."

"I'll be in touch once I hear from him," Tina said.

"Do you know when that will be?" the woman asked.

"No earlier than tomorrow," Tina said.

"I'll keep calling, then," the woman said, and Tina pressed her lips.

"I understand. I'll tell him, anyway. I hope your son turns up in the meantime."

"Thank you," the woman said, and Tina wrote some extra notes on the paper, then frowned at it.

There was enough there to *start* on, at least.

Wasn't there?

And this was a missing kid, not Marcus Calloway and a mysterious missing item.

No elementals.

No Imps.

She looked at her notes and then around the office.

What was so special about this place?

Miriam Lane's son was missing, and Tina could help.

Maybe not anywhere near as much as Tell, but if he decided to take the case, she could give him a starting place.

Couldn't she?

She picked up her purse and went out.

Jack Lane lived in an apartment off of campus on his own. He had a girlfriend - a new one, from the sound of it, though Tina knew better than to trust a college-aged boy to tell his mother about a girl in his life when it actually started - who hadn't seen him, but she lived in a dorm on campus.

Tina had the information on his car, there on her post-it note, and she scanned the parking lot, but she didn't see anything that matched it. She went up to his apartment, finding nothing interesting about the door. A young man walked past with a basket full of laundry and looked at her.

"I'm looking for Jack," she said. "We were supposed to meet to work on a project."

And there it was. Lying as easy as breathing. The words just came out.

"Haven't seen him," the man said.

"It's really cold out," Tina said. "Do you know if anyone has a spare key I could borrow?"

"You can come sit in my place while you wait," he said, and she gave him a quick little head shake.

"Thanks, but I don't know you."

He shrugged.

"Let me see if Ella has a key."

She nodded and he disappeared into the apartment across the concrete walkway, coming back out with a cell phone pressed to his ear with his shoulder and a ring of keys.

"Silver?" he asked. "That's not helping any."

He looked at Tina.

"What did you say your name was?" he asked.

"Tina," she said.

"Tina," he said into the phone. He pushed the keys apart with his thumb, trying one and then another one in the door.

"What class is it for?" he asked.

"English," she said, random stab in the dark, but there was a good chance he'd be in an English class, sophomore year, right?

The third key opened the door and the young man pocketed the keys.

Tina rubbed her arms.

"Thank you," she said, going in.

"Just don't, like, steal anything, okay?" he asked,

and she nodded.

"Thanks," she said again, standing as he closed the door.

The apartment was a wreck, but no more of a wreck than most of the college apartments she'd been in. There was no sign of recent activity in the kitchen, either on the counters or the table, and she looked in the bedroom, not seeing a backpack or anything that looked like it had been recently packed or unpacked.

He hadn't made it here.

She checked the mail sitting on the counter, not finding anything exciting, then she went through his room once more.

He seemed like a nice kid. Pictures of him and a few other people, any number of whom might have been his new girlfriend, textbooks sitting in a crate next to the bed, a stack of handwritten letters from a girl that Tina had to assume was a high school girlfriend.

Nothing weird, nothing gross, nothing illicit.

Just a boy who didn't come home.

Disappointed that she hadn't turned up more than that, Tina left, knocking on the door across the way.

"I'm not sure I got the time right," she said. "If you see him, would you ask him to call me?"

The young man gave her a little salute with the piece of paper where she'd written her number, and she went down to the car, feeling… very satisfied, for not having accomplished much.

She'd *done* it. Yes, the kid was missing, and that was sad. And she had no idea what to do *next* to try to track him down. But she'd eliminated something.

And that felt good.

She sat down in the car and was about to start the engine when her phone rang.

It was a number she didn't recognize, and she frowned, thinking maybe the kid across the hall had called her for some reason.

"Tina Matthews?" a woman asked.

"This is she," Tina answered.

"This is Glenda Mitchell," the woman said. "We need to speak."

Tina swallowed.

Her mother's friend from school.

"I thought you were still in Europe," Tina said.

"I…" the woman said. "We need to speak."

"All right," Tina said slowly. "Where should I meet you?"

"Can you be at the food court at the mall in an hour?" Glenda asked, and Tina nodded, writing it down just to have done it.

"Yeah."

Nothing would be open, yet, but presumably that wasn't the point.

"Okay," Glenda said. "I'm so sorry, dear."

"Thank you," Tina said.

"I'll see you in an hour," Glenda said, and the line went dead. Tina set her phone down in the other seat, staring at it for a full minute, unable to make heads nor tails out of what had just happened.

Two of the fast food places in the mall now served breakfast.

That hadn't been the case, when Tina was in high school and had met with her friends at this very food court, and nothing smelled particularly appetizing, but she bought herself a cinnamon roll and a soda, anyway, just to have a tray in front of her as she sat and waited.

Glenda was another fifteen minutes, the woman very much a figure from Tina's youth.

Glenda Mitchell had come to many of the Matthews family parties, helping Tina's mom with everything in the kitchen, and then helping to clean up, afterward. Tina's mom had done the same, for Glenda, though Glenda's son was estranged and much older than Tina, so the Mitchells had had many fewer parties, in comparison.

The woman sat down, fingers nervous on the sides of the table, and Tina frowned.

"Mrs. Mitchell," she said.

"Tina," Glenda answered. "I'm so sorry."

"Thank you," Tina said.

"How are you, dear?" Glenda asked, and Tina shook her head.

"Things have been… strange, ever since. I don't really know."

Glenda reached across the table to cover Tina's hand, pressing her lips.

"I wish…" She shook her head. "I wish I had been here. I know your mom wouldn't have… Do you have friends looking after you?"

Tina stretched her mouth to the side.

"I'm doing okay," she said. "I've met a couple of people, through all of this, who have been taking good care of me."

Okay, that wasn't entirely true, but it was as much as Tina was ready to admit to.

Glenda nodded.

"I feel awful," she said.

"I'm sorry," Tina said. "I mean, you lost a friend, too."

Glenda shook her head firmly.

"No, don't do that, no. I'll…" She sighed. "It's all my fault."

She put her fingers in front of her mouth, and Tina frowned.

"What are you talking about?" she asked, and Glenda shook her head, looking around quickly.

"I… Maybe I shouldn't have done this."

"What's going on?" Tina asked. "What are you afraid of?"

"What do the police say happened?" Glenda asked.

"The last update I got, they thought it might have been a robbery that went wrong," Tina said, and Glenda nodded.

"That's good," she said, and Tina tipped her head.

"Mrs. Mitchell, please tell me what's going on," she said.

Glenda shook her head, then reached across the table again.

"You're your father's daughter," she said. "He never could leave a puzzle to sit, undone."

"No," Tina agreed slowly. Glenda nodded.

"You need to let this one be," she said. "Please. Your mother… She would turn over in her grave, if she knew…"

Tina grabbed hold of Glenda's hand and pulled it in between her own two.

"Mrs. Mitchell, what are you afraid of?" she asked.

"If it can just stay…" Glenda said. "If they just let it *lie*, it can all be *over*, do you see? But if you… If you upset things, it won't be over."

"No," Tina said, finding her tone steely. She liked that noise, in her own voice. "No. It can't just be *over*. I want it to be *done*."

Glenda looked at her with panic in her eyes.

"You won't let it be," she said, and Tina shook her head.

"You need to tell me what's going on," she said.

"I *can't*," Glenda whispered. "They'll kill me."

"They already killed my parents," Tina said. "You need to go to the police and *help* them. Doesn't my mother deserve that?"

"They…" Glenda said, her voice strained, low. "No. I can't. I *can't*."

Tina sighed.

"Please," she said. "Do this for my mom."

Glenda shook her head, standing.

"Just leave it alone," she said.

"You weren't in Europe, were you?" Tina asked.

Glenda looked around quickly, then started walking.

Tina stood, prepared to go after her, but a hand gripped her elbow.

"Easy," a soft voice said. Slick soft, unconcerned. "I can find your kidney and be out the door before you even start bleeding."

There was the point of something uncomfortably sharp just beside her spine and Tina drew a slow breath.

She could elbow him.

Maybe not with the arm he held, but the other one.

The back of her head was suitably *hard*.

If she knew where his nose was…

The pressure of the knife grew.

"If you think that I'm kidding, you should ask your father."

"Who are you?" Tina asked.

"Let's go somewhere more private, where we can have a *real* conversation," the man said. He smelled sweet and woody, cologne over top of a human scent Tina didn't think she would ever forget.

She swallowed.

"I don't know anything," she said.

"You'd be surprised how much people *do* know, when you sit them down and tell them what it is you *want* to know," he said, pulling her arm gently back.

"There are people everywhere," Tina said. "I'm not going with you."

"Take a slow look around," he said. "You see if *anyone* makes eye contact with you."

"Security cameras," she said. He laughed.

"I turned them off," he said. "Not so hard. Call security and tell them that my boy is missing, then slip in behind them and flip a switch. I've got at least ten more minutes before anyone is going to notice."

There was a breath-space of a pause, and then the pressure on her elbow again.

"Do you know how long it takes to bleed out from a good, clean knife wound that severs a renal artery?"

"No," Tina said.

"You *will* find out, if you don't move your feet," he said, his voice rising ever so slightly, gaining a slight grit. "Right now."

She moved along in front of the knife blade, looking around, trying to find the way out.

She could scream.

He'd killed her parents.

He'd searched her apartment.

She *believed* him.

She *believed* him.

He would kill her, rather than let her go.

She walked.

They got to the doors.

"Open them," he said, and Tina put her arms out, pushing the doors open ahead of her, one set and then another. They walked across the parking lot, and she scanned for cameras, closing her eyes with a sense of desperation at his laugh.

"The blue van," he said. "Open the sliding door."

"Cliché much?" Tina asked, and he laughed once more.

"The classics are classic for a reason," he answered. She opened the door and he waited for her to climb in. There was a single captain's chair, there, and she turned to look him in the face.

"Sit," he said.

He had pale skin, dry and damp-looking at the same time, a fully-bald head, and dark eyes.

Maybe in his fifties.

And the knife in his hand, the way he held it, the way his body postured around it, felt like a tool he was comfortable with.

"Sit," he said again. "Quietly."

She sat down in the captain's chair, once more thinking about the various things she would hit him with if he gave her a window, but he tossed two pairs of handcuffs at her.

"Put them on," he said. "One per arm, then lock your arms down to the chair."

The arms on the captain's chair had posts that connected to the seat. Tina didn't think it was a common configuration, but it felt like she'd seen it before. She did as he said, then put her head back against the headrest as he closed the sliding door. A moment later, the driver's door opened and he got in.

"I have friends who are going to come looking for me," she said.

"Everyone does," he said, starting the engine and turning around. He held the knife up with a thumb across and open palm and set it over in the seat next to him, then reached back, closing something around her ankle with quick fingers.

Velcro?

It didn't matter. It held her leg fast, just like that, though she kicked at him with the other foot. He caught her shoe and put his weight down, wrapping her other ankle and settling back into his own seat again.

"You need to know that I have no problem just killing you and getting rid of you," he said. "At some point, that's how this is going to end, no matter what. You don't walk away alive. You aren't going to appeal to my pity."

"You're doing it wrong," Tina said. "You're supposed to try to make me cooperate by promising to let me go, after I cooperate."

He laughed.

It was chilling.

"You will tell me what I want to know when you are ready to *embrace* your death," he said. "I don't expect you to, any time before."

He pulled out of the parking spot, and Tina looked over her shoulder, at the blacked-over windows at the back of the van, back where her car was parked, where Glenda Mitchell was walking away, where Tell would come to look for her.

Wouldn't he?

Wouldn't he?

They drove for about thirty minutes, maybe a little way out of town, maybe just to the far end of the north side. Tina didn't recognize much of the drive after the first ten. He pulled into the driveway of a sixties-era single-level house, shutters falling off and gutters clogged with leaves, even this far into the winter.

He shut the engine off and looked back at her.

"You look like a fighter, to me," he said, and she nodded.

"I am."

He smiled.

"I like those, but not yet."

He opened the glove box and pulled out a bottle and a cloth, dousing the cloth and reaching back with it. Tina fought, but his hands were merciless, and her range of motion was too limited. The strength sapped out of her and the world went dark.

She had no idea how long she was unconscious.

It was dark, when she woke up, a windowless room, musty-smelling.

Cellar.

She lifted her head, finding her hands bound behind her back and her feet tied to a chair.

There was the sound of metal across stone, and she turned her head to look over at it.

A small lamp, obscured by a body, and a workbench.

"What time is it?" she asked.

"Doesn't matter," he answered.

"Does to me," Tina said.

He laughed.

"Won't for long."

If she'd been out a *long* time, it would be getting closer to dusk…

She should have played possum.

Too late.

"You killed my parents," Tina said. "I've been looking for you."

"I hardly noticed," the man answered.

"Who are you?" Tina asked.

"Nobody," he said. "I'm nobody."

"I don't believe that," Tina said. "There's a name on the deed for this house. Is it yours?"

"No, that would be poor Regina," he said. "She died in her sleep a few weeks back. Natural causes, from all appearances."

"Appearances can be deceiving, can't they?" Tina asked, and the man laughed.

"What a silly girl you are," he said.

"What do you want?" Tina asked. "Why did you kill my parents?"

He came to kneel in front of her, playing the point of a long knife against his thumb.

"How well do you think you knew them?" he asked. "Your parents?"

"They weren't complex," Tina said. He smiled.

"You have no idea," he said it. "They got themselves tangled up and in over their heads, and they wouldn't have ever told you, because they were in so much denial."

"No," Tina said. "No. They were teachers."

"They thought that they could keep things from me, protect that fluffy cow from the mall. I'm going to take her, when this is all done, and I'm going to kill her just for having set me back this far."

"I don't know what you're talking about," Tina said.

"No, you don't," the man said. "But you do know where it is."

"What?" Tina asked. "What do you want?"

He brought the knife up to eye level, letting the light glint off of it, then he went to put it away on the table again.

"I'm going to go get lunch," he said. "I find that some time alone in the dark helps people realize how *dire* their situation is."

"Is that what you did to them?" Tina asked as he started toward the shadow of a stairway.

"Yes," he said, looking back at her, just a pale line of his face and silhouette. "They tried to rescue each other, in the beginning. They held hope for a long time."

He turned his face forward again and went up the stairs.

There was a bright shaft of light that flooded the cellar for just a moment, then he walked through the door and closed it again, leaving Tina with just the hooded desk lamp for light.

She worked at her ankles, her arms, but nothing had any sense of give to it. The chair didn't wiggle underneath her at all.

And then.

And then he was right.

Without him there to engage her curiosity, she saw where she was for *what it was*.

She thrashed with a crashing sense of panic, lifting her head and looking around again.

Be smart.

Be smart.

Tell had gotten out. He'd gotten a call to Hunter.

The problem was that both of them were asleep, and she didn't have either of their phone numbers.

She worked at her wrist, wiggling it back and forth, looking for anything that would wear or give.

Leverage.

She just needed enough leverage.

She could break anything with enough leverage.

Tape.

He'd used tape on her.

With enough twisting, she'd gotten just the front edge of it off of her skin, oiled the tape enough that it wasn't re-sticking again, but the problem was that it twisted with her, and she didn't have enough range of motion to get it off of her, all the way around.

She tried to force her eyes to get used to the dark, to look for tools.

Even if she couldn't reach them, she could be ready to use them, if she got an opportunity.

Tell had warned her.

Warned her that *bad things happened*.

She knew that.

She'd been the one to find *them*.

And yet.

For just a *minute*, she'd forgotten.

Sweeping through town with Hunter, it had felt like a game.

It *was* a game to him, she thought bitterly.

Immortal.

Incredibly hard to kill.

It was all just a game, and she'd gone along with it because he was having so much *fun* at it.

She'd let herself get sucked into it, just the way Tell had told her she would.

The *romance* of it. Covering up the dark.

She sat in the dark.

Working at her wrist, she sat in the dark and she waited.

Hoping for night.

The man came down some time later.

She had no sense of it, but that it had been a *long* time.

It was a long time to sit, her shoulders aching, her hips aching, her wrist *burning*, waiting.

He went back to the workbench, picking up the knife and looking at her again.

"I want you to tell me about your mother."

"She loved kids," Tina said. "She loved art. She loved life."

He laughed quietly, kneeling in front of her and sliding the knife, flat-sided, down her thigh.

"You know the fluffy one, don't you?" he asked. "She called you because she cares about you."

"Is that how you found me?" Tina asked.

Of course it had been.

"What do you want?" Tina asked. "What's so important that…"

She could see it, there in his eyes.

The cold glee, the way they just bored into her.

He felt *nothing*, killing people. They didn't have to be *worth* killing.

Like a little boy pulling the wings off a fly, he was doing it because it interested him.

"The fluffy one," he said. "She's going to be interesting. That much *soft*, you can just peel it away, bit by bit…"

He leaned forward, mesmerized with watching her face, and Tina gritted her teeth.

Glenda may have been involved in what happened to Tina's mom, and she may not have told Tina what was happening when she *should* have, but it wasn't because she was a *bad* person. She was afraid.

She was afraid of *this man*.

Tina would have been. Well, she was. She was *very* afraid of him. But she would have been petrified, *stupefied*, if not for the past couple of days.

She didn't hold that against the older woman, and the idea that *this man* was going to get his hands on her, hurt her for pain's sake…

It made her angry.

He slid closer, serpentine, uncoiling his knees to

look her closer in the face, his weight propped on the knife on her thigh. He smiled.

"You're going to be a fun one to break," he said. "They cried. Both of them. From the beginning. Told each other how much they *loved* each other. No fun at all."

The chair was secured to the floor.

Leverage.

She didn't just have her own muscles, her own mass.

She had the entire *house*, the entire *earth* to use against him.

Legs, arms, back, all of them bracing, pulling against the chair, she slammed her forehead into his nose, feeling a crack that she wasn't sure whether it was her or him.

It hurt.

Her vision went red for several moments, and she heard him scuffle and scramble back, then fall.

Well.

Even if that was all it was, she'd nailed him once, and that felt *good*.

She shook her head as her vision cleared, and she blinked, trying to find him on the floor.

The knife had fallen on the floor next to her. She could just make out the metallic glint, there, but there wasn't anything she could do about it.

Her arm wasn't free.

Nothing was any more free than it had been, two minutes ago.

Well.

No.

She was.

Tell had told her that justice wasn't going to fix it.

And it wasn't.

She could see that, now.

Nothing was going to bring her parents back. Nothing was going to fill in the hole that it had put in her life.

Nothing.

But.

She'd hurt him.

She'd *hurt* him.

She had taken the power back from him, for one instant, and she could *breathe* like she hadn't since before…

Since before.

He rolled onto his side, groaning, and she wondered just how good a hit she'd gotten.

There was a hole in the human skull, where the air that came in through the nose went into the sinuses.

You could poke cartilage through that hole, if you did it right, and there wasn't anything *hard* between there and the brain. Nothing to stop a shard of hard nasal structure from killing you.

If you did it right.

"There's more than one kind of monster in the world," a voice said quietly, and Tina sat up.

"Tell," she said.

"Are you okay?" he asked.

She could have cried.

Maybe she did; she was too busy to think about it.

"Get me out," she said. "I want to kick him."

"Let me do this," he said gently, fingers on her arm, tape ripping. "You don't want to be this kind of monster."

"Like hell," Tina said, pulling her arms around to the front, feeling the relief on her shoulders. Tell knelt in front of her, tearing tape on her ankles.

"Is Hunter here?" she asked.

"Why?" he asked and she shook her head, not sure why she'd asked. Maybe she'd thought he would care.

"What time is it?" she asked.

"Ten," he said.

"At night?" she asked.

"It's not in the morning," he said, running his hands up her arms. "Are you sure you're okay?"

"He didn't hurt me."

She rubbed her shoulders, glad for the feel of his fingers, there.

Powerful.

He was powerful.

She was safe.

On the side with *power*.

"I'm going to go kick him," she said. The man slid away, along the floor, and Tell held Tina's elbow.

"Defending yourself is one thing," he said. "Attacking a man as he lays on the floor? Are you sure you want to *be* that person?"

She pulled her arm away, going to the workbench and tipping up the lamp so that it lit the room.

Oh, the gruesome that was living on that bench.

It turned her stomach and made her even angrier.

"Never again," she said, hauling a leg back to kick the man as hard as she knew how in the stomach, then she turned away.

Swallowed.

"I'm done," she said. "Do what you need to."

There was a scraping noise on the floor as the man tried to drag himself away, coughing, and Tina turned to watch as Tell propped him up against the workbench.

"I admire your skills," Tell said. "If I weren't *me*, I'd have never known you were there. But I need to know what you were looking for, and what value it had."

The man coughed a few times, the side of his face bloody and his hands clutching at his stomach as he looked into Tell's eyes.

And then.

There.

There was the flicker of mania that Tina had seen.

"You're something new," he said to Tell. Tell reached out, putting his palm to the man's forehead.

"As are you, friend," Tell said. "You could lie to me and I wouldn't ever know, because your body doesn't know the difference between a lie and the truth, does it?"

The man laughed.

"They're going to enjoy you," he said, lifting his face to look at Tell with a twisted smile. "Oh, yes. They aren't going to see you coming, but when they catch you? You have it, don't you?"

"Have what?" Tina asked, and the man's eyes darted over.

"Why her? She's paying you, isn't she? How

much? They'll pay you more."

Tell shook his head.

"My services aren't for sale," he said, "though I charge dearly."

He ran his fingers across the man's bald scalp, drawing a breath, then nodded.

"This is going to be work," he said. "You shouldn't be here for it."

"I'm staying," Tina said. The man on the floor laughed, coughing again and spitting up blood.

"Much as I'd love to stay and see you work," he started, and Tell jerked, but too slow. The man reached up to the underside of the workbench. Tina couldn't see what he brought back down, between the shadow and the fact that he didn't *seem* to have *anything*, but he covered his mouth with his hand and laughed again. Tell went into the man's mouth after it, but whatever had happened was done.

Tell stood.

"What?" Tina asked.

"What *in the world* are you into?" Tell asked. "This isn't just some guy from a pawn shop."

"Is that what you thought?" Tina asked. He shrugged.

"Seen that one before. What *is* this?"

She shook her head, indicating.

"Ask *him*."

"He isn't going to talk anymore," Tell said, coming to stand next to Tina and turning, crossing his arms. As Tina watched, the man convulsed and began to foam at the mouth.

She covered her mouth with her hand.

"What's *going on*?" she asked. "It was supposed to just be a robbery…"

Tell shook his head.

"How did he find you? You weren't at the office or the diner. I *know* you weren't…"

"My mom's friend called," Tina said. "Glenda Mitchell. She was in the file. She said we needed to talk…"

"So you left the office to see her?" Tell asked.

Oh.

"Um," she said. "I was already looking for a missing college kid," she said. Tell's eyes went wide.

"You were *what*?"

She shrugged.

"I thought I could help," she said. "And it wasn't like that was how he *found* me. He found me because he followed Glenda. The kid is *missing* and his parents are frantic, and no one is looking for him because he's an adult, but he never made it home, I went and looked around his apartment…"

Tell held up a finger.

Tina fell silent.

He licked his lips and shook his head.

Opened his mouth.

Closed it and looked away again.

Finally drew a breath and spoke.

"I'm not going to tell you that you can't do things. It's not who I am. And I'm dearly trying not to be overprotective, but… I mean, they tried to *kill* me two nights ago. And… *this*, whatever it is…"

He paused, shook his head.

"No. You were in an unexpected place and investigating a mundane human problem." He looked down at the sociopath on the floor and shook his head. "You probably weren't wrong. If he was missing long enough for his parents to notice, time matters, and maybe you could have put me ahead looking for him today, if I did it. Yeah." He looked at her again. "But you *have* to stay away from people that you *knew*, and *anything* related to my world. For now."

She nodded.

"I wasn't thinking."

"It was a mistake," he said, and she nodded, then he frowned, shaking his head.

"No," he said. "I mean, *you* made a mistake, but *they* made a bigger one. I was at a dead end. He didn't leave a trail because he wasn't *tied up* in any of it. He was work-for-hire, and *really* good at it. If he'd killed you before I got here and burned the place, he might have gotten away from me, again. But I've got him, now, and…" He sucked on a back tooth, beginning to smile. "Oh, I've got them, now. You don't… No, you don't, and expect me *not* to come at you with everything."

Tina swallowed.

"You're terrifying sometimes," she said, and he nodded without looking at her.

"I know."

"Why didn't Hunter come?" Tina asked.

"I never said he didn't," Tell said.

She looked at the stairs and then back at Tell again, exasperated.

"*Is* he or *is he not* here?"

"Why does it matter to you?" Tell pressed, and she shook her head.

"I thought we'd kind of had a… a meeting of the minds, looking for you. I thought…"

"That there was no way he was going to let me come looking for you without him tagging along?" Tell asked. "He's upstairs, watching my back."

Tina nodded.

"Yeah."

Tell grinned, squatting.

"You should let him take you home."

"It was just *afternoon*," Tina said. "How did it get so late so fast?"

He glanced at her, standing and sniffing her shoulder, then turning away again.

"Knock-out gas," he said. "Your system is pretty weak. I expect he dosed you a lot harder than he meant to."

She felt weak, as he said it.

"He's upstairs?" she asked.

Tell nodded, approaching the sociopath's body once more.

"I have work to do," he said. "Tell Hunter to stay with you until you eat. You've got the shakes."

She nodded.

"You've got a way to get home?" she asked.

"You shouldn't worry about me," he said. "Get

some food, get some rest, and I'll talk to you in the morning."

"Will you find her son?" Tina asked. "My notes are in my car…"

"At the mall," Tell said. "I'll find it."

"Keys," Tina said, patting her pockets. "Where are my keys?"

"With your cell phone," Tell said. "I found them."

She looked at his back.

"Will you find the woman's son?" she asked. He glanced over his shoulder at her.

"Do you want me to do that, or do you want me to do this?"

She took a slow breath and nodded.

"He could be in trouble," she said. "My parents aren't getting any deader."

It shocked her, how easily the words came out.

"I'm not letting this go," he said. "There are going to be clues around here that are time-sensitive. But I will look into it before dawn, and I will leave you a list of things to follow up on, if I don't make it until you wake up."

She had been started for the stairs, but she paused.

"Really?" she asked. "You're okay with me doing that?"

"It will mostly be phone calls and online work," he said. "But you're good. And I'd be an idiot to not use that. But you *need* to make sure that you don't go anywhere that someone who *knows* you is going to expect you to be there. For a little while longer, at least."

"I have friends," Tina said. "I don't want to just

ignore them forever."

He shook his head, his focus returned to the body.

"Not forever," he said. "Just for now."

Hunter was sitting on the front stairs, passing a gun from hand to hand.

He stood as she came out.

"You're alive," he said.

"Yes," she answered.

"Tell wouldn't promise," Hunter said, looking her up and down like he wasn't convinced.

"I'd accuse you of not being used to being around *fragile* humans, but you literally drink them, so what's your excuse?" Tina asked, starting down the stairs.

He grabbed her elbow as she went past.

"Are you okay?" he asked.

"We're all running a little thin…" she started, but he shook his head.

"Don't do that," he said. "Are *you* okay?"

She shook her head.

"No."

He looked her up and down again and she dropped her head against his shoulder.

She had *no idea* why she did it, but he was there and he was solid and then she had her forehead against the soft spot by his ribs.

Her head hurt, where she'd hit it against the man's nose, injury over the beating from Bellet, which she was definitely feeling again. Hunter put his hand on the back of her neck, and she felt his chin come down to brush through her hair.

"What can I do?" he asked.

"Take me back to Viella," she said. "Sit with me while I eat dinner."

"Are those your orders, or Tell's?" he asked with humor.

"His," she said.

"What can I do?" he asked again.

"I thought I was going to die," she said.

Did she?

She wasn't sure it was true, though the way her body felt, it certainly wasn't a lie either.

"Not with Tell being who he is," Hunter said.

He took a step down to stand on the walkway next to her, pulling her in against him.

He smelled earthy in a way that she wasn't sure if she liked it or not, but he *felt* safe, and that was…

That was exactly what she wanted, right now.

"Tell is scary," she said, wrapping her arms around his waist, realizing that she actually was shaking.

Hunter laughed silently, nodding.

"He is. He gets paid a lot, for that."

"I mean, he's maybe a hundred eighty pounds, soaking wet, and… He's too *thin*. To be scary. You know?"

"It amplifies it," Hunter said. "If he was a big dude, it'd be obvious. It's that it comes up on you, by surprise, that really drives it home."

"You've had a lot of time to think about this," Tina

said, turning out so that she could walk alongside him.

"I have, actually," Hunter said. "And appreciate it, too. People know that he's my friend, and, while he really couldn't care less about people screwing me over in business deals, I've yet to have a heavy show up at my door and try to force me into a deal that I didn't want. And that's not unheard of, for us."

She shuddered and he squeezed her shoulders.

"You want to, like, talk about it or something?" he asked.

"You are such a frat boy," Tina answered, and he laughed.

"You know, they didn't have frats where I came up, but I think I really would have liked them."

"You're lying to me if you're trying to tell me that you've never done the frat thing," she said, and he laughed again.

"Busted."

She nodded.

"You have blood on you," he said quietly.

"It's not mine," Tina answered.

"I know."

She looked up at him, then shrugged out of his arm as gracefully as she could.

"I'm sorry," she said. "I'm just a little off right now. I don't mean to imply…"

He held up both hands.

"Just walking a girl to the car," he said. "You know me. None of this means anything."

She nodded, not sure why that disappointed her,

and not sure what she was hoping to see in his face.

It was Tell's car parked on the side of the street.

"Did you get your car back?" Tina asked.

"Paid a guy to go get it today," Hunter said. "But Tell was already moving when he called me, so this was simpler."

"I didn't get his keys," Tina said.

"I have them," Hunter answered. The keyring hadn't been on his finger, a moment before, but it was there, now.

She paused, but he went around the car without getting her door.

She waited for him to get in and lean across, to unlock it, and she got in, hugging her arms.

"You cold?" he asked. "I have no clue how you feel, so if you need the heater, you should just do it."

She nodded.

"I'm cold, but that isn't going to fix it."

She sat up, patting her pockets again.

"Tell said that he found my wallet… didn't he? I don't remember."

"He did," Hunter said.

"I don't have my key," she said. "The one to his apartment."

"Vince will let us in," Hunter said. "Believe me, I crash that place all the time."

"Why?" Tina asked. "Don't you have some fancy-schmancy place here in town all to yourself?"

He shrugged.

"I do. But it's much more fun to take dinner over

to Tell's place and make a party out of it."

"Ah," Tina said.

"Do you want to get drive through or something?" Hunter asked. "I mean, Tell's a good cook, but it's kind of like ice sculpture, to us, you know? I don't… *do*… that."

"Then how do you know he's good?" Tina asked, looking out the window.

"All the girls want to go to his place," Hunter answered with humor. "Seriously, do you want something hot to eat?"

"Yeah."

"Preference?"

She shook her head.

"Just whatever's easy."

He pulled into an all-night drive through and ordered a burger and fries for her, handing them across. She tore into the bag like she was starving, shocking herself with how *calming* salt-covered French fries were. The entire meal was gone by the time they got to Viella, and she felt a lot more confident over her own feet, going up the stairs to the lobby, where Hunter waved Vince over.

"She's misplaced her key," Hunter said. "Can you let us in, upstairs?"

"Of course," Vince answered. "Should we re-key the elevator, as a precaution?"

"Like anyone would ever be able to sneak in past you," Hunter laughed.

"I think Tell has it," Tina told Vince. "If it's actually missing, I'll let you know."

"Thank you, Ms. Matthews," Vince said.

They got to the penthouse and Vince took the elevator back down as Tina went to put her shoes by the closet.

"Why do you do that?" Hunter asked, wandering in toward the kitchen.

"It's too nice for street shoes," Tina answered, and Hunter laughed.

"If these *floors* could talk," he said. "Are you still hungry?"

"He knocked me out," Tina said. "I didn't know what time it was, or if Tell was going to get there before he killed me."

"And yet, he's the one who lost blood," Hunter said.

"He got too close and I head-butted him," Tina said, and Hunter sat down at the island counter, grinning.

"Tell does know how to pick them."

"The man killed himself," Tina said. "Before I came upstairs."

"Tell's a scary beast," Hunter said.

"But he said that the people he was working for were going to keep… trying to find me…"

Hunter shook his head.

"You're safe here. You know that, right?"

She nodded.

"And it's night. And Tell is *on it*. There aren't many people in the *city* who are safer than you. You know that?"

She nodded again.

"Now actually believe it," Hunter said. "Because

it's the truth."

"I don't…" Tina started, then went to sit on a couch, crossing her arms on the back and resting her chin on her wrists to look at him. "I don't know how to feel."

"You're looking at the wrong guy, to talk about feelings," Hunter said. "I'm pretty notorious for not having any."

"I noticed," Tina said, and he grinned.

She wanted to go back and kick him once more, just to have done it.

He was dead.

For everything she'd been through, the past couple of months… The man who had killed her parents was *dead*. And she'd been there to see it.

And it solved nothing.

"It's, like, time for you to sleep, now, isn't it? I mean, I don't even *remember* a time when the sun didn't dictate when I had to go find a place to lay down. You getting to choose…"

Hunter shook his head, standing up.

"So I fed you. Right? Now I tuck you in?"

"I guess so," Tina said.

He came over and offered her a hand. She took it, and he closed his other hand around hers, squeezing her fingers tight, then leading her up the stairs and into the guest room.

"You should do something with all of this," he said, motioning. "Make Tell give you a renovation budget. You can't possibly *like* it."

"It's beautiful," Tina said. He snorted.

"It's… bland," he said. "And you are nothing *like* bland."

He squeezed her hand and let go, backing toward the door.

"Shower, teeth, bed," he said. "No playing around on your phone, oh, wait, you don't have one."

He grinned, pulling the doors closed as he backed into the hallway, and Tina stood, alone.

Alone.

The room was comfortable.

Warm.

Snug, despite how high the ceilings were and how spare the furniture.

Something about the curves and the textures, it just made her feel bundled in and cozied.

It wasn't the room that felt empty.

It was *her*.

It was *done*.

Not all of it. Tell still had to figure out what the man had been looking for, and who had sent him. There was mystery - risk - left, aplenty.

It was that the single thing that had been driving her was over.

She didn't know if Tell would call Detective Keller and tell him… *anything*.

She didn't *care*.

She sat down on the bed, the comforter coming up to her elbows on either side, and she tried to toe her shoes off, remembering late that they were downstairs.

She looked around the room, blinking at it,

mesmerized by *nothing*.

Tina didn't know what she was doing here. Or what she would do tomorrow. Or ever again.

Tipping over onto the pillow, she shuffled her body just enough to get the blanket over her, and she tucked her head onto her elbow, staring at the floor.

The sobs came as a shuddering, aching surprise. She didn't even know what they were about, just... pain. Pain inside coming out, in coughing, racking sobs.

She hadn't cried like this since the week after her parents had died, falling down on the floor and just *being* in pain.

The doors opened again, but she didn't look up. They closed a moment later, just an awareness that the light had changed, and she continued to cough up pain out of her chest.

A body came to lay down on the bed behind her, a chest against her back, an arm pressed firm down on her shoulder, a face against the back of her head.

She didn't turn.

It could have been anybody.

But it comforted her, and some time later she finally fell into a deep and dreamless sleep.

She woke in the bed alone, her face matted over with hair and her body aching from being exactly how she had lain when she got there.

Tina looked around the room, seeing it as if a stranger, then went into the bathroom and showered.

For a long time.

She wanted to talk to Tell, to find out what he'd determined, what he needed her to do, just to *talk* to him, but she stood there until any reasonable water heater would have given up before she finally got out and dressed.

She needed more clothes from her apartment.

Or just new ones.

Maybe.

She didn't think about it much, but for the fact that she was reusing clothes more than she normally would have.

She went looking for her phone, remembering late that it was still missing, then went out into the hallway. Tell was sitting on a couch in the second-story atrium - mezzanine? - reading a book.

He glanced up as she came out of the hallway, giving her a tight-lipped smile.

"I wasn't sure," Tina answered. "It's a little hard to tell. Aren't you up late?"

"I'm an expert on this, and I don't think I've ever seen Hunter any closer to head over heels than he is, now."

He sat with two fingers on his temple, not looking up from his book.

Tina nodded slowly, going to sit on another couch.

"Too bad he's a vampire," she said, and Tell nodded sagely, putting his book down.

"Too bad."

"First one of you who gets a twinkle in his eye thinking I might like to be one of you, I'm gonna kick him in the balls," Tina said, and Tell lost control of a smile for just a moment.

"I see."

"Good."

"I thought that you would want to know that your cleaner's name was Edward," he said.

Tina shook her head.

"That's not creepy enough," she said. "I'm going to call him… *Victor*. No. *Thaddeus*. No. *Griswold*. I don't know. I give up. Edward. Whatever."

"You feeling okay?" Tell asked.

"No."

"Fair enough. Well, he was good at what he did, if what he did was keep things secret."

"You didn't find anything," Tina said.

"I didn't say that," Tell protested.

"You kind of did," Tina answered, and he shook his head.

"I said he was *good*," Tell said. "I didn't say he was *as good as me*."

"All right," Tina said. "What did you find?"

"Not a lot," he admitted. "I've got some paper trails to chase down, when I get up tonight, but I'm going to get them."

"I believe you," Tina said. "What about the kid?"

"You've got a hospital run to do," he said, taking a slip of paper out of his book and handing it across to her.

"Oh, no," Tina breathed, and he shrugged.

"Sometimes the job is harder than others. This is what you signed on for. Finding him. I found him, I think. I'll leave it to you to confirm before you call his mom."

She nodded, looking at the paper.

It was a hospital in a little town about an hour away.

"I'll go after I eat," she said.

"I know that it needs to happen today," Tell said. "It's a big part of the reason I stayed up. You need to take care of yourself today. Between yesterday and the day before… Anyone would have a hard time making good decisions. You're sort of in a bad place, to begin with."

She nodded.

"I think I'm safe to drive, but I need my car and stuff."

"All of your personal items are on the counter downstairs, and your car is parked in the garage," Tell said. "Stay close, when you get back. I don't know what the people he was working for are capable of, nor what he told them."

"Yeah," Tina said. "Okay."

He nodded, standing.

"Look, I know a lot of this… There's not a lot that you can do, to make it easier. And I don't actually know anyone who's been through *everything* you have, but if you want to talk to one of the girls, or something…"

"The fountains?" Tina asked incredulously, and he gave her a sheepish half-grin.

"Yeah, I see your point. Just… Hunter and I are kind of… immune. I don't know how to help you."

She held up the slip of paper.

"I'm going to go tell a worried woman what happened to her son," she said. "It's going to suck. But I'm going to be okay."

He nodded, rubbing his face.

"I've got to go crash before it drives me into the couch permanently," he said. "I'll see you here tonight?"

"Yeah, so long as I don't get abducted by a sociopath again," she said, and he held out an arm as he walked away.

"Yeah. Don't do that."

She watched him as he walked away, then she went to get her things, which were just where he'd told her they would be. Her phone was dead, so she went to get her charger, plugging it into an outlet in the kitchen island and making herself a breakfast of toast and orange juice.

She wasn't actually hungry, though her body felt fatigued in a way that told her that she needed to eat. She forced the toast down, then drank an extra glass of juice, checking the charge on her phone.

It would work fine, navigating, and she could finish charging it in the car.

She put her charger away in her purse and pushed the button for the elevator, wondering passively if Hunter was around here, somewhere, unconscious.

She stopped off in the lobby to tell Vince that she'd found her keycard, then went down to the parking garage, where she found her car.

The one piece of *home* that she hadn't completely lost.

It felt good, smelled right, getting into her car and starting the engine, putting her purse down on the passenger seat and looking over her shoulder to back out of the spot.

Yes, she was going to a hospital to confirm that something awful had happened to a college student with a promising future and a mother who loved him.

But.

She was alive, and it felt like being *her*, in a novel way. A *new* way.

She turned on the radio and sang with it as she drove, finding the hospital and asking about the unnamed young man who had come in two nights before.

"Do you know who he is?" the nurse asked, and Tina nodded.

"I think I might. I'd like to confirm it before I call his mom. Can I see him?"

The nurse picked up a clip board and walked her back to look through a window at a man hooked up to various machines, tubes taped to his arms and mouth.

"What happened?" Tina asked. The nurse shook her head.

"I can't discuss that with you," she said. "Is that your boy?"

Tina winced her mouth.

"It's hard to say," she said. "Can I go in?"

The nurse gave her a quick nod.

"Just for a minute."

Tina went through the door to look down at the young man's face, what she could see above the respirator.

The shape of the nose.

It was distinct.

She nodded.

"That's him."

"It's a relief," the nurse said, turning to walk back out with Tina again. "Hate to see a kid like that, in here all by himself. He's old enough they wouldn't look for him, isn't he?"

Tina nodded.

"Traveling back to college from home. He's a long way from either, right now. I'm going to go call his mom."

The nurse walked her back to the front lobby, where Tina sat on a couch and dialed the number on her phone.

"I found him," she said to the woman, giving her the hospital name and location.

"What happened?" the woman asked.

"They won't tell me," Tina said. "He's unconscious, but you knew that. You knew that if he was missing, it was because he couldn't tell you where he was. He's *alive*. This is about as good as it could be. You come here, and then you go from there."

"Thank you," the woman said. "Thank you."

"I'll be here, when you get here," Tina said.

"Thank you," the woman said again, and Tina hung up, resting her head against the couch and passively watching the television for the next forty minutes.

A heavy-set woman in a purple sweater bustled in, seeing Tina and coming over. Tina stood.

"You're the one from the investigator?" the woman asked, and Tina nodded.

"Yeah. Go find out. I'll be here."

Tina waited again as the woman went to talk to the nurse, then got buzzed back into the hospital. It was almost an hour before the woman came back out. Her face was red and puffy, and she hugged Tina for a long time, just sitting on the couch next to her.

"Is he bad?" Tina asked. The woman laughed, digging a wet tissue out of her pocket and putting it to her eyes and then her nose.

"He woke up," she said. "I went in and he woke up and he held my hand. He couldn't talk, and I don't think he knew where he was, but the doctor said it was a really good sign."

Tina gave her a genuine smile.

"I'm so glad."

The woman nodded, touching her eyes with the tissue again.

"They don't know what happened to him. Or where his car is. They said that he got hit in the head, and it doesn't look like it was an accident… Someone attacked my son, but you found him. And… He woke up."

Tina nodded again.

"I'm glad," she said once more.

The woman squeezed her hands.

"Thank you. I'm…" She motioned back toward the desk and Tina nodded.

"Go."

And that was that.

She'd done something good.

Something *really* good.

She smiled, going back out to her car and driving into town, getting lunch at a drive through on her way to the office, where she spent her day reading about what it took to become a licensed private investigator.

A whole day where nothing that remarkable happened.

Sure, she went to a hospital, identified an unconscious young man, and told his mother where to find him, but no one put a knife to her throat or punched her or threatened to kill her or anything.

She went back to the penthouse, stopping at the concierge desk on the way by with a grocery list.

"I feel really bad," she said to Vince, "but I'm not supposed to go grocery shopping as long as there are men out there who might be trying to kill me…"

"Ms. Matthews," Vince said. "You insult me. Give me your list."

She'd handed it over, and thirty minutes later, she had a well-stocked refrigerator for making anything she wanted to.

Unfortunately, her mother had never been much for cooking, so Tina looked up online how to make a lasagna, because that sounded good. Homemade noodles? Not hardly.

Tell got up about ten minutes into the process, and he glanced once at the recipe then shook his head, but helped with assembly without comment.

"How are you feeling?" Tina asked.

"Better," he said. "I'll go out with Hunter again tonight to see if I can't get a little more caught up, but I don't think that Bellet's guys would have beat me, if they'd caught me out, tonight."

She nodded, and he leaned his hips against the counter, crossing his arms.

"And how are you?"

"I found the kid," she said with a smile, still sprinkling cheese across the top of the pasta. "His mom was there when he woke up."

"Do you want me to find the people who hurt him?" Tell asked. She glanced over.

"You knew?"

He nodded.

"I did."

She sighed, then shook her head.

"They can call back if they want to hire you to do that. She just wanted to find him, and she did."

"All right," he said.

"Is this how it's going to be?" Tina asked as she put the lasagna in the oven, checking the time, and then leaning against the opposite counter to look at Tell. "You up all night, me up all day, and we just cross paths for a few minutes at dawn and dusk every day?"

He snorted.

"If you're going to hold the day shift at the office, I don't see a lot of wiggle room. Wait until summer, when I'm sleeping sixteen hours a day."

She hadn't thought of that.

"I want to hang out with you," she said. "Do you ever just stay in?"

"Not very much," he said. "I mean, we have parties, and I stay in for those, but mostly I'm out. Even as old as I am, I've never found that there's enough time to do everything that's worth doing."

She nodded, checking to make sure the oven was on, then went around the counter to sit down at one of the bar stools.

"I guess," she said. "Maybe I'm just lonely, or something, but I'm jealous of all of the going out and doing things that you and Hunter do."

He grinned.

"You want to be our human sidekick?" he asked.

"Better than Alfred, back at the manor," Tina answered, and he laughed.

"Give it time," he said. "I'm not going to tell you how any of this is going to go, because it could go any way you want, but for now…"

"Yeah, yeah, for now I've got people who would prefer I be dead," she said. "So I have my list of approved places…" She paused. "Why won't you tell me why it's safe at the office?"

"Because you still wouldn't believe it," he answered playfully.

"Why not?" she pressed.

"Because," he said. "I look like you and I think like you and I used to *be* you. The things in this world that have *never been* human are an awful lot harder to swallow."

"You bit me," she said. "You drank my blood, and you went from being a broken man on the floor to beating people up, outside."

"And you're completely used to stories about sexy men in dark clothes who bite women's necks and drink their blood," he said, motioning to himself with a handflip.

"I love you for your self-confidence," Tina said, and he grinned.

"It's so much easier, when I can just be myself," he answered, still teasing. "No, there are people there - and I use that term to describe sentient life forms of a quasi-humanoid shape - who have been watching my back for decades. I return the favor. That's a small part of why I go out every night. People *need* me. So I go do what they need me to do, because if I don't, no one will. But they know that I'm *down* during the day, and they step up. Some of them, in really *real* ways."

"So when you went missing, they were the ones I should have gone to?" Tina asked. He narrowed his eyes, then shrugged.

"Some of them... *maybe*. But only during daylight, when they really have an advantage over the vampires. The kinds of trouble I have the ability to get into, you really don't have access to the skillset to dig me back out."

"So what am I supposed to do?" Tina asked.

He shook his head.

"I still owe Hunter some severe comeuppance for taking you out, that night. You don't get tangled up in it. I *appreciate* you doing what you did, but there was no reason to expect you would *survive* that. It was just all luck that it worked out like it did. And that's not good enough. You need to stay *away*, and let me take the consequences of my own decisions."

Tina paused.

"Nope."

He raised an eyebrow, and she shrugged.

"I'm never going to do that, so you need a better plan."

"Do I?" he asked, and she nodded.

"You do."

He closed his eyes and drew a slow breath.

"I don't think there is one," he said, humor gone, his tone dry. "If you push at this, you'll end up dead, and… It took me a long time to forgive myself for what happened, last time. I'd rather die, than do it again."

She nodded.

"I don't want to die," she said. "I really reaffirmed that, yesterday. I was afraid of dying. But I can't sit back and just… wait. Tell. I can't do that. You need to help me figure out what to do instead."

"The only real alternative is you let me turn you," he said. "It wouldn't be *enough*, but it would give you enough resilience to at least *hope* that you'd survive."

She crossed her arms.

"This isn't over," she said. "I don't want to just hide away all the time."

"I'm not asking you to," Tell answered, giving her a quick smile again. "I'm just asking you to not die."

"Thank you for coming to get me," Tina said, and he nodded.

"It's a full-service outfit I'm running here, it would seem."

"It would seem," Tina agreed, then he nodded, walking past her toward the elevator.

She went to sit on one of the couches in the den,

waiting for the timer on the lasagna to go off, then eating exactly one piece of it and putting the rest into the refrigerator.

This was why she didn't cook for *herself*.

No one else to eat.

She was actually living with someone else, now, and there *still* wasn't anyone else to eat.

She scavenged Tell's shelves to find a new book to read, then took it to bed with her, falling asleep just a few pages in. It had been a long couple of days.

For a few days, things fell into a rhythm. Tina worked days at the office, coming back to the apartment and spending a brief window of time with Tell. After three days, she mentioned that she might want to get certified as an investigator, and he laughed.

"I'm not," he said.

"Aren't you?" she asked, and he shook his head.

"You have to show up and provide a lot of evidence that you're a real person," he said. "I don't have that skillset among my admirable collection, so I do what I do off the books, as it were."

"I still can't believe I called you," Tina said, and he grinned.

"I completely understand that. I don't get many phone calls, and that I was even *there* to take it…" He shook his head. "Dumb luck."

"I guess."

"Do you want to go out tonight?" Tell asked. "Are

you feeling recovered enough?"

"What's going on?" Tina asked, and he shrugged.

"Hunter keeps asking about you, and you've already been to Partridge. I figured I should at least show you that not all establishments catering to the night crowd are quite that… focused.

"I didn't notice," Tina said, and he shook his head.

"You will, if you get to see what a *normal* place is like."

"Oh, you're talking about the back rooms for drinking blood," Tina said, and he shook his head.

"No, those are standard issue. Just… do you want to go out with us?"

She considered.

She was bored, that was true.

And she was sleeping way more than she had in a long time.

There weren't any compelling reasons *not* to go, other than that she didn't trust Tell and Hunter to have an entertainment venue that wasn't completely messed up.

"Yeah," she said. "Let me get changed. What should I wear?"

He shook his head.

"It's not that kind of a night out," he said. "It's not like Partridge."

She looked at her jeans.

"Are you sure?"

He nodded, and she shook her head.

"You're dressed better than me," she said. "Just… just give me a minute."

He held out a hand, only just not touching her as she started toward the stairs.

"I don't want you too flashy," he said. "The girls... the fountains... they all compete with each other. You shouldn't let anyone confuse you for that."

She swallowed, then nodded slowly.

"Who's going to be there?" she asked.

"Night folk," he answered.

"Vampires?"

He nodded.

"Some."

"What else?"

He shook his head.

"It's not something I want to discuss with you. It's going out for drinks. At a club where we hang out. That isn't like Partridge."

She pursed her lips.

"All right."

She went to get her stuff and followed him to the elevator and the car.

"Where does Hunter live?" she asked. He shook his head.

"Not going to tell you that."

"Why not?"

"Because it's his home," he said. "Information like that... It should always come from the person who owns it."

"Says the private investigator," Tina said, and he grinned.

"I didn't say you shouldn't ask. Or even that you

shouldn't *try* to find it. Just that I shouldn't tell you."

She settled down lower into her seat.

"Tell," she said.

"Yeah?"

"Is that really your real name?"

He glanced over.

"Now, that's even more personal than where I live," he said, and she nodded.

"But *I* live there," she said. "So clearly the line is somewhere further along, yet."

He sighed.

Nodded.

"I see your point."

She waited, and he glanced over again.

"Tell," he said. "I had a name, before. It doesn't matter, because it doesn't mean anything. I thrive, uncovering secrets, understanding things. Tell me. I said it so many times, those first few years. Tell me. It stuck."

"Tell," she said, and he nodded.

"Yeah."

"What did you do with the man who killed my parents?" she asked.

"Are you sure you want to know that?" he asked, and she nodded.

"I put him in a freezer in a storage locker I own, just outside of town. When the time comes, I'm going to thaw him out and send pieces to people."

"Which people?" Tina asked.

"The ones who need to know that I'm serious." He laughed quietly. Darkly. "You just don't want to get that one wrong."

"Do all vampires look at humans as food?" she asked.

"What now?" he asked. "Where did that come from?"

"As *less*?" she asked. She wanted to ask… Wouldn't. Wouldn't do it. She had too much dignity for that.

"Less in what way?" Tell pressed, not understanding.

"Like fountains," she said. "Like… Vampires are vampires and humans are humans, and the relationships that go between are… *transactional*."

He nodded out at the road.

"I see."

She waited.

And waited some more.

"Um…" she prompted, and he laughed quietly.

"I'm thinking. A lot of vampires have almost no interaction with humans of any *significance*. I think that they would view humans as less, if you asked. I mean, you met Leopard."

She nodded.

"Yeah, no, I'm not talking about the snobs. I'm talking about vampires in general."

Or in specific.

Whatever.

"You've got to let go of the idea of vampires being a monolithic culture," Tell said. "I know vampires who run very successful businesses, and there isn't another vampire there. I know vampires who *hate* vampires and avoid them religiously. I know vampires who think that humans have a definitive odor that they have to bathe to get off. I know a group of vampires out west who believe that humans are vampire deities. Self-loathing is actually pretty common. And then there's Bellet and his lot... There's no rule to it."

She squeezed her elbows in against her hips and nodded.

"That said," Tell said slowly. "When you're out with vampires, you have to *assume* that some of them are going to hit on you as a fountain."

"So you're saying I shouldn't take it that they're calling me pretty?" Tina asked, and he chuckled.

"It brings the idea of *meat market* to a whole new level, believe me."

"Did Helen deal with that?" Tina asked, and his face closed over for a moment.

"Sorry," Tina said, and he shook his head.

"She didn't," Tell told her. "It was a different time. They would make inquiries, sometimes, but... Nothing was like it is now. Now? It's cool for a girl to go home with whoever. For whatever. No one blinks. Back then, she'd have gotten a reputation with the humans, any of them would have, so it was a lot more discrete. Passing notes and whispering. Setting up times and places... Everything was secret. I think a lot of humans got the worst of it, for that. Now, if a vampire hurts their fountain, word goes around."

They pulled up outside of an apartment building

some distance away and Tell looked over at her.

"I wouldn't be doing this, if I didn't think that you were perfectly strong enough to stand up for yourself. So if you need to, do it. You shouldn't worry about offending people. Yeah?"

"Okay," Tina said, getting out and locking her door. She waited as he came around, then put her arm through his, walking up the stairs and into the little foyer. He walked past the base of the stairs, going to a door that looked an awful lot like a janitor's closet. He jiggled the door knob, finding it locked, and Tina took a step back.

Closed?

He jiggled the doorknob again, and then let his hand drop. The door opened and a man stepped out of the way.

"Tell," he said.

"Henry," Tell answered, putting an arm back to Tina.

The doorman sniffed her on the way past.

"New blood," he said, and Tina looked him in the face as she went past, wondering what he was thinking.

"Can you tell?" Tina asked. "Who's human and who's vampire?"

"Vampires don't have a heartbeat," Tell answered, turning to go down a set of stairs. "So that's easy."

They reached the bottom of the metal stairs, coming into a dim room with waitresses and tables and… nothing much remarkable.

Tell motioned.

"Hunter beat us," he said, leading her across the

cement floor to a round booth where Hunter was sitting with an amber-colored drink.

"Jackie's here," Hunter said as they sat.

"So?" Tell asked.

"She asked about you."

"So?" Tell asked again.

"Has a *job*," Hunter said.

"Busy," Tell said, and Hunter whistled, low.

"Can I be there when you tell her that? She's sure she owns you, these days."

"Not her who *would* own me, if someone did," Tell said. "Would be Mortimer."

Hunter grinned.

"You know she thinks that Mortimer's chits are hers."

"I'll be sure to be very clear and use small words," Tell said, bored.

Hunter grinned, sipping his drink.

"So how are you recovering?" he asked Tina. "Got some good normal humaning in, the last few days?"

She looked over at him, but Tell nudged her before she had formed an answer.

"What do you want to drink?" he asked. "Wine? Beer? Spirits?"

"Old man," Hunter mocked. Tell shrugged, keeping his eyes on Tina.

"Wine," she said. "Red."

He raised an eyebrow, then stood.

"You're a philistine, aren't you?" he asked, and she grinned.

"Surprise me."

He shook his head and left.

Tina sat back against the leather of the booth, watching the room.

"How many of these people do you know?" she asked.

"More than you," Hunter teased, sliding over to sit next to her. "They all know who you are, though. Walked in here with Tell. His new toy."

She looked over, offended, and he grinned wider.

"You don't think that's what you are, to these people? A passing fancy. You'll get older, he won't. They think in decades, most of them."

It hurt to hear it, but she could see how it was true.

Somehow it hadn't come into clear focus just like that, before.

"Why did you take me back into the back at Partridge?" Tina asked. He frowned.

"It's all over," he said. "Why do you want to talk about it?"

"Because," Tina said. "You acted weird, and I want to know why."

He stretched, slouching in the booth and putting a leg up across the other knee and his arms across the back of the booth.

He looked at her, brazenly, then out at the room.

"There's nuance, here," he said. "May not look like it. May look like one century-long party, but everyone knows everyone, knows how they act. Someone caught wind that I was worried about Tell, puts both him and me in a worse position. Bringing you in there was a signal, and I wanted to control what signal it was."

"That I'm yours," she said, and he shrugged.

"Could be worse," he said.

"Could it?" Tina asked, and he grinned, still not looking at her.

"Better than *Tell*," he said. "With me, there's some competition. Puts you in better stead with the rest of the fountains, that I took you back on your own. *Brought* you."

She gritted her teeth, shifting and trying to keep from going completely stony.

He looked over and snorted, his eyes teasing.

"You didn't think it was… Look, it was a good time. Show you off to all the big bads with their big egos, go bite Bellet good and hard, burn his place down. And I'm not ever going to underestimate what you did for Tell. But you can't read that much into it. He goes missing again, I'll come track you down, but other than that? It's just cover, babe."

Tell came back with a wine glass and a snifter. He put the glass down in front of her, glancing over at Hunter.

"That didn't take you long," he commented, but before Tina could ask what it meant, a pair of men came up to the table, shaking hands with Tell.

"Heard you might have some free time coming up," one of them said, glancing at Tina.

"You heard wrong," Tell answered. "I'm involved in some private affairs for the time being, and I'm not interested in distractions."

The second man looked over at Hunter.

"Still slumming it?" he asked.

"Which one of us?" Hunter asked, and the man grinned.

"Both of you. No one can figure you two out."

Hunter shrugged, sipping his drink again.

"Suits me."

"I'm not sure that I'm willing to take no for an answer," the first man said to Tell. "This is important, it's urgent, and you *owe* me."

"As far as I recall, we've exchanged funds for services at each junction," Tell said. "The very definition of not owing each other *anything*."

"You available, sweetheart?" the second man asked Tina.

"No," she answered. He grinned.

"Oh, come on, you can't tell me you're here wasting your time with just the two of these guys."

She glanced over at Hunter.

"Seems I've already won the prize," she said, and the man laughed.

"Is that what he's telling you, sweetie? You haven't been around here long enough to know what he really is."

She turned her head to look at him, leaving her face still. Office workers telling her their social problems. Everyone was the hero of their own story, and they were *all* immature beyond measure.

It only made sense that immortals would be the *most* immature, as she looked at him.

"You're free to inform me," she said, shifting under Hunter's arm. He let his hand drop casually onto her shoulder, and she lifted her chin a fraction higher.

"He's a playboy," the man said. "No loyalty to him at all. You think you've won it, tonight, but tomorrow he's off with another girl. Forgets you. There are men around here, loyal ones, like having a steady stable of girls so they don't have to *come* to places like this to go fishing for a new one. You just turn up on schedule, they'll make your life go *easy*."

She frowned thoughtfully.

"Like you?" Tina asked. "Or are you one of the ones down at the fishing hole?"

The man looked at the one who was only momentarily distracted from talking to Tell.

"Bradley, here, he's one of the ones who sticks with his fountains."

She tipped her head to look at the other man, who gave his friend a dark look.

"This isn't what we came here for," he said.

"You came all the way down here in hopes I might turn up?" Tell asked. "Or are you here for something else, and I'm just serendipity?"

"It ain't just girls a man like me goes fishing for, at a place like this," the man said, glancing once more at his friend. "You behave. I'm not here to poach."

"Yes you are," Tell said. "You're just never that upfront about it."

Tina swallowed, watching the man who had spoken to her at first as he licked his lips.

"Don't know what he sees in you, anyway. You got hips like a breeder."

Tina only just narrowly avoided looking down into her lap.

She did *not*.

She gritted her teeth, waiting for something clever to come to her, but the business man had turned his attention back to Tell fully again.

"I want to play nice, but I seen you now, and it means that you're the one I want on it. You do this, or you're going to have trouble."

"When do I *not* have trouble?" Tell asked. "Everyone and his brother trying to run me. Don't know how many necks I have to break before people start taking me seriously that I don't *play* that way."

"You call me when you aren't so drunk and you're thinking clearly," the man said, patting the table. "We'll forget this unpleasantness. Good money in it."

"Money, I have," Tell answered, watching the pair of men walk away.

"I'm a prize," Hunter said cheerfully. Tina could see the eyes around the room, the way they dodged across the table, seeing what was going on. She couldn't just spurn him.

"Oh, you're a prize, all right," she answered, reaching for her wine.

He leaned his head over against hers, touching her ear with his nose.

"You're a natural," he purred. "Hidden daggers are more useful than swords."

She turned her head slightly.

"You know how to use a sword?"

"I know a lot of things you might not expect," Hunter said, and she shook her head.

"That isn't an answer."

"Yes," he said, humored. "Yes, I was quite *good* with one, a century ago."

"You're supposed to say that you're *still* an expert with a sword," Tina answered darkly and he tipped his head back with laughter.

"Bad luck, ending up with him," Tell said. "You're never going to shake him loose, now."

"All I have to do is get poached," Tina said. "You have a harem, Tell?"

He gave her a piercing look, half a smile.

"It's a lot more casual than that, unfortunately."

"He hasn't got *anything*," Hunter said. "He just counts on me to bring the girls, and they all come running because of mysterious, brooding Tell."

Tina read Tell's face, a confirmation.

"You guys are worse than the kids I work with," she said. "Using each other and never understanding why no one really cared about them."

Okay, it hadn't *actually* gone that way. Some of them invested emotionally in every person they ever went on a date with.

But still.

The worst of the egos were dwarfed by the two men here at the table.

"Ouch," Hunter said playfully. "Words hurt, Miss Matthews."

"No, *elbows* hurt," Tina said. "Shall I show you?"

He laughed again, finishing his drink and standing.

"Don't run off with the next vampire who wanders by, okay? I'm kind of enjoying this."

She looked over at Tell.

"What was that about?" she asked.

"What part?" he asked, and she shook her head.

"You know what I mean," she said, and he shook his head.

"I honestly don't. Hard to say which part of the evening so far you've found least expected."

"The man trying to extort you into doing work," she said, still convinced it was obvious. He nodded.

"Right. His name is Bradley, and he wants me to do some work for him."

She crossed arms, glaring at him, and he ducked his head slightly, sipping his drink once and looking around the room.

"I don't know what he wants, but I do have a reputation for being able to handle *delicate* situations. Odds are good that he's got something political going on, and he wants me to come unstring it for him."

Tina drew her head back.

"No," she said. "Nothing I've seen so far suggests that you are *delicate*. You blew up everything with Marcus Calloway just to see who showed up with the bait. You took a body and hid it in a freezer. And I've *seen* your apartment."

"What's my apartment got to do with it?" he asked with humor. "No, for one, that *is* delicate, for us. Hunter would have paid an elemental to just go through all of them and pulverize them, once he knew where his stuff was and who was watching it. For two… Yeah, that's just how we work. We play hard, because no one ever tells us no."

"How do you not get in trouble with the police?" Tina asked. "Bodies and guns and… stuff."

He shook his head.

"On this side of the gray line, there aren't police. No one calls for external justice, because justice would take *all of us* away. No. It's a power balance that defines who takes and who loses."

"No one has ever *lost* a body?" Tina asked. "I mean… You *know* Detective Keller."

"I do," Tell agreed. "I take on some human work. Keeps me fresh, working with people with such… different motivations." He narrowed his eyes and nodded. "The people here… they're about as *diverse* as you're going to find anywhere, and vampires, man. A vampire will do *anything*, for reasons you wouldn't even guess at. But at the end of the day? Okay, if I get another cheating spouse call, I'm going to throw someone out a window, but some of the other stuff…" He shook his head. "You just don't see it, around here. People are twisted, they're dark, they're greedy. Predictably. But humans? With short lifespans and a society based on justice and law? Some of them are…" He paused. "That's why I took your case. You were *good*. Not *clever*. You were honest, and what you wanted… I still don't think you're entirely sure what it was you wanted, but I knew. You just wanted to believe that the world was governed by a force of justice that always *wins*. I kind of feel bad, taking that from you."

She crossed her arms, sending Hunter a sharp look as he landed back in the seat next to her again.

"Don't patronize me," she said. "I know that the world isn't a pretty pretty princess land where the fairy godmother sets everything right by the end."

"Wait," Hunter said, looking around quickly. "What? When did that change? Am I at the right table?"

Tell smiled at his drink.

"And yet, you believe it," he said. "There's a difference between what you *know* and what you *believe*."

"I do not," Tina protested. "The world is a wretched place full of terrible people who…"

Who walked away when a mass murderer turned up standing behind her.

Glenda Mitchell.

Tell nodded.

"I saw it in your eyes," he said. "But I *really* saw it in your binder. I'm never giving it back, by the way. The quality of work is just too inspiring. I'm going to keep it with the things that remind me why I'm not *him*."

"Hey," Hunter said. "I might be offended by that."

Tina looked over at him and shook her head.

"No, you're not."

He grinned.

"No I'm not."

He drained his drink.

"Do you want to dance?" he asked.

"No one's dancing," she said. "This isn't dance music. I *don't* dance."

"All great reasons," Hunter said. "I accept."

He dragged her around the table, as Tina's thrashing grab at Tell's shirt missed, and he pulled her toward a section of the floor where there weren't quite as many tables, tucking her hand in against his shoulder and holding her waist with a firm, flat hand.

"That's not how this works," Tina said. "What are you *doing*?"

"Staking a claim," he said. "They saw me at Partridge, but some of them are going to be thinking I was sneaking around behind Tell's back. He's here, now."

"But I'm not yours," she muttered. "I'm not *anyone's*."

"I know that," he said. "And you know that. And Tell knows that. But that's not how we work. Humans? They don't come hang out because we're cool kids. If you're here, it's because you like the blood game."

"So?" Tina asked. "There aren't any *rules*. Tell keeps telling me that."

"Tell makes the world out to be more simple than it is," Hunter said, and Tina scoffed. "I'm serious. Yeah, there are too many different species here to count, and vampire politics are a dirty mess, but he thinks that anyone can do anything they want. *Be* anything they want. He exists in a bubble, my friend. One that's likely to get you killed if you believe that that is *your* bubble, too. And you aren't willing to do the things it takes to earn you a bubble of your own." He pulled his head back to look her in the face. "Believe me."

She nodded, letting him tuck her head in on his shoulder again.

"It's not so bad, is it?" Hunter asked. "I don't smell bad, I'm not bad to look at. I'm fun."

"Right, because that's what I'm into, as a faux blood slave," Tina answered, and he laughed, silent, just the feel of his chest against hers.

"I want you to be okay," he said.

"And I'm glad that you're watching out for Tell," Tina said. "But it's clear that you are not interested… not *able* to treat me like a human being."

"Or that I *do* treat you like a human being," he answered quietly, turning his face into her hair. "That's what you are."

"And that's all I am to you?" she asked.

"I told you that," he said. "I want you to be okay. I want them to think that you belong to me, because I'm not to be trifled with, and they all know that. They can try to poach you all they like, and you can even be an *actual* fountain for one of them if you want, but it puts you in the game in a way that has *rules*."

"It makes me a cow," she said. "Dumb, meaningless, and someone that they can overlook."

"Hidden dagger," he said again. "I'm going to bite you now."

"Don't you dare," Tina breathed as he pulled her hair out of the way and put his mouth onto her neck. It was just for a moment, and he didn't *actually* bite her, but she froze anyway, feeling out of control and defensive without being able to do anything about it.

"Why?" she whispered as he kissed under her ear and put his face back against her hair again.

"It is what it is," he said. "Sometimes it's a big game and you play it out, and sometimes it's just a snack."

"But *why*?" she pressed. "Why are you *doing* this?"

"Because Tell won't," Hunter said. "And I want you to stay alive."

She drew a breath, not understanding, but not wanting to talk about it anymore. Not wanting to *touch* him anymore.

She pulled away a moment later and went back to the table, sitting down next to Tell.

"Master of theatrics," Tell said without looking at her.

"I want to go," she said. "This is stupid."

He nodded.

"I need to have a conversation," he said.

"Wait," she said, putting her hand out.

"We can talk later," he answered, standing and walking away, still without looking at her.

She let Hunter put his arm around her again as he sat down, and she took a long drink of her wine.

"You ever do that again, I'm going to stab you with a nail file through the ribs."

"You carry one?" he asked.

"I will, from here on," she answered.

"You know that doesn't kill us," Hunter said, leaning in closer.

"Exactly," Tina said. "I can inflict a *lot* of pain without even *worrying* about killing you."

He laughed and shifted his waist and hips over until his clothes touched hers.

"You're fun," he said. "And pretty. You don't smell bad, either."

"Are you hitting on me?" Tina asked. "I can't keep up."

"I'm going to Thailand tonight," he said. "Plane takes off in an hour. I'm going to go find another one of my girls and top up."

She looked at him, and he looked her up and down, playfully.

"You're leaving?" she asked.

"I have business to deal with," he answered.

"What if something happens to Tell?"

"You think I'm his body guard?" Hunter asked. "Dumb luck I was even here, when it happened, with Bellet. No. Tell takes care of himself. I'm just hoping he remembers to take care of you, too."

"Says the one who took me to see Leopard and Pyro," Tina said, and he grinned.

"I'm not saying you're ever going to get it," he answered.

"I'm not sure *you* get it," Tina said. "You're some Puck Loki character in your own head, and you do whatever the hell you feel like all the time, and then try to wave it away with some mystic all-knowing crap."

He slapped his chest with an open palm.

"You got me," he said. He kissed her cheek. "Been fun. I'll see you next time."

She spread her hands as he stood, moving away across the dim room and weaving himself around a skinny woman in a fitted dress and stilettos.

Tina shook her head, finishing her wine and moving to the edge of the booth, looking around for Tell.

She found him in a corner, sitting down next to a man in a gray suit and a fedora.

She waited, just out of earshot, watching the room, then Tell came and put his arm around her waist.

"Did Hunter go?" he asked.

"I guess so," Tina answered, and he nodded.

"That's how he is. Are you ready? I'll drop you off at home."

"At the penthouse," Tina corrected, and he swiveled over quick feet to walk backwards for a step, reading her face as she stopped walking again.

"Do you wish I hadn't brought you?" he asked. "This is my life. These are my people. Like them or not - and I usually don't - this is where I *belong*. I thought you'd want to see it."

"He bit me," she said, and he shook his head, coming to walk alongside her again, escorting her back up the stairs and into the foyer of the dingy apartment building.

"Come on," he said, going out the door and down the cement steps. They walked the two blocks to the car, and he let her in, coming around and getting in without starting it.

He drew a breath, and Tina waited.

"Hunter thinks he's doing right by you," he said, and she shook her head.

"He's a sociopath," she said. "He doesn't feel anything, and everything is about tactics and getting what he wants."

Tell looked over at her.

"If you believe that, then nothing I'm going to say is going to change it, but I don't think you actually believe it. I think that you got scorned tonight, and that you're coping with both that *and* everything else, tonight, and that's a hell of a lift for anyone, not to mention you, after what you've been through, the last few days."

"Scorned," she said. "He's a jerk."

"And the two of you went through something together," Tell said. "I've seen it more times than I can count."

"The guy was telling the truth about him," Tina said. "Being a player."

Tell shook his head.

"That's not what I'm saying. I've *seen* it more times than I can count. Not that I've seen it happen to Hunter. He's pretty clean about not establishing attachments."

"Oh, that makes me feel better," Tina said.

Was she admitting being attracted to him? She didn't think so.

No.

No, she hadn't.

She wasn't.

Tell was watching her quietly, and she shook her head.

"He bit me," she said.

"Did he really?" Tell asked, and she frowned, shaking her head.

"But he acted like it was no big deal," she said, and

Tell shrugged.

"It isn't. He's trying to do right by you."

"He said it's about *you*," Tina said, and he nodded.

"Yeah, he would."

"What does that even *mean*?" Tina demanded, and he shook his head, smiling.

"I'm not asking you to understand two-hundred odd years of history in a night. I wanted you to see it, and… I knew Hunter would make a scene, somehow, and you just need to learn to roll with it, if you're going to be around us."

"What are you doing tonight?" Tina asked, and he shook his head.

"Doesn't concern you," he said.

"Do you know who wanted to hurt my parents?" she asked. "Who hired that man and what he was looking for?"

"Would have loved to ask him that myself, but I'm still working on it. I've got leads, though, and it's just a matter of time before something pans out."

"You said they made a mistake," she said. He nodded, starting the car and pulling away from the curb.

"They did," he said. "And I'm not going to let it go. I promise."

She nodded.

She still felt so *strange*, so out of place and out of herself.

"Why not fly during the day, when he's already going to be sleeping?" Tina asked.

"Planes don't give us enough protection," Tell

answered. "You put a vampire in a plane during the day, unless it's a really special one, he's going to cook alive."

She frowned.

"You can't get to Thailand overnight, can you?"

"They'll go over the North Pole to make the night last longer," Tell said. "But, no, he's probably got a day, landed somewhere between here and there."

She shook her head.

"The logistics of what you do are exhausting, aren't they?"

He nodded.

"On the other hand, I don't have to *eat* three times a day, so I've got that going for me."

She smiled at the road, tipping her head back.

"Regrets?" Tell asked a moment later.

"No," she admitted. "I mean, I'm mad. You keep everything from me and he treats me like some casual hookup in the middle of everything… But no. No regrets."

"Good," he said. "I've got to admit that I like having you around."

"Just not while you're off on your super-secret vampire stuff."

He glanced over at her.

"That really bothers you?" he asked. "That I don't drag you into the worst of our underworld?"

"That you don't *tell* me about it," she answered. "I'm perfectly fine going back to the apartment and going to bed. I'm *tired*. I just don't like that you don't want to tell me what's going on."

"I'm not sure that I see there's a difference, but I'll think about it," he said.

Several minutes later, as Viella came into view, Tell pulled off to the side of the road, parking the car.

"What's going on?" Tina asked. He shook his head.

"I told you that they made a mistake," he answered quietly. "They just made another."

Tina sat up.

"What?"

"You really want answers?" he asked.

"Yes," she told him, feeling like that was obvious.

"You trust me?" he asked.

A pair of men got out of a car ahead of them and started walking back towards them.

"Do I have a choice?" she asked.

"I can take them, here and now," Tell said. "But if I do, they'll probably take their answers with them."

She couldn't have gone back into the apartment building for this part?

Why did he stop out here?

"I want answers," she said, and he nodded. Why had she said that? She wanted answers, but much less than she wanted to avoid *pain*.

Didn't she?

"Hold tight," he said. "I don't know where this one goes."

One of the men knocked on the glass of Tina's

window, bending down to look in at her.

Big nose, dark eyes, creases along his cheekbones that looked like knife cuts, they were so deep and so sharp.

She glanced over at Tell.

"Come on out, Ms. Matthews," the man said. "We need to talk."

Perhaps until that very instant, she hadn't felt like it was real, like it was *happening*, like it had anything to do with her.

He knew her name.

He *knew* who she *was*.

"Last chance," Tell murmured, and she would have taken him up on it, but for the other man looking in Tell's window at the same time.

"Tell," she breathed, and he turned his face.

"Damn," he said.

"What is that?" she asked.

"Unexpected," he said. "Go along, do whatever they say. Give them anything they want. Okay?"

"What?" she asked.

"Promise me," he said as the other man ripped the door open and pulled Tell out into the slow-slushy street.

He had had fangs.

Long fangs that parted his lips both on his bottom and top jaws, like a saber-toothed tiger.

Tina opened her door carefully, leaving her purse there after barely a moment's consideration.

Maybe it would still be there when she got back.

If she got back.

"What do you want?" she asked.

The man shook his head, grabbing hold of her upper arm with a stony hand.

"Not here," he said. "Come with us."

She tugged away.

"The last time I did that, it didn't go so well for me," she said, and he looked back at her.

"If you don't do it, it won't go so well for *either* of you," he answered. "Get in."

She looked over at Tell, but the man was walking toward the car, his head down, his arms behind his back.

Broken.

It was a front.

A game.

A tactic.

The man on her side of the car grabbed her arm harder and pulled her toward the lead car, and she let him throw her into the back seat next to Tell. The man with the fangs crossed sides to get in on the passenger side, looking back at her. The corner of his mouth came up in a snarl, showing a huge, yellowed canine.

"I'm going to tear your pretty throat out in front of him, when this is all done," he said.

"What are you?" Tina asked as the other man got into the driver's side and started the car.

"He's a werewolf," Tell said.

"Bane," the man said. "I'm a vampire killer."

Tina looked quickly from the driver to the werewolf.

"What do you want?" she asked. "What is this about?"

"A conversation," the driver said. "If everything goes well, we'll think about leaving the two of you alive."

She looked at Tell, but he shook his head.

She sat back into her seat, putting on her seatbelt out of a sense of habit, and waited to find out what was going to happen next.

The car slid through the darkness, away from the still-populated part of the city near Viella and into darker parts of downtown, where the streetlights were unreliable and people on the sidewalks scrambled out of the way as they went past, just shadows and ideas of people.

Tina looked at Tell again, wondering when his plan was going to spring into action.

Surely a two-hundred year old vampire wasn't going to get captured by people who had a legitimate chance of killing him twice in a week.

Right?

Right?

They pulled into a garage in a soot-stained brick building, the door sliding closed behind them and leaving the car in complete darkness.

The car door opened and someone pulled Tina out by the arm, finding her secured and pulling harder. She scrambled to get her seatbelt undone, sliding onto the slick cement floor and trying to get her feet underneath her as the hand dragged her.

She didn't even know which direction she was going.

"Tell?" she called.

Another door opened, casting a bolt of dim blue light across the garage floor, and a shadow stood, waiting for them.

"Is this her?" the shadow asked.

"Yes. He was there, like they said."

"Let them have him," the voice said.

"No," Tina said.

"Excuse me?" the man asked.

"You… He has to come with me," Tina said. "Or else I won't help you at all."

The man laughed.

"My dear, I'm *rescuing* you, don't you see that? You got yourself tangled up in this world because you were trying to make things right. Surely now you see that you *can't* make things right, and the simplest path forward is to cut your losses, and walk out the front door without ever looking back. No more running, no more looking over your shoulder, no more mysteries. Don't you want that?"

No.

"Maybe."

"We'll give you some time to think about it," he said. "But not forever. You've cost us a lot of time and resources, already, and our patience is not infinite."

"What's going to happen to him?" Tina asked.

"That isn't your concern," the man answered, putting an arm out. She let him put his arm around her shoulders and escort her forward into the building, where the man holding her arm let go.

"What is this about?" she asked. "He never did tell

me, the one you sent."

"Edward had his own way of doing things," the man said, leading her into a windowed room and sitting her down at a dusty but well-built table. "We found his results spoke for themselves."

"Right up until he got himself killed," Tina said.

"Indeed. He was someone we found valuable. No matter, though. We'll find another."

"I can't help you unless you tell me what you want," Tina said. "My parents weren't interesting people. They didn't… They wouldn't have been involved in *anything* that had to do with vampires and… *werewolves*."

The word still felt strange on her tongue, the idea that she actually *believed* in such a thing.

"Oh, no," the man said. He sat down at the table a few seats away from her, tapping his fingers across the surface. "No. I had no idea about any of this, a scant few days ago. And then a man came to me and said that we might have a mutual problem that he would be willing to cooperate with me in order to find a solution. Apparently he was a confederate of Edward's, but he is also so much more…"

He looked down, tugging at the arms of his gray suit and then looking up at her again with a pleasant expression.

"He explained to me that the boogeymen of the stories, that many of them are *real*, and that one of them was defending you for no reason that any of us have been able to discern. He said that he could help us, if we would… meet some specific demands about the things that happened next."

"If you would hold me hostage while he kills Tell," Tina said. The man gave her a cool smile.

"You're much sharper than your parents," he said.

"Why doesn't he do it, himself?" Tina asked. "If he's strong enough to hurt Tell…"

Why not just kill her?

Werewolf.

Someone strong enough to make Tell just *surrender* like that.

Hunter was gone.

Tell had no allies, according to both of them.

And this man.

This man had paid the sociopath to kill her parents.

"What is it that you want?" Tina asked. "Just a straight answer."

He gave her a little frown.

"A young man in my… employ… took work home with him one evening, and he left some of it at his mother's house by mistake."

"Glenda?" Tina asked. "His mother is Glenda Mitchell?"

"Yes," the man said. "And she had the misfortune of finding it and looking at it. It seems that she didn't want to call the police outright, because her son was implicated, so she gave a jump drive to your mother for safe keeping while she decided on what she was going to do."

"A jump drive," Tina said. "You killed my parents over a *jump* drive."

He shrugged.

"Human life has very little value to me, unless it does," he said casually. "They must have refused to hand it over, because otherwise I am quite certain they would still be alive."

That hit Tina hard.

Very hard.

Somehow she hadn't thought about it like that before that moment.

"A jump drive," she murmured. "What's on it?"

"Oh, I'm quite certain that you would not want to know," he said. "It's much easier to turn over something when you aren't aware of the stakes."

She crossed her arms.

"You're telling me that I *wouldn't* give it to you, if I knew what was on it, but that you're going to *tell* me that, and then expect me to hand it over, anyway?"

He gave her a wan smile.

"That is exactly the size and shape of things," he said.

"What if I don't know where it is?" Tina asked.

"Then that is very unfortunate," he said. "My people have been through the house, they have been through your apartment, and they have been through various other locations that might have served as a hiding spot for such a thing, and they have not found it. I *will* keep looking, but I can't simply let you go to find it and turn it over to the police."

"And what happens to Tell?" Tina asked.

"To tell…" he said slowly, raising his eyebrows.

"The vampire," Tina said, and he frowned, shaking

his head.

"Oh, no, no, my dear," he said. "You have nothing to do with him, anymore. What will happen to him is… Well, I'd wager that it's already done."

"How much do you know about… them?" she asked. He gave her a frightening smile.

"I am hoping to find other business opportunities with mutual benefit," he said. "Quite a useful skill set, when you're in my business."

Tina didn't ask what business that was.

She didn't want to know.

They needed this man to hold her here.

It meant she had some kind of power against them, or else they wouldn't have needed to involve this man at all; they just would have taken Tell and left her in the car. Or dead.

How do you kill a werewolf?

Vampires didn't conform to any of the archetypes, outside of the whole *sun* thing. And blood.

Blood.

They were going to bleed him, and it would take a long time.

Were they afraid she would go for reinforcements? Hunter was gone.

Hunter was gone.

That made tonight an *excellent* night to take them.

The man in the suit shifted.

"I should tell you that giving me the information I need, the key to walking out of this room and never seeing me again, this is a very limited-time offer. When I lose my patience, I will simply end you. No messy bodies, like your parents. You simply won't ever be found. But that's not going to be a surprise to anyone, is it? You disappeared weeks ago from your own life. Maybe you moved away. Maybe you couldn't bear the grief and you killed yourself. Your friends, your co-workers, they'll never know."

That one hurt.

He was right.

"All right, and if I know where it is and agree to tell you, what are you going to do to help Tell?" Tina asked.

He shook his head.

"Not a part of this negotiation. The sooner you forget he ever existed, the better."

"No," she said. "Not good enough. He's a good man, and I'm not leaving him to be tortured to death. Not when he saved *me* from the same thing."

The man shook his head.

"My dear, I'm afraid I do not have the *power* to help him. We have an *agreement*, but the people that I'm working with? We are a mere inconvenience to them."

"Then why did they need you?" Tina asked, and he smiled.

"Sometimes the inconveniences are able to remove *themselves*," he said. "The clock is ticking. Your mother gave you the jump drive, but perhaps you didn't notice at the time that that's what she was doing."

She frowned.

Had her mother given it to her?

She wanted to argue with him, but there was no point. Convincing him that she didn't know where it was

was just telling him that he ought to go ahead and kill her.

She looked around the room, just taking everything in.

Was he wearing a gun?

She couldn't tell.

She didn't see anyone outside, in the hallway, but there had been people in the dark of the garage.

If he didn't plan on killing her *with his bare hands* - and he didn't seem the type - someone else was going to have to step up and do it.

Which meant she had a moment.

Maybe only one, but a moment.

"Maybe I know where it is," she said. "Maybe my mom gave it to me and I'm not remembering, and if I went home and looked around, maybe I'd remember."

"You aren't going to leave this room," he said.

"So you'd rather have to kill me than get your jump drive back?" she asked. "You know, the guy who could probably *find* it is out there getting tortured to death? I mean, did your new friends ever tell you that? He's *amazing* at finding things. Can track them by *smell*, I kid you not. All you had to do was hire *him*, and all of this would have been… nothing."

It didn't strike her how true it was until the words were out.

If this man had known Tell, had been willing to pay his fee and Tell had been willing to do it, her parents would still be alive.

Maybe.

Or maybe he would have killed them out of fear

that they'd looked at whatever it was that Glenda Mitchell had to hide away.

More likely.

Yeah.

She didn't think Tell would have been the one to kill them, though.

It probably would have changed nothing.

Didn't make it *not* a compelling story, though.

"You think he could find it?" the man asked, and Tina nodded.

"You're letting them kill your best asset because he has enemies like them."

"I'm quite happy with the business arrangement I've come to," he said. Tina shrugged.

"Then you should accept that your data is going to be out there, wandering around in the big, wide world, where someone might someday plug it into a computer and have *no hesitation* turning it over to the police."

He pursed his lips.

"You make a valid point," he said. "I think my better solution is to make you show me where it is."

"And if I don't know?" Tina asked.

"Then you're expendable, either way," he answered with a thin, grim smile. She nodded slowly.

"I'm seeing that," she said.

"Well then," he said, slapping his knees and standing up. "If it's all but inevitable, let's just get it over with, shall we?"

He was hoping she was going to start spouting ideas, doing whatever she could to save herself.

Instead, she got up and hit him with a chair.

It was heavy and awkward, and all she really did was get him in the side and knock him back some, but it was enough. She pushed it into him again, and then swung it once more, as he put his arms up to defend himself.

"Jamie," he called. "Jamie."

Tina hit him high enough the third time to knock him down, and she landed on his chest with her knees, grabbing him by the hair and slamming his head against the ground with a sense of angry mania as a set of arms pulled her up and off of him.

"What the hell?" the man asked, throwing her back behind him and kneeling to check the man in the suit.

There was another man in the doorway, and Tina charged into him, shoulder first.

His arms closed around her and wrapped her in against his chest as he staggered backwards, and she jerked away, toward the hallway, but he was stronger than she was - bigger than she was. He smelled of cigarettes and unwashed man, and his hands were rough as he untangled her, grabbing her throat with one hand and wrapping his arm around her waist with the other.

"What do you want me to do with her?" the man asked. The man in the suit sat up groggily, waving them away with the back of his hand.

"Get rid of her," he said. "More trouble than she's worth."

Tina struggled as the man started toward the hallway with her.

"Tell said you made a mistake," she said.

"The vampire did?" the man in the suit said as he pulled himself up on the table. "What was that?"

"If you hadn't sent your sociopath after me, he might never have found you. By my count you've made two mistakes. You let him get a new lead, and then you doubled down and brought him into your own building. On purpose. You're going to regret doing that."

The suited man put his sleeve to his nose and waved them away again.

"She stopped being fun ten minutes ago," he said. "And she was never going to be useful. She doesn't know where it is."

The man holding her walked her down the hallway toward the door into the garage, shoving it open and closing it behind him.

Dark.

She heard feet move, and voices that she couldn't make sense of. Other noises that she couldn't understand at all.

"What are you doing?" someone asked.

"Boss is done with her," the man said. "Handing her back over to you."

"You aren't supposed to be here," the other voice said. "You're supposed to keep her."

"Not my problem, anymore," the man said, dropping Tina onto the floor.

She stayed low, listening to his feet as he headed back toward the door, then when it opened, she faced the rest of the room, trying to take in anything she could.

There was a body in front of her, a set of legs in

jeans that she could just make out, but beyond that, everything else was too shadowy.

"All right, let's get this over with," the man said, grabbing her by the collar. Tina didn't help at all, and he started dragging her across the garage floor.

Somewhere in the back of her head, she was remotely aware that she was probably going to die, now, but with the forefront of her mind, she was trying to figure out where they'd taken Tell. If she was going to survive this, it was going to require finding him and fixing whatever they'd done to him so that… So that he could Tell.

Whatever that entailed.

"Where's my friend?" Tina asked.

"The meat doesn't talk," the voice at the end of the arm answered.

"Are you a vampire?" Tina asked. The man paused, let go of her, and then after a brief sense of motion, something very knobby and hard smacked her across the face.

"You are not permitted to speak," he said.

"Werewolf," Tina said, putting her hand to her face and trying not to cry.

There was just such a visceral shock to it, knowing it had been the back of his hand, knowing that he considered her on the level of an animal, and not being able to see the blow coming…

There was a thud.

The sound of flesh giving way under impact.

That way.

That.

Way.

The man grabbed her by the shirt again and Tina twisted, letting her arms go and slipping out of her sweater, then getting up and running as hard as she could in the direction she'd heard the noise.

She felt fingers rake down her arm, but they didn't find grip on her skin, and she pulled her arm forward, across her body.

She slammed *hard* into something, spinning and seeing bright lights in the total darkness for several seconds, and when she finally got her feet under her again, she realized that she had no idea which direction she'd been going.

The man grabbed her elbow, long fingernails digging into her arm.

She jerked once again, but he was too strong.

Werewolf.

If she had to make a wild guess about what their weakness was?

Probably not silver. That seemed too obviously fake.

Vampires, it was sun.

Were werewolves strongest at night, too, maybe? Or by the phase of the moon, like the tides?

That didn't help her at all.

The man started dragging her again, holding her by her elbow and letting her hips slide along the concrete.

There was another smack and Tina reached up, finding the man's feet and tangling her arm in them. He stumbled, giving her just enough slack to jerk at her arm once more. One of his nails tore through the soft skin on the inside of her elbow, but she landed rudely on her shoulder, her arm tangled underneath him as he fell to his knees, and she was up again, running again.

She had blood on her face. She hadn't noticed it, before, but the breeze from moving that fast made the side of her face cold.

Either that or she'd been crying asymmetrically.

She bounced off of something hip-high and sharp-cornered, but it was only a glancing blow, and she managed to keep her feet under her as she kept going. The man behind her shouted, nothing more than a growl, and she ran face-first into a wall, stumbling backwards as more fingers grabbed at her. She slapped back at them, punch drunk and out of fear response.

"Helen," a voice said, raspy and soft, but familiar.

"Tell, it's Tina," she said. She shoved a shoulder into someone's stomach, then slid along the wall. "How do I hurt them?" she asked.

"You *don't*," Tell said. "Duck."

She squatted and something thudded into the wall above her. It might have been a body, but she didn't feel it attached to any knees.

"I didn't mean this to happen. I tried to protect you. Forward," Tell said, and she scrabbled forward on her toes and her fingers, her knees up at her shoulders.

"You shouldn't have come back," he said, closer now. "I made a mistake."

"Wasn't my choice," she said. "But I would have chosen it. Tell me what to do."

"You can't *see*," he said. An arm went around her waist, hard and final, and she clawed at it, kicking and throwing her head around violently.

This was her moment.

She needed to come up with something they weren't going to anticipate. Something that was going to fix it. Clever, creative, systematic.

Like a binder.

What did she know?

What were her options?

What was the option she was overlooking?

She bit him.

Deep into a hairy bicep, not quite furry, but certainly not a normal human skin, she sunk her teeth, hanging off of him as he pushed her shoulders away, trying to get her to let him go.

There was blood in her mouth, and for a moment she wondered if she was going to turn into a werewolf and be Tell's mortal enemy from here on out, but there was something satisfying about causing the man *pain*.

He howled and jerked his arm away, kicking at her, and she fell onto the floor, spitting and crawling away.

"She bit me," he yelled. "She bit me."

She found the wall again.

"Are you tied?' she asked.

"You did what?" Tell asked.

"Are. You. Tied?" she asked again.

"Iron cuffs that have pins that go through my wrists and ankles," he said. "I'm sorry."

Damn.

If it had been rope, she might have had a chance.

"Did you seriously just bite him?" Tell asked.

"Is that a problem?" Tina asked, finding his side and running her fingers up along a disaster of a ribcage to his arm, where she found a point of bone under his shirt and a long section of dripping wet fabric. At his wrist, she found a tight-fitted band of warm metal, and more blood.

"What do I do?" she asked. "How do I help you?"

She stepped in front of him, looking out at the black.

Why weren't they attacking her? They'd been *beating* him… Right? There were more than one of them? Why weren't they coming *after* her?

"I made a mistake, letting them take me. I'm sorry."

"Shut up and tell me how to fix it," Tina answered.

"It was werewolves who killed Helen," he said quietly. "I couldn't save her. They had you."

"They haven't got me now," Tina said through gritted teeth. "Tell me."

"I need blood," Tell said after a pause, his voice changing.

"Where did they go?" Tina asked.

"They're afraid," Tell said, very, very quiet. As she stood next to him, his head came to rest on her shoulder. "If I can get enough blood out of you to break these chains, I'm going to go through them like wind through chaff."

"Then do it," Tina said.

He shook his head.

"They're waiting to see if I will. If I can."

"Tell," she said. "If you don't do this, they're going to kill me, too. This is not optional. Do it."

"I fed on you too recently," he said quietly. "It might kill you."

She closed her eyes, feeling the *idea* of monsters in the dark.

"Probably better that way than theirs," she finally answered, taking one more step across him. "Why not just pull me away?"

"They won't come that close to me," he said. "You were their leverage."

"Tell," she whispered. "I trust you."

He sighed.

"You shouldn't."

The motion he made, putting his face against the curve of her neck, it was familiar, the way that Hunter had done it at the club just a few hours earlier, but when he opened his mouth and put it against her skin, there were teeth. Twin points, sliding through her skin like it was made for them, and she swallowed, putting her hand up on the back of his neck, to steady herself as much as anything.

There was a strong pull and the feeling of warm flow across her skin, his tongue on her neck, and she tipped against him, eyes closed, afraid and delighted and… safe.

She'd told him she trusted him, and it was true.

Hunter had simply kissed her, and she'd wanted to punch him in the stomach for it. Tell… It was so much more personal and so much less.

She put her hand against the wall as he pulled again,

feeling herself go light-headed and tippy.

Her knees wouldn't hold her up much longer, like this.

His neck arched, more physically confident, controlled, pulling her against his chest, and she dropped her head onto his shoulder, her brain going foggy.

"There are other humans," he growled. "I can smell them on you."

"What?" she asked, blinking.

Where was she?

Why was it so dark?

She should have been in bed.

"Humans," he said more forcefully. "Where?"

"Door," she said. "Through."

"They're just right there?"

"Maybe."

There was a sharp cracking noise, and then a pinging, and an arm under her knees. She heard barking and howling as she put her head against Tell's arm, feeling sleepy, a sharp breeze stirring at her hair, and then she was on the ground in the dark, by herself.

She curled up against the wall, pulling her knees in against her chest, and moments later, a hand grabbed her forearm, starting to drag her away.

Hard hand.

Claws.

She pulled against it, but she had nothing left, and she let it drag her full out across the floor, a rag doll with a lolling head.

There was a rude slamming noise, loud, and a bolt

of blue light that washed across her, and then one hard jolt and the hand was gone.

She lay on the floor on her back, fuzzy and drifting, almost gone, listening to the sound of *nothing* around her.

Wind.

She shivered, finding her exposed skin against cold cement, and she rolled onto her side, curling up and trying to stay warm.

There was a dull thud, flesh giving, and then again.

If Tell lost this fight, she was going to die.

Her muddled brain remembered the feel of the *pull* on her neck, and her fingers found the spot. There was nothing there to find. Just her own skin.

She let her head rest on the floor and she closed her eyes, more throbbing color there with her eyelids down than up. Arms went under her - soft, smooth skin and warm fingers - and she let Tell settle her in against his shoulder.

"It's done," he said quietly.

"You're warm," Tina answered.

"That much blood, I'm going to be warm for a couple of days," he answered.

"Are you okay?" she asked, and he pulled her in tighter against his chest.

"I have friends with resources," he said. "I'd prefer you get a transfusion, but you at least need IV fluids."

"He told me," she said, rapidly falling asleep.

"Who told you what?" Tell asked and she struggled to remember what she'd been about to tell him.

"Jump drive," she said. "Glenda Mitchell gave my

mom a jump drive, and she wouldn't give it to him."

"I'll find it," Tell said. "But he's dead. I drained him."

She sat up, her head swirling and swimming and her brain threatening to lose its grip on the dark room entirely. She struggled, blinking hard and keeping her mind latched down until the spinning stopped some.

"You what?"

"I won't apologize," Tell said. "I'll pay to have it cleaned up, but I won't apologize. He intended both of us to die, tonight."

She thought about this.

"I hit him with a chair," she said, and she heard Tell smile.

"Good girl."

She put her head back against his shoulder again, and she felt him shift, and then there was orange light, too low to see his face.

"Where did your sweater end up?" he asked as he slid her into the back seat of the car.

"I lost my jacket, too."

"Your jacket is there," he said. "I'm going to go find your sweater. I won't be a second."

She sat up, bracing against the back of the driver's seat, to look at the car.

She didn't know this car. Where was she?

Was this Tell's car and she was just confused? She blinked and Tell was in the doorway again, pulling her sweater on over her head. She wrestled her arms through the sleeves, finding the cut down her arm, and then let him do the same thing with her jacket.

"This isn't your car," she said.

"It's theirs," he said. "You remember. They drove us here."

"I don't have the keys," Tina said, and he gave her a sideways grin as he pulled her seatbelt on.

"You remember how good I am at finding things?" he asked. He looked up at the overhead light and switched it, then closed the car door. The light stayed on, and Tina put her arm against the window as a pillow for her head, leaving the other arm tucked against her stomach. The front door opened a few moments later and she opened her eyes to make sure it was Tell.

"I don't understand," she said. "What just happened?"

"I killed them," he said. "I'm confused why that's unclear."

"Why didn't they just kill me?" Tina asked. "Why do *any* of this?"

"Ah," he said. "They underestimated me at the beginning. Thought that they could just threaten you and destroy me, but… They figured out what I was, after the other men took you away. And once they figured that out, they realized they had cause to be afraid. You walked into the middle of that. Why they participated? Werewolves will do anything for money, more often than not. I suspect they were paid muscle, in this case. What's important is that I believe you're safe, now, from the threat that killed your parents."

She nodded her head into her elbow, not tired or

drowsy so much as spinny and exhausted. The car started and Tell drove forward.

After that, Tina lost track.

She woke up on a soft leather table of some kind, bright lights overhead.

"Tell," she said, sitting up.

"Woooo," a voice said, not a word so much as a calming noise, and a gentle hand pressed her back down onto the table. Tina found herself looking up at a woman's face, though there was something odd about it that she couldn't quite put her finger on, at first.

"Where is Tell?" Tina asked.

"Next room, darling," the woman said. "Harley's talking to him. Not like him to over-drain a young woman."

"He," Tina started to argue, then put her arm across her eyes. "Not his fault."

The woman laughed.

"It's entirely his fault," she said. "We take in the emergency cases, but we don't put up with anyone abusing their meals. If they bring them in as low as you were, they're going to get a talking-to from Harley, and… I'll be honest, miss, we ain't like to give you back to him, and you ought to find yourself a new companion."

Tina shifted, finding tape on her arm, and she looked.

"IV," she said.

"Some of the vampire fountains have a particular

aversion to carrying around someone else's blood, so we prefer to ask, if it isn't a life-threatening situation."

Tina propped herself up on her elbows, looking around.

"Where am I?" she asked.

"Our office," the woman said. "I'm Pippa, and I run it with my husband Harley. Taking care of the specials and their people."

"Specials," Tina said, looking harder at the woman's face. Something about the shape of her nose, her eyes. Just not... normal.

"Specials," the woman said again. "Like us."

"What are you?" Tina asked. The woman smiled.

"You're new."

Tina nodded, and the woman gave her a little head shake.

"It's a bit of a coarse question, in our circles, though it doesn't offend *me*. We're Niddles."

"I've never heard of that," Tina said. The woman shook her head again, looking over at a monitor for a moment, then returning her attention to Tina.

"No, and you aren't likely to, outside of us," the woman said. "Keep to ourselves, mostly, and there aren't that many."

Tina put her hand over her eyes again.

"My head hurts," she said.

"Let me get you something," the woman answered. "It would, after what he did to you."

"Wasn't his fault," Tina said. "They were going to kill him."

The woman paused, coming back to the table.

"Who was?" she asked. Tina shook her head.

"Werewolves, I think, but... it was really dark."

"Which club were you in?" Pippa asked, and Tina shook her head.

"Kidnapped, in a garage," she said.

Pippa crossed her arms.

"Harley is talking to Tell right this minute, and if your stories don't match up, you aren't going to manage to cover for him, so you ought to tell me the truth."

"If he says something different, it's probably because I didn't understand what was going on," Tina said. Maybe she'd said too much, already, with the werewolves. "He saved my life."

She wasn't very good at this, right now. Secrets and figuring out whose side anyone was on.

Maybe they'd gotten caught on the way out, and this was just another ploy... a feint...

She rubbed her forehead again and the woman came back with familiar-looking tablets. Tina twisted her mouth to the side, then struggled to sit up.

"I need to see Tell," she said. "Or I'm leaving."

Pippa stuck her jaw out for a moment, then nodded.

"I'll go talk to Harley. But if you pull out that line, I'm putting it back in your dominant hand, see if I don't."

Tina believed her.

She swung her legs over the side of the table, finally recognizing the doctor's chair, though it didn't have paper on it like she was used to.

She looked at the IV and something peevish in her seriously considered pulling it out, but she also didn't like the idea of sitting there for the woman to stick it back *in* her hand, which would certainly happen whether Tell was sitting in a cage down the hall or on his way into the room right now.

So she left it.

The door opened again and Tell came in, glancing back over his shoulder as a huge man with a distinctly marble-ish shape followed him in.

"I'm still so grateful to the two of you," Tell said, turning to look at Tina. "Did they hit you?"

"Oh, yeah," she said, putting her fingers up to her face and actually feeling the new bruise, now. "I'd forgotten."

Everything was bruises right now.

He frowned hard, shaking his head.

"It was one of the beasts," he said.

"She said werewolves," Pippa said, following the man who had to be Harley into the room. Tell glanced back at her.

"They were," he said.

"You clear them out?" Harley asked.

"As many as I could catch before they got out of the building," Tell said, still inspecting Tina's face.

"Why didn't they kill me?" Tina asked. "*Clearly* any one of them could have broken me in half."

"You're squirrellier than you think," Tell said. "And they don't see that well in the dark at new moon."

"Moon," Tina crowed. *"I'd guessed that. Couldn't*

figure out how it might be useful, but I wondered if they might have a relationship with the moon."

He smiled.

She frowned, remembering more details.

"Am I going to turn into one?" she asked, looking for the scratch on the inside of her right arm. It appeared Pippa had bandaged it.

"No," he said. "That's not how it works."

Pippa made a ripping motion across her body, like she was throwing something invisible on the floor.

"Deviants," she spat.

"Why were they afraid of you?" Tina asked. Tell glanced at Pippa and Harley and shook his head.

"That's personal," he said.

"Because he gives 'em hell," Harley said.

"When can she go?" Tell asked.

"No long-term damage," Pippa said, stepping forward and checking a monitor once again. "You promise to take good care of her and bring her back if she's still woozy tonight, I'll get her packed up, now."

"You have my word," Tell said.

Harley offered Tell his hand.

"Glad to hear you hadn't fallen off the wagon, friend," he said as Pippa drew the IV needle out of Tina's arm and pressed a cotton ball against it, doubling Tina's arm over it.

"Keep pressure on that for a few minutes, all right, dear?" she asked, and Tina nodded.

"Thank you."

"Any time," Pippa said. "We're all neighbors

here."

Tina gave her a smile and hopped down off of the table, holding onto it for a moment and then nodding.

"I'm okay," she said. Tell came and put his arm around her after he shook Harley's hand, walking her out the door, down a short hallway, and through a small and very cozy lobby. He opened another door and Tina frowned, recognizing the hallway outside.

"This is your office building," she said, and he nodded.

"It is."

"I've never seen them before," Tina said.

"They live here," Tell said. "They get their supplies delivered, and what doesn't come by currier, the rest of us make sure they get it. They take care of us."

"She sounded like vampires drinking too much blood wasn't uncommon," Tina said. He shrugged.

"Sometimes they just lose track," he said. "And some of them are jerks. It actually takes a special set of skills to drain a human that far. It's a big city with a lot of vampires in it. Things go wrong, and Pippa and Harley put the pieces back together more than everyone else in the city combined. But they won't do repeat offenders, and they make sure that the fountains find out who's doing that kind of stuff."

"Are you going to get in trouble?" Tina asked, and he shook his head.

"No, they know me. That's most of it. But everyone knows that I'm deep in conflict, so it's not like either of them were exactly *surprised* that you got caught up in it. Not that Harley didn't tell me I needed to drop you off at the nearest bus corner and get you out of my life forever."

"You aren't going to do that?" Tina asked, just to hear the answer.

"I promised I'd look after you, at least for today," he answered with a smile. She frowned.

"It was because of *me* that they were there," she said. "They can't blame you for that."

"They aren't the police," Tell told her. "I don't get in *trouble*. I've just got a friend who's going to give me an earful every time he sees me, because he thinks I'm endangering you. And he's right. It's just none of his business."

"Except that they just saved my life," Tina said. "Didn't they?"

"Hard to say if you were in real danger, or just really weak," Tell said. "But they did right by you and they did right by me," Tell said. "So I guess it is his right to tell me what he thinks about it."

"It's *my* decision," Tina said, and he shrugged.

"It's the two of us, at least," he said. "Do you want breakfast, or just sleep?"

He opened the door and winced against the rising sun.

Tina took a step back into the building.

"Are you okay?" she asked.

"It's hardly a surprise," he answered. "I could feel it, even before. Just keep moving."

She nodded, walking with him out to the car.

"Do you want me to drive?" she asked.

"Worst thing possible is getting into a wreck because you pass out, and being *stuck*," Tell said. "It's only a few minutes. Stop worrying about me. I *do* this."

"I felt your ribs, last night," she said. "They broke you."

"And I fed *hard* after that," he said. "I'm not in top form, but it's only a matter of time between here and there. Stop worrying about me."

She nodded, putting her head back against the headrest and watching as the buildings slid past the window, just a blur of brick and cement.

Not long after that, he pulled into the garage under Viella, taking off his sunglasses and coming around to get her.

"You need to get to bed," she said, and he shook his head.

"You first, then me," he answered, helping her onto the elevator.

Leaning against the hand-holds in the elevator, she was loathe to admit how much she'd *needed* his help.

"Red meat and lots of fruit," Tell said. "Iron and vitamins. And salts. Basically everything. You're going to be short on everything for a while. I shouldn't have fed on you twice so close together."

"No, you definitely should have let me die," Tina said, then looked over at him. "Or let them turn me."

His face went hard and he shook his head.

"I would have killed you," he said. "Before it was over."

"It's that bad?" she asked.

"They would say no," he told her, "but they're… I wouldn't want you to be one of them. They're mostly animals."

"Are you like, a really *powerful* vampire, then?" she asked, and he smiled gently at the doors, shaking his head.

"It's more complicated than that," he said as the elevator opened. He walked her into the atrium and seated her on a couch, kneeling in front of her.

"Vampires are like humans," he said. "They don't come in *kinds*, and while you can kind of group them up, it's only until the one comes along to prove that the groups don't work. But they do have strengths and weaknesses, and those come from both their natural being as well as their training. What they *don't* do is evolve. Humans *live*. Vampires do not. Which is part of why we're *so* political. The only way to get a leg up in our world is through political alliances. I can't work out and get stronger, I can't run and get faster. There are very few, very specific exceptions. I am what I am, and my leverage is only in how I use it."

He paused, looking around the room.

"I am a very strong vampire. I was an archer, in my natural life…"

"An *archer*?" Tina asked, and he grinned.

"Don't underestimate the physical capability it took to be an expert archer, back in the day. I was fit, I was fast, and I was clever. And I retained those things when I became a vampire. Not everyone does. But I have some paradoxical strengths that… Being around humans, being *involved* with humans makes me stronger. Some vampires get stronger by eliminating all contact with humans entirely - most of them, actually, weaken by virtue of even being around fountains, which is why they only do it to feed - but the more involved I am with humans, the stronger I get. And they killed Helen for that. And they're going to try to kill you."

"Just to be clear," Tina said, holding up a finger. "Because I'm still kind of foggy right now. You are or are not hitting on me, right now?"

"I most *certainly* am not," he said. "Honestly, you're a lot of fun, but my kind of girl is a lot softer and a lot quieter than you. I'm just…" He waved a palm at her in a window-washing motion. "Just no."

She grinned.

"Back at you," she said.

She lay back on the couch as he shifted up to sit next to her.

"Marcus doesn't even *know* how many people are going to come after you, because I've… Because I'm letting you be around me, because I *care* what happens to you. I've been avoiding it for a long time."

"How do you kill a werewolf?" she asked. He closed his eyes and shook his head with a smile.

"Silver," he said. "Through the heart or the brain."

"Seriously?" she asked. "I ruled that out."

He nodded.

"They're fast, they're *strong*, but with you there, they weren't as strong as me, and they knew it."

"So I need to carry a silver knife," Tina said, and

he shook his head, looking over at her.

"No. If you want to stay here, you need to know that there are very, very few creatures who would come after you that you could successfully defend yourself from."

"So I shouldn't even try?" Tina asked, and he shrugged.

"I told you that you needed to carry a gun," he said. "And learn to use it. I still mean that."

"I've kind of been busy," she said, and he nodded.

"I've noticed."

Can I turn *into* all of the stuff that you're talking about?" she asked.

"No, you can't turn into a Niddle. They're a species. A lot of them, you can, but it's *hard*. It's not like some virus that casual contact can infect you, or else the world would have known about us for a *long* time."

She nodded, crossing her arms across her chest.

"I'm going to science the snot out of you, you know that," she said, closing her eyes.

"Only if you can catch me," he answered, happily enough. "Can I get you anything to eat or anything?"

"A tea," she said. "Iced, I think. And then sleep. I can barely lift my head."

"If I wake up before you do, I'm going to your parents' house to see if I can find a jump drive that's special. And then I'm going to take it to Detective Keller."

She opened her eyes to look at him.

"You won't even look to see what's on it?" she asked, and he shook his head.

"The man who was after them, he's dead, and Keller isn't ever going to find him. If Keller can use the information on the drive to lock up some other bastards, that's great, but…" He shrugged. "This is all I took on, for this case. I'm going above and beyond the call of duty, tracking down the guy who *paid* the guy who killed them."

She nodded, swallowing.

"He wanted me to tell him where it was, and I couldn't," she said. "I don't know if I *would* have, if I'd known where it was."

"If you want me to read you, I'd say no," he said. "You came to me angry, but that was after they hit you. I can't tell you with certainty what you would have done."

"They were going to kill Glenda," Tina said. "Is she safe, now?"

"I'll look in on her," Tell said. "Her information is in your binder. If I smell anyone who doesn't belong around her house, I'll track them down and make sure they aren't going to bother her. Once the jump drive is with Detective Keller, the incentive to go after her is just punitive."

She nodded.

Looked at him, sitting down by her feet.

"I never called work," she said, and he nodded.

"I know. I did. The first week. They paid out your outstanding vacation, and I think by now you're on your own."

"You *quit* for me?" Tina asked. He smiled.

"You weren't ever going to go back, even if you didn't stay with me," he said. "You want to split a box of cereal?"

She felt her eyes go wide.

"Yes," she said. "Yes, yes."

He nodded.

"Stay."

He slid up and around the arm of the couch and disappeared, coming back maybe a minute later and carrying her into the den, where they sat down side by side on the couch facing the television.

"You need to go to bed," Tina protested and he shook his head.

"No more than you do," he said. "But we did a thing, tonight. You and me. I exterminated a pack of werewolves and you faced down the man who killed your parents. Hit him with a chair, I hear."

"I did," she said.

He handed her a box of cereal and a glass of tea and she sipped at it, finding that her throat absorbed almost all of it before it even hit her stomach. She drained half the glass, then sat with her head back against the couch for a moment.

"You did it," she said.

"We did it," he answered.

"You're going to get fed up with me before too long," she said, taking out a handful of corn puffs and handing the box back over to him.

"I loved Helen," Tell answered. "I never got tired of how dynamic she was, and how she smiled when she saw me. You're different…"

"See," Tina interjected, pointing.

"But I'm hoping that they're going to find you a lot harder to kill."

She stuck her lips out as she chewed, happy like she couldn't remember being.

"Damned straight," she answered.

THE END

Tell It Like It Is

Being a detective's assistant goes from dull to DUCK! fast.

Being the assistant to a supernatural detective takes it three steps further. But Tina is too curious and too hooked on the adventure of it all to walk away.

She is bound and determined to figure out Tell's world, and Tell himself, but danger lurks everywhere for a human who doesn't understand the lay of the land. This becomes even more evident as Tina and Tell start a search for a young woman who has gotten in over her head with a group of paranormals that stole a literal pile of gold. A chance encounter with a Djinn while chasing a lead gives her some unexpected answers and a lot more questions. She's never going to look at anything about Tell or his world the same again.

Hop back in as Tell finds out how it really is.

More Fiction by Chloe Garner

Tell, The Detective

Tell Me A Secret
Tell It Like It Is
Show And Tell
Time Will Tell

Anadidd'na Universe (Urban Fantasy)

Rangers
Shaman
Psychic
Warrior
Dragonsword
Child
Gorgon
Gone to Ground
Civil War

Book of Carter

Surviving Magic
Unveiling Magic
Real Magic

Gypsy Becca: Death of a Gypsy Queen
Gypsy Dawn: Life of a Gypsy Queen
Gypsy Bella: Legacy of a Gypsy Queen

Other Urban Fantasy

Hooligans

Science Fiction

Portal Jumpers
Portal Jumpers II: House of Midas
Portal Jumpers III: Battle of Earth

Space Western

Sarah Todd
Sarah Todd: Rising Waters
Sarah Todd: Clash of Mountains

About the Author

Chloe Garner is a wanderer with a host of identities in her head fighting each other to get out. Chloe writes about the things that go bump in the night, the future, and all things fantastical. Find her on Twitter as BlenderFiction, on Goodreads and Facebook as Chloe Garner, or at blenderfiction.wordpress.com.

Printed in Great Britain
by Amazon